HIS TO LOVE

SIERRA CARTWRIGHT

HIS TO LOVE

Copyright @ 2019 Sierra Cartwright

First E-book Publication: December 2019

Line Editing by Jennifer Barker

Proofing by Bev Albin and Cassie Hess-Dean

Cover Design by Once Upon An Alpha, Shannon Hunt

Photo provided by Depositphotos.com

Promotion by Once Upon An Alpha, Shannon Hunt

All rights reserved. Except for use in a review, no part of this publication may be reproduced, distributed, or transmitted in any form, or by any means, electronic or mechanical, including photocopying, recording, or by any information storage and retrieval system, without prior written permission of the author.

This is a work of fiction. Names, characters, places, brands, media, and incidents are either the products of the author's imagination or are used fictitiously, and any resemblance to any actual persons, living or dead, is entirely coincidental.

The author acknowledges the trademarked status and trademark owners of various products referenced in this work of fiction. The publication/use of these trademarks is not authorized, associated with, or sponsored by the trademark owners.

Adult Reading Material

Disclaimer: This work of fiction is for mature (18+) audiences only and contains strong sexual content and situations.

It is a standalone with my guarantee of satisfying, happily ever after.

All rights reserved.

DEDICATION

Especially for the fabulous Flamingo Posse! Keep dazzling and brightening the world with your beauty and talent. My life is so much fuller now that you're in it. I appreciate you so very much.

CHAPTER 1

"I want your submissive."

Stunned, Shelby Salazar sucked in a frantic breath. "What?" From her place, kneeling on the floor, she glanced up at Master Trevor Lawton.

The stunningly handsome Dom thumbed back the brim of his cowboy hat and met her gaze. The makeshift poker room of the Quarter—New Orleans's elite dungeon—swam beneath her.

Though decorum dictated that she look away and refocus on the wooden planks beneath her, she was helpless, ensnared in the compelling trap of his steel-laced blue eyes.

She'd had a crush on the mysterious billionaire for at least a year, since she first saw him brooding and alone in the club's bar area. With his dark hair and unyielding jaw, he was the stuff of her submissive dreams. But Shelby was smart enough to realize her fantasies were safer from a distance.

He had a reputation as an exacting Dominant, and she was relatively new to the scene. As much as he fascinated her, he also terrified her.

For a flash of a second, she saw something in his eyes. Pain? Longing?

At her fanciful thought, she shook her head.

Trevor severed their silent connection, and her breath whooshed out. Just the brief interaction unnerved her.

Instead of looking away, he swept his gaze down her body, lingering for a few seconds on her chest. In keeping with the Western-themed night, she'd selected a white demicup bra. As much as she wanted to be bold, her innate shyness had won out before she left the house, and she'd slipped into a studded leather vest. Her sterling silver bolo tie with its beautiful mother-of-pearl conch had been a rare indulgence. She'd spent over a month shopping for it, and the way it caught the light when she moved made it worth every penny.

Trevor continued his slow perusal and paused again at her pelvis. In addition to white leather chaps, she wore a pair of pink panties. Though she was covered, she shivered, as if completely exposed to him.

When he looked at her face again, his slow smile told her he found plenty he liked.

Her breaths threatened to strangle her.

When he finally turned his focus away from her, she momentarily grabbed hold of the poker table to steady herself.

"What do you say, David?" Master Trevor asked.

She was absolutely certain her friend and occasional escort would say no to Master Trevor's outrageous suggestion.

Instead, stunning her, David walked one of his few remaining poker chips through his fingers. "I'm not sure I heard you correctly, Lawton."

His response made her reel.

"I'm quite certain you did. I want your submissive."

Wide-eyed, she shook her head. She wasn't David's sub and never had been, but Trevor couldn't know that.

In the sudden, tense silence surrounding them, Master Trevor continued in his calm, confident manner. "I'd like a month, but I'm willing to start with a week."

A month?

"You'll have to make this a little more interesting to me," David responded.

What the hell was going on here?

A small voice inside her urged her to shout out her objection. Instead, a deep, feminine part of her blossomed. For a wild moment, she pictured herself naked and humbled in front of him.

Shaking, she pushed the unnerving—if exciting—image aside.

"I'm listening," Trevor replied.

This can't be happening.

"If I win, you make a twenty-five-thousand-dollar contribution to the Shaughnessy Community Law Offices."

She swayed forward before catching herself.

"One moment, Sirs." The dealer signaled to one of the dungeon masters. Presumably, he wanted to summon Mistress Aviana, the club owner.

What was normally a fun game at the club's annual Western theme night had taken a stunning, outlandish turn.

David Shaughnessy, one of a group of people she'd hung out with since college, was an attorney with an overly generous heart. He accepted cases others wouldn't, and he took on a significant amount of pro bono work. His offices were borderline derelict, and he'd never met a sob story that didn't tug his heartstrings or hurt his wallet.

Because she helped out at his law center from time to time, Shelby knew he had spent months, if not a year, trying to get an appointment with Master Trevor. Along with mentoring entrepreneurs, the billionaire was a renowned philanthropist. But it wasn't easy to get past the layers of people who protected him from the thousands of requests he received each year. There was a formal process in place. So far, David had not made it to the second round of selection.

Time dragged, and Trevor checked his high-tech Bonds watch before settling his gaze back on her.

When nerves were turning her inside out, Mistress Aviana finally swept in, electrifying the air with her larger-than-life personality. This evening, she wore cowboy boots emblazoned with turquoise-colored sugar skulls. Her booty shorts and matching leather mini-top were decorated with fringe that glimmered when she moved. In addition to an oversize hat, she'd selected a turquoise duster jacket. As always, she was the most stunning woman in the place.

Out of respect, Trevor stood, and his dull silver spurs scraped the hardwood floor. He stood well over six feet tall and had impossibly broad shoulders. His tailored shirt showed his trim waist. But there was something even more compelling. The man was cloaked in an undeniable aura of command. In a club filled with Doms, he was the ultimate alpha.

Following suit, David, too, pushed back his chair. Unsure what she should do, Shelby remained in place, her heart thundering.

"Evening, Milady." Trevor kissed the Domme's hand.

His gentlemanly manners made Shelby want to swoon.

"Mistress Aviana." David acknowledged Mistress Aviana with a nod.

Several people had followed her into the area, and a few others wandered over to see what was happening.

"I understand an unusual bet has been proposed." She glanced first at David and then at Trevor.

"Indeed, Milady. Master David appears to be alarmingly low on funds."

Aviana looked at David.

He shrugged.

"I'm guessing he had an ulterior motive for sitting down at this particular table." Master Trevor angled his head to one side.

Earlier in the evening, there had been eight people playing Texas Hold'em. Now it was down to just David and Master Trevor.

"Master David?" Mistress Aviana asked.

David shot the imposing Domme a wry smile.

Shelby blinked. Could Trevor be right? Had David invited her to join him with the intention of wagering her?

"As I suspected." Trevor gave a sharp nod. "Nevertheless, I'm happy to continue the game, under David's terms."

"Most unusual." Mistress Aviana glanced at Shelby. "It's my understanding that Shelby is not an owned slave."

Aware that everyone was looking at her, Shelby raised up a bit and shifted uncomfortably. "That's…" After gulping down her nerves, she tried again. "That's correct, Milady."

"Therefore, it's not Master David's right to wager you."

"Unless Shel is willing," David added.

What? The scoundrel *had* planned this.

"Why don't you ask her?" David's voice was steady, as if he were confident in her answer.

Damn you. From conversations their group had shared, David knew Master Trevor fascinated her. And because she was friends with David, she knew how desperate he was for money.

"I agree with David," Master Trevor said into the pulsing silence. "I'm all about consent. Let's see what the sub wants."

A shiver of fear mixed with desire raced up her spine as

she and the terrifying Dom made eye contact again. He'd obviously noticed her sneaking peeks at him all night.

Intuition screamed at her to end this madness. But something more primal drove her. She was enjoying this. An unfulfilled part of her wanted all of his focus on her.

"Please come with me, Shelby." Mistress Aviana crooked her finger. "We need to have this discussion away from the table."

Swimming in confusion, Shelby looked toward Trevor—rather than David—for guidance.

He offered his hand. After a slight hesitation, she accepted. With restrained strength, he helped her up; then he pulled her toward him to capture her chin.

What would it be like to be in his arms?

She inhaled his barely tamed scent, drowning in his masculinity.

Then, so quiet that no one else could hear, he said, "Make no mistake, if you agree and I win, you will be mine for a week. Be careful with your decision, Shelby."

"Ah, I have work." It was an excellent excuse, but her traitorous mind spun with possibilities. "Well, I can reschedule some of my clients or get a colleague to cover for me so that I can have a couple of days off." There was one case, the Lemieux divorce, that no one else could take. This would be their third—and hopefully last—session. "Friday I have to be there."

"Understood. I'm not far from the city. You can commute from my house."

"Shelby?" Aviana prompted. "With me, please."

With seeming reluctance, Master Trevor released Shelby.

After shooting David a fierce scowl, she hurried after the club's owner.

Mistress Aviana, flanked by her most trusted dungeon monitor, Tore, strode past the bucking bronco that had been brought in for tonight's event, then pushed through a door leading to a more intimate part of the club. Then she continued to Rue Sensuelle—known by the regulars as Kinky Avenue. There were numerous small settings, separated by partitions, each designed to cater to a particular kink. A schoolroom, a boss's office, even an examination room. When they reached one that was unoccupied, Aviana waved Shelby inside.

Aware of the church pew in front of her, she squirmed.

"I'm not in the business of bartering submissives between two Doms who are indulging in a pissing contest."

Shelby grinned at Mistress Aviana's bluntness. "I understand, Milady."

"And I'm guessing you're not accustomed to being swapped between men?"

"Me?" The suggestion was ludicrous. Men did not vie for her attention. "No, Ma'am." She resisted the urge to draw the lapels of her vest even closer together, as if it could shield her from this uncomfortable meeting.

"Tell me how you'd like to proceed. If you don't want to be a pawn, I'll put a stop to their nonsense."

"I'm…" She twisted her hands in front of her. If David won, the money would be huge. And if Trevor won, she would have an experience she'd never forget.

Did she have enough courage to be bartered by two Doms?

"Shelby?"

"Yes." She bit her lower lip. "I'm willing."

"This must be a very exciting evening for you, in that case." The woman smiled. "I can vouch for Master Trevor. If he's out of line, he will answer to me."

"Thank you, Ma'am." Nervous about the evening's outcome, her feet leaden, Shelby followed Aviana as they returned to the table.

Tore stood off to one side. The dealer hadn't moved. David had pulled his few remaining chips closer to him. Master Trevor had a leg propped on top of the other, at ease, relaxed.

Now that she was back, she didn't know what to do.

As if intuiting her confusion, Master Trevor nodded toward the floor, about midway between himself and David.

Taking a breath, reassured by her potential Dom's confidence, she knelt.

Aviana glanced between both men. "I've spoken with Shelby, and I'm satisfied that she's agreeable."

"I can't tell you how delighted I am," Master Trevor said, the sound of his deep voice dancing shivers across her nerve endings.

Aviana folded her arms and nodded to the dealer. "You may proceed."

"Do we have a bet?" David asked.

"Indeed." Though he spoke to David, Master Trevor looked at her. "Indeed we do."

The dealer burned the next card before turning over the fifth—and final—one.

Shelby held her breath.

The jack of spades.

A couple of the spectators in the room whispered. There were three spades showing. Definitely the potential for a flush. With the jack, a straight was a possibility.

She looked at David. His eyes were wide, and a quick grin flashed across his face before he schooled it away.

She released her breath. David's work meant everything to him and many people in the New Orleans area. And it appeared he was going to get just that.

The dealer nodded to David. He turned over his pocket cards. The eight and nine of spades.

Yes. She grinned. His flush was likely unbeatable. No doubt, by tomorrow, he'd be planning his building's remodel.

Then, aware of the silence pulsing around them, she hazarded a glance at Master Trevor. Unlike David's, his face was set in unreadable lines.

"Sir?" The dealer signaled for Master Trevor to show his pocket cards.

Steady, betraying nothing, he flipped the two cards lying facedown on the felt.

Ace and queen of spades.

Royal flush.

She gasped as the room spun. David clamped a hand on her shoulder. *This...* She couldn't comprehend it. The odds against Master Trevor prevailing had been astronomical.

Seeking understanding, she looked at him.

He captured her gaze. In his eyes, she read reassurance and promise, two things she desperately needed.

"Well fucking played, Lawton." Then, seeming to draw on the same composure he used in the courtroom, David extended his hand toward Master Trevor. "Congratulations."

"Thank you." He stood. "I'm honored to have Shelby as mine."

Her tummy dropped.

David crouched in front of her. "Fuck, Shel. I'm sorry. I really thought I'd win."

For a moment, so had she.

"If I'd have thought…"

"I know." Which one of them was she trying to reassure? "It's okay."

"This could be a great opportunity for you," he added quietly.

"I'll take good care of her," Trevor promised.

David stood. "You're damn right you will." After another reassuring squeeze on her shoulder, he left.

"Game's over, everyone!" Mistress Aviana clapped her hands. "I invite you to partake in the unique pleasures of The Quarter."

Tore extended his arms wide to encourage the stunned spectators to walk away.

Because Master Trevor had yet to give her any instructions, Shelby remained on her knees, her gaze downcast as the noise in the room diminished.

At this point, she realized it was probably a good thing he hadn't given any commands. Adrenaline raced through her body, and she doubted she'd be able to follow any direction, no matter how simple.

"You're free to go," Mistress Aviana said to the dealer and Tore.

With sharp nods, they did as she said.

Mistress Aviana strode toward Trevor. "I trust this is only about you wanting to play with Shelby," she said to Master Trevor.

"She's under my protection."

"I expect nothing less," Mistress Aviana said. "As I told Shelby, this transaction happened at my club, so I have an obligation to her." To Shelby, she added, "If you need me, call."

"Thank you, Milady."

"We'd like to use a private room," Trevor said.

The words sent tiny shockwaves through Shelby. The private rooms were upstairs, and nudity was permitted. The club's safe word was always honored, and scenes were monitored. But the distance from the dungeon meant the players had much more intimacy.

"I'll have Trinity arrange one," Aviana replied.

"With your indulgence, I'd like to spend a few minutes here with Shelby first."

"No more than fifteen. We need to reset the area."

"Of course, Milady."

There was respect in Master Trevor's tone, but also finality. For him, the conversation was over.

The spiky heels from Mistress Aviana's boots clicked against the wooden floor as she left.

The sudden silence, the realization that they were alone and that for the next seven days she was his submissive, made Shelby's pulse echo in her ears.

"Before I take you upstairs, there are a few things I want to know about you."

Commanding, broad and beautiful, he loomed over her.

"Tell me about your relationship with Master David."

"We're friends, and there's never been anything more. We've never slept together or scened together. He's part of the group I went to college with. I've only been here a few times, and mostly it's for special events. Theme nights, in particular. I've never come by myself."

"Go on."

"Really? You want to hear all this."

His silence was unnerving. He'd told her what to do, and he'd meant it. "Anyway, we—my group of friends—make an evening out of it. Dinner. Then we sometimes go to breakfast before heading home." Shelby paused to drink in a breath. He continued to wait. "I guess I'm trying to say that David looks out for me." And he'd represented her during her divorce. "In the interest of full disclosure, I've done some work at his law center."

"Have you?"

"When possible, he likes to use mediators. It can sometimes resolve things quicker and less expensively than going to court."

"That's what you do?"

"Yes. I wish I could volunteer more time."

He drew his eyebrows together. "Volunteer?"

"Maybe you didn't know. Almost none of his clients can afford to pay him, which is why he's in a ridiculous amount of personal debt. The building he's in is old and crumbling. He puts in sixty-hour weeks and works harder than anyone I've ever known. He's… I don't know. Feels a personal obligation to be a savior. Most often, he's the last hope for most of his clients." Realizing she'd gone on too long, said too much, she exhaled. "What I'm trying to say is that I know how much winning the bet meant to him."

"I appreciate your loyalty and your honesty." Master Trevor crouched in front of her, then tipped back his rakishly perched hat. "So tell me this, my bold little sub. Would you have agreed to go home with any Dom who'd been prepared to make that kind of wager?"

"No," she admitted with some reluctance. "No, Sir."

He placed his finger beneath her chin, compelling her to look at him.

"Then it's personal?"

He was relentless in his quest for answers. She didn't have the courage to tell him the truth…that she was incredibly attracted to him or that she'd fantasized about him a thousand times. Frantically she searched for a safe answer. "You have a reputation as a Dominant who is demanding but fair."

"That's probably an accurate assessment." He lifted a shoulder in a shrug. "But that's hardly enough to put your life in my hands for a week."

His words sent a shiver through her. That was exactly what she was doing. "I've seen you play."

"Have you? Often?"

Every chance she had. "You seem confident. I don't know, maybe in tune with the women you play with." Focused and relentless. Swoonworthy. "I don't have much experience. Although I'm guessing you might have figured that out."

"The way you squirmed while David and I were playing the game? Your impatient sighs?"

He'd been studying her that closely?

"The way your gaze strayed all over the room?" He cracked a smile, transforming his features, taking any sting out of his words, and devastating her all over again.

He dragged a chair over. Not surprising her, he sat, but left her kneeling helplessly before him. "Tell me what you've done, what you'd like to repeat. What you'd rather not do again."

Because it made the conversation easier, she glanced down at his boots. Even though they appeared to be hand-tooled, they were marred, scratched by the years. The dark color of his jeans had faded slightly, meaning the denim had broken in, and now it hugged his strong thighs.

When she met his gaze again, she realized he'd never looked away from her. "Most times, I end up watching rather than participating."

"Are you a voyeur?"

"No. It's the dynamic that keeps me watching. There's a formality, isn't there? Or there can be." *The elegance by which you exert your control.* "The surrender." *Sometimes even passion.* She sighed. "Does this make any sense?"

"Anything you have to say, I want to hear. Keep going."

"The best way I can explain it is that there's a psychological dimension to BDSM play that I've never experienced. Fiona and Hannah—my friends—talk about it. Turning control over to someone else."

"I'm honored that you'd choose me."

Time stretched and twisted into a vortex of possibility. "I'm scared." She paused. "Nervous, a little. And..." Oh God, she was going to blurt it out. "But I don't know why you want me when you can play with anyone here."

"Woman, once I saw you, I had no other choice. I'm

attracted to everything about you." His quick smile softened him and calmed her fears. "Even your misbehavior."

In that moment, nothing existed but him. He was her whole world.

After a few seconds, he cleared his throat. "You've played privately?"

"No. Just here at the club."

"Impact play, then, I take it?"

"I've tried a paddle and a flogger." She paused, debating whether or not to go on. "I haven't told anyone else this…"

"You're safe with me. I appreciate your trust."

She lifted each knee in turn, fidgeting from mental, rather than physical, discomfort. "You asked what I didn't like. One Top used a tawse on me. It hurt like hell, and I didn't enjoy it." While she struggled to express herself, Trevor remained quiet. He steepled his index fingers and regarded her in a way that told her he'd wait forever if that was what she needed. Shelby sipped from the cup of courage he offered. "It comes back to the psychological implications that I was talking about. I was being daring, and I expected something wonderful. But it was awful. Then it was over. I was in some pain the next day. You know, as if you've worked out too hard. And I had bruises that lasted for days. Instead of pleasure that I'd had before, I was disappointed." She sucked in a breath. "I'm rambling."

"Not at all. Did you have any aftercare?"

"He had someone else waiting for his attention, so I thanked him for the scene, then went and changed. I went out to eat with Fiona and Master Andrew before driving home." She'd been unable to fall asleep, even after a long soak in a hot bathtub. "I haven't played since."

"You haven't…? At all?"

"No."

"Did you talk to anyone? The friends you mentioned?"

She shook her head. "I'm hoping that wasn't a typical experience. So I want to give it one more chance."

"You really *are* bold."

"Am I?" The gruff praise woven in his voice sent her pulse into a frenzy. She wanted more and more of it, even if she pretended nonchalance. "Maybe I just want to find out if it can be as good as some people insist it can be. I've heard of subspace. In fact, I've seen people who seem lost in a scene."

"Once again, I'm honored you chose me. Thank you." He stood and extended a hand toward her.

After fighting back the sudden knot of nerves in her tummy, she reached for him.

CHAPTER 2

When Shelby slid her palm against his, the electricity of her trust—hot and powerful—arced through Trevor.

She blinked up at him, and she took in a sharp breath. Did the connection rock her as much as it did him?

Jesus.

What the ever-living fuck was happening here?

Life had taught him to be cool and calculating. He didn't make ridiculous wagers. And he never allowed his dick to do his thinking for him.

But from the second Shelby had awkwardly knelt near the table, he hungered for her.

It wasn't a maybe. It was a driving, consuming need.

She'd been fidgety, and not nearly close enough for him to touch her, even though he'd wanted to. He'd known he could reassure her by lacing his fingers in her hair or simply caressing her shoulders.

As the evening progressed, he caught the beautiful wannabe sub looking at him. There was innocence in her wide green eyes, captivating him, grabbing him by the jugular, refusing to let go. That—maybe—he could have ignored.

But when her beautiful lips parted slightly, he imagined her beneath him, her hands pinned above her head. Her surrender to his demands would be total and oh so damn sweet.

For the first time in his life, he shoved aside his rules—about women, submissives, money—just to spend some time with her.

And now, she was his. *For one week.*

Trevor helped her up. She was so damn small, lighting up his protective synapses. "Do you want me to call you Shelby?"

"Yes."

With a small grin, he cocked his head.

"I mean..." She cleared her throat. "Shelby is fine, Sir. Thank you."

"Is it a scene name?" For numerous reasons, protecting their identities, or because it gave them more mental or emotional freedom, some people selected alter identities for their time at the club.

She shook her head. "No. Shelby Maria Virginia Salazar, if you want to be formal." Then she smiled, dazzling him. "My parents couldn't decide which grandmother's name to use as my middle name, so they selected both."

"Wise choice, I'm sure." He took a moment to drink her in and savor the way her thick dark hair flowed down her back. Though he appreciated her very sexy outfit and soft pink leather boots with spiky heels, it was her feminine curves and slightly open mouth that crashed testosterone through his bloodstream. It had been months—years—since he'd had such a raw reaction to a woman. "I'd like to look at you." With reluctance that surprised him, he released her. "Will you turn for me, please?"

She did, exposing her bottom to him. When she faced him again, her eyes were downcast, as if uncertain of his reaction.

"You're captivating, Shelby Salazar."

"I'm…" She shifted her weight from foot to foot. "Thank you, Sir."

He waited.

Without prompting, but with vulnerability making her tremble, she met his gaze. "Being looked at makes me a little uncomfortable. I want to be bold, but then I can't seem to make myself take the actions."

With the way she watched, rather than participated, he should have guessed that. Suddenly he was glad he'd asked for a private room. "I hope that after we've played together, you'll be able to see yourself the way I see you."

"I… Maybe. Sir." Her half smile was forced and perhaps disbelieving.

That, he hoped to change. "If you're ready, I'd like to get you upstairs."

"Uhm… Yes. Of course, Sir." Her voice wobbled.

"We'll need to collect my toy bag from the coat check." Because he wanted everyone to know she was his, he offered his elbow.

After blinking away her obvious surprise, she accepted.

They emerged from the makeshift room into the thunderous noise of the main dungeon.

This evening, there was a lasso competition, with squealing, giggling submissives as the target. A mechanical bronco situated among large crash pads was the dungeon's main feature.

Shelby stopped and pointed. "My friend is next in line."

"Would you like to watch?"

"Really? You don't mind?"

"Not at all."

They joined the circle of spectators. "That's your friend? Master Andrew's new submissive?"

"You know him?"

He leaned in close to hear her over the thumping music.

"Wait." She held up a hand. "Of course. You probably know most of the people here."

Trevor knew that Andrew was besotted with the woman. Over drinks at the club's bar one night, he'd confessed to wanting to collar her. So far, Fiona had resisted the idea, much to Andrew's utter frustration.

Until tonight, Trevor hadn't been tempted to claim that kind of responsibility.

Shelby moved in closer to him to watch while Andrew accompanied Fiona toward the contraption.

The operator gave directions, and then Andrew assisted Fiona into position, and she tucked her hand beneath the strap.

In response to something Andrew said, she scooted forward.

After Fiona nodded, Andrew stepped aside, and the operator turned on the machine.

People cheered as she threw her free arm in the air to counterbalance the bronc's rocking and spinning.

One of Fiona's breasts, the nipple covered with a sparkling pasty, slipped out of her bra cup.

"Yee-haw!" a man shouted.

Fiona held on for a few more seconds before being tossed unceremoniously into the air. She landed on the thick crash pad with an oomph and a giggle. Before she could stand, Andrew was there to help.

"Eighteen seconds!" the operator called. "Well done!"

While blocking her from view, Master Andrew adjusted her top to safely tuck away her breast.

The next sub climbed aboard the piece of metal, and

Shelby rose up on her tiptoes to talk to him. "That looks like fun," she said.

"Maybe you should try."

She looked at the bronco, then back at him. "I'm not sure I have enough courage. And the whole thing with being the center of attention."

Now that she'd mentioned it, he was intrigued by the idea of watching her shift her weight as the operator turned up the speed on the ride, making her writhe and twist.

Fiona, face flushed and grinning widely, pointed toward them. When Master Andrew nodded his permission, she made a beeline toward them.

"You did great!" Shelby said.

"It was a total blast." Fiona grinned. "Except for the chafing on my inner thighs."

"Good thing you're a masochist, pet," Andrew commented as he joined them.

"Yes, Sir." She giggled.

Trevor shook the other man's hand.

"Have you met my…" He paused and cleared his throat. "Fiona?"

"A pleasure," Trevor said.

She offered a cute little curtsy to go with her big smile. No wonder his friend was intrigued by her.

"We saw David and heard what happened. With the card game." Fiona ignored both men in favor of focusing on Shelby. "You look like you're okay with this. Are you?"

"A bit nervous." Her voice wasn't as unsteady as earlier. "But yes."

"Meet me for brunch tomorrow?" Fiona squeezed Shelby's hand. "I want to hear all about it. Like, everything."

Shelby looked up at him. And he liked that she'd consulted him. "Perhaps next Sunday might be better?" he suggested.

She flushed. "Uh…yes. I'll be with Master Trevor this week."

"You can't be serious! I thought it was just for tonight!" Fiona's mouth opened into a wide O. "David didn't tell us that. Rat bastard. How dare he do that to you? A whole week?"

"Why don't you visit us?" Trevor suggested to defuse Fiona's growing ferocity. "Tuesday? Wednesday? After work? Evening cocktails on my pontoon boat?"

"Really?" Fiona blinked. "That sounds awesome." Then she hesitated for a moment. "Would you like to go also?" she asked Andrew.

Andrew nodded.

"Bring a swimsuit if you'd like to jump in the pool or the lake," Trevor suggested.

After settling on Wednesday night at six, he lightly touched Shelby's spine. "If you'll excuse us?"

She shuddered, something he wouldn't have known if his fingers weren't on her bare skin.

Fiona gave her a quick hug and whispered something into her ear.

"I promise," Shelby said as the hug ended.

Andrew and Fiona remained where they were, watching as the next volunteer walked toward the innocent-looking mechanical horse.

"Thank you for inviting them out. That was really nice of you," Shelby said when they neared the coat check. "I know it will make Fiona feel better too."

Shelby's happiness was worth anything to him.

After picking up his play bag, they made their way to the second floor where they checked in with the dungeon monitor standing behind a podium.

"You're in number six, Master Trevor. Mistress Aviana scheduled you for an hour."

Which wouldn't be nearly long enough. "Thank you."

Trevor guided Shelby toward the end of the hallway. When they reached the correct room, he closed the door behind them. The sudden silence wrapped them like a cocoon.

While he placed his bag on the metal side table, Shelby wandered to the middle of the floor and folded her arms around herself. When he turned toward her, she cast a nervous glance at the spanking bench, then back at him.

The sturdy piece had a tall, thin center beam and two other beams, one on each side, so her knees would be supported. Red vinyl covered the horse, and it was artfully decorated with two dozen metal rings. There was no limit to the ways he could secure her.

He opened his bag and removed a small flogger that she eyed warily. "Do you have a safe word?"

"You'll laugh." She tore her gaze away from the implement to meet his eyes. "Tangerine."

"Tangerine?" he repeated. Despite his attempt to remain neutral, he grinned. "It's unique. You'll actually remember it during a scene?"

"I hate tangerines," she said. "I'd never forget that."

He laid the toy on the table. "And how about a word for slow?"

"I'll go with yellow."

"Did you use either the evening you were subjected to the tawse?"

"No."

He walked toward her. "Is there a reason for that?"

"I know this is ridiculous, but I was afraid of disappointing him."

"Listen to me, Shelby." Gently he took hold of her shoulders and rubbed his thumbs in tiny circles. Her skin was like silk, and she deserved to get what she wanted. "You will never disappoint a Dominant by using a safe word. We're not assholes. I don't want you to do something or act heroic because you think it will make me happy. It won't. In fact, it will piss me off."

She scowled.

"I mean it. Scening together, playing, isn't meant to torture you. Yes, I may encourage you to try things, do things that push your comfort zone. But I never, ever want you to cross your boundaries. Not for me. Not for any man." He stopped moving his thumbs. "Tell me you understand."

"I'll try."

He needed more than that. "Shelby, the scene won't be fun for me if you suffer needlessly. It won't deepen our relationship, and in fact, it will destroy trust. Hearing your secrets is an incredible turn-on. That takes more guts than remaining silent. Is that possible?"

"You ask for a lot, Master Trevor."

"I do. Your emotional honesty. Your vulnerability." Maybe there was nothing more difficult.

"I..." She twisted her fingers together. "I'll do my best. That's all I can promise."

His pulse accelerated. "I'll be watching you, but I don't have psychic powers."

"There goes my whole fantasy. Up in smoke." Her words were light, laced with a teasing air. "Trying to defuse the situation? I thought Doms were all knowing, all powerful."

Negotiating was too serious for joking. "This is a two-way relationship, Shelby. You have to be an active participant."

Her slender shoulders trembled a little, showing she understood what he'd said and revealing her trepidation. Despite that, she tipped back her head. Her beautiful eyes, the color of uncut spring grass, were wide, unblinking with no pretense, no artifice.

Trevor had told her he appreciated her trust, but it was so much more than that. She humbled him. The emotion plowed into him, hard. He'd worked hard for everything he had, sacrificing years of his life in pursuit of his dreams. He'd been driven, allowing nothing to get in his way.

But now the weight of the responsibility he had for Shelby settled over him. He waited for the obligation to chafe. It didn't. Instead, he wanted it. Embraced it.

Silently he vowed not to fail her.

Very slowly, he released his grip on her. "Is there anything I need to know? Medical or physical conditions, perhaps?"

"None."

He nodded. "How about your limits? Hard and soft."

"To be honest, I don't really know. That's embarrassing, right?" She wrapped herself a little tighter. "Canes terrify me. I can't even watch those scenes. There's something about the sound of them, even." She shivered. "And I don't want to do anything that will break my skin."

"Understood. And is the tawse a limit?"

"Actually it's…" A small line formed between her eyebrows. "No. I might be willing to try it again, with you. But…"

He waited, giving her time to sort through her answer.

"I guess I want to be more than a random sub who gets spanked and forgotten."

The soft pain in her voice gutted him. "I'll tell you this, Shelby. You are not the type of woman to be easily forgotten."

She gave him a half smile. Trevor was suddenly a greedy man. He wanted a dozen more.

He extended his hand, and she finally lowered her arms. "Come with me."

She slipped her hand into his, and he drew her toward the side table. He liked having her close, her scent, that of innocence and unconscious seduction. Trevor wanted to wrap his hand in her hair and kiss her deep. Later, he planned to do exactly that. "I want you to unpack my things. As you take each toy out, talk to me about it. Let me know if you're interested in trying it. Place it off to the left if you're not. If you're unsure or it's a soft limit, place it in the middle of the table. We can discuss those at another time. The things you want to start with should go on the far right side." He picked up the small flogger and dropped it back in the bag. "Whenever you're ready."

"I think I'd prefer if you just showed me what's in there."

"Why is that?"

"This seems too personal."

"Ah, Shelby. Everything we do for the next week is going to be personal." To the extreme. "I intend to explore every part of you, excavate your deepest secrets."

She shivered as she looked up at him. "Should I be scared?"

"Should you?"

For a second, neither of them blinked.

Her eyes darkened, as if a storm approached. "You might not like what you find."

Shelby's words were light, but the apprehension hiding behind them was real. Suddenly he wanted to take away anything in her past that had hurt her. "Maybe I will." He lifted a shoulder in a shrug. "It's a risk I'm willing to take."

"I hope you're not disappointed, Master Trevor."

He liked the way she said his name, with respect, maybe a hint of admiration. Holy hell. She was stunning. "I won't be."

"Uh, we didn't discuss sex." She knotted her hands into tight little fists at her sides.

"Go on."

"Will you expect us to sleep together?"

"You are utterly desirable."

At his words, she trembled. He liked that he had that power over her. "But I want to make it clear that I don't expect you to engage in intercourse. I'd never demand that from you. Sex and scening do not have to go together, and as you know, very often they don't. But if you'd like it, I'm more than happy to make love to you. Take you. Make you mine."

"I'm...not on birth control."

"Understood. I will always protect you, Shelby."

"Well, then, if it works out, we can. I mean, that is, if we both want to."

Trevor winced. He'd never lacked for willing romantic partners. Her nonchalance was nearly a mortal blow to his ego. "I promise you this—when, if, we have sex, you will desire me every bit as much as I desire you."

"I didn't mean to imply that I didn't..." She blushed and turned away. "I mean, you're a very handsome man."

Her hesitant, honest words soothed him, making him grin. Oh yes. Most definitely, he intended to have her. "Whenever you're ready, please continue."

After nodding and uncurling her hands, she opened his bag wider.

The first thing she picked up was the small flogger. "I think I'm interested in trying this."

"Excellent choice."

After a soft breath, she pulled out a Wartenberg wheel. "I saw one of these at a vendor show a couple of months ago."

At theme nights, the club often allowed members to showcase their wares. "Curious?" When she didn't respond, he suggested, "Try it. On your palm. Then if you like it, on your arm."

She did. "It's not as intense as I thought it would be."

"It can be, depending on the amount of pressure used. May I?"

She blinked but dropped it into his open hand.

"Will you take off your vest?"

After a slight hesitation, she shrugged out of it, and he placed it on the side table. Then he drew the spiky metal wheel across the enticing flesh of her right breast, above her bra cup.

Her gaze followed his action.

"Harder?" His question was soft and inviting.

"Uhm…" After a moment, she nodded. "Yes."

He liked her boldness. He retraced his motion, this time with enough force that she sucked in a shallow breath. "Yellow?" he asked. "Tangerine?"

"No. In fact, it's amazing." She frowned, as if searching for the right words. "As if my skin is alive. On fire."

He offered the handle back to her.

Without hesitation, she laid the medical toy next to the flogger before taking a breath and pulling out a set of lightweight tweezer nipple clamps. She tipped her head to the side, as if considering.

"Well?"

"Maybe."

He nodded.

Next she fished out his most serious pair of Japanese clovers meant for advanced players.

"These are an absolute no. No, nope, no. No. Hell no, even." Shelby shook her head so furiously that he grinned.

"Good to know."

She dropped them, and the strike of metal on metal jarred the silence.

Hurriedly she reached in again.

With a frown, she placed a bottle of lube in the middle of the table. Then she withdrew a small metal butt plug. "Oh. God."

He watched her reaction—a wrinkled nose, and again, that curious tilt of her head.

"I don't know what to say about this." She studied it, then looked at him.

"Soft limit?"

"I don't know."

"Meaning?" When she hesitated, he asked, "You've never played anally?"

She pushed out a soft breath. "No."

"As in zero experience? No fingering? Tonguing?"

"Absolutely not."

Shocking him, a small blush crept up her cheekbones.

Trevor was captivated. In that moment, he realized how jaded he was. He scened with women who knew what they wanted and were forthright about it. This—being the first to introduce her to certain experiences—would demand something new from him. Patience. And it gave him a thrill he'd never found outside of his financial pursuits.

Realizing she was still holding the toy and looking to him for some sort of guidance, he brought himself back to the present. "Is it something you want to place off-limits, or would you be willing to try, given the right circumstances?"

Her blush deepened. "Can we talk about that later?"

"Of course. For now, put it in the consider pile?"

Rather than drop it, she placed it carefully before pulling out a blindfold. Unhesitatingly that went on the yes side of the table.

She fished around until she found his dragon's tail. "Maybe."

"We'll have plenty of time in the next week to explore everything." The two sets of restraints were an immediate yes. *Interesting.*

When the bag was empty, she hugged her shoulders and dug her fingers into her skin. Nervous tension radiated from her in heated waves. "Now what, Sir?"

"First of all, take a breath. Wait on my direction." He tucked a strand of hair behind her ear. "Practice stillness."

She puffed out a gentle scoff. "I don't think you have any idea what you're asking for."

"Perhaps I do." Intensifying her emotions. Heightening her physical responses. Engaging her emotions. Expanding her psychological awareness. "I want to see more of your body. Look at it. Touch it. Begin to explore it. I appreciate that it may be difficult for you. But it's going to happen, unless you need to refuse."

Her eyes were unblinking. She was going to push through this. His heart responded with several rapid thuds. "You're doing great. When you're ready, please drop your hands to your sides."

Slowly she did as he asked, her chest rising and falling in shallow motions.

"Concentrate on me. The sound of my voice. Block out anything—everything—except what I instruct you to do."

"I'm not sure I can hear anything over the sound of my heart racing."

He offered a reassuring smile. "I'll repeat my commands if necessary."

"Thank you, Sir."

Her voice, tremulous, deep from a combination of anxiety and anticipation, was like a drug in his veins. "Please turn around and spread your legs as far as you can and bend over."

She hesitated before complying. "This is more difficult than anything I've done with any other Dom here."

"Because I'm really seeing you? There's no one else waiting for my attention. You matter to me."

"That's the problem." Her voice trembled with vulnerability. "I don't want to disappoint you."

"You won't." He remained where he was.

"Nerves are killing me."

"That's okay. It means the scene matters to you too."

She nodded. Then, quickly, as if scared she might change her mind if she thought too long about it, she turned and bent into the position he required. Her dark hair cascaded onto the floor, and her pink panties stretched taut over her derriere.

"Can you spread your legs a little farther?" It would expose her more, and she would be concentrating on following his order rather than anything else. "Shelby?"

"Yes." She wiggled on those sexy heels, and he enjoyed every moment spent watching.

Trevor took a step toward her and outlined the tender spots where her silky panties snuggled the tops of her thighs. Her breathing increased. "Lovely. Now reach back and part your ass cheeks for me."

It took her so long to respond that he wondered if she actually would.

Gently, he placed his hands on her hips. "Over the next week, I want to learn everything there is to know about you. I'm suspecting some of it will make you uncomfortable. But if my guess is right, you want that as much as I do, even if it's scary as fuck."

She nodded.

After several seconds and clenching her buttocks tight, she reached back.

"I won't touch your ass while we're here."

Slowly she relaxed.

"That's right. Give yourself to me." Anal play would take discussion and plenty of preparation. In the end, though, he would claim her there as fully as he did everywhere else.

He bunched the gusset of her underwear and moved it to the side. Then he took one of her hands and moved it to the thin scrap of fabric. "Hold it there."

Though she trembled, she did as he said.

"Everything about you is gorgeous." Her fingernails were a striking shade of hot pink. The sight of the bold color nails against her gorgeous olive skin made his cock throb. He hadn't had a sub, or any woman, in months. Suddenly he wanted to take her fast and hard, possess her, claim her, mark her as his for the entire damn world to see. What the hell had gotten into him?

Trevor shook his head. He couldn't let the sweet, sexy image of her make him react as a caveman. After clearing his throat, he tried to regain control. "Stand up slowly and turn toward me."

Her motions had a bit more elegance to them than they had a moment ago, thrilling him.

After she faced him, she instinctively looked down.

"So beautifully done, Shelby." He'd studied her after the poker game. Now he allowed himself the time to appreciate her.

Her unruly hair fell over the feminine curve of her shoulders. She had a lovely, kissable neck, and the mother-of-pearl concha lay alluringly against her throat, making him think, for a dizzying moment, of seeing her in his collar.

Where the fuck had that idea come from? He'd never put a collar on a woman, even temporarily.

Realizing she was waiting for him with no idea of his inner turmoil, he forced his focus back to her. "Please remove your bra." For now, for his sanity, the chaps, panties, and the tantalizing little boots could stay.

She reached behind her to unfasten the clasp, then shrugged off the straps and allowed the silky fabric to fall to the floor.

Her breasts were lush, and her beautifully dark nipples were hard. "And your bolo tie, so it's not in the way."

After she removed it, she shook her head, tumbling the riotous mess of her hair over her shoulders.

When he arrived this evening, he'd thought he might opt for a short scene with a willing submissive. He had no idea he'd be thoroughly ensnared by a woman who knew nothing about her own power.

She handed over the bolo, and he placed it in a side pocket of his bag.

When he returned to her, he cupped her breasts and lifted them before flicking his thumb pads over her nipples.

Her knees bent. "Oh, Sir."

Because her breathing had increased a little, he did it again, this time a little harder. "You like this."

"Yes." The word was half whisper, half moan.

He left her for a moment and returned with the Wartenberg wheel. "Keep your hands by your sides. If it's easier, you may fold them behind you. In fact, do that. It will pull your shoulders back." Which would force her breasts out. "That's it."

Trevor held one of her breasts in a cupped palm, then bent his head to suck one of her nipples. The bud stiffened as he swirled his tongue around it, and she swayed toward him.

When he eased back, she moaned.

"I'd take more of that, Sir."

"Would you? Seems you can be a greedy little submissive." He grinned.

In return, she gave him a small smile.

This was unique and welcomed. Teasing with a play partner, watching the tension drain from her body as they formed a bond with each other.

He circled her nipple with the spikes of the wheel, guiding it with his purposeful touch, methodical and light.

Her mouth parted a little.

With a small nod, he applied a little more pressure and went across her taut flesh.

"Damn." Shelby made no attempt to pull away. In fact, she moved in a little.

Taking his time, he went a little deeper. Her eyes glazed over as she surrendered.

After a minute or so, she closed her eyes. Trevor used that opportunity to stop what he was doing.

Instantly, she blinked, then tipped her head to one side to study him.

"We're just beginning," he promised.

They had most of an hour still ahead of them, then days for him to awaken her senses.

Suddenly that thought was all-consuming.

CHAPTER 3

Shelby tingled with the awareness of Trevor's power. Beneath those terrifying but delicious spikes of metal, her nerve endings had lit up. Her nipples were harder than she ever remembered.

When she agreed to be part of the wager, Shelby had no idea of what she was getting into.

Even though she knew of Master Trevor's reputation, she hadn't been prepared for the effects he would have on her.

Surprising her most, he was kinder than she'd anticipated. She expected him to waste little time getting to know her or her likes. Of course, he'd ask about limits and safe words. That much she expected.

But he hadn't stopped there.

It was as if he wanted to know all of the things that pleased her. His probing questions broke down her defenses, stripping her bare. It wasn't just physically, in the way he'd exposed her pussy to him; it was so much more. His firm gentleness chipped away at her emotions. Her fear crumbled beneath his patience. And that made him much more dangerous than any Dom she'd ever met. Any *Dom?* Any *man*.

"We'll play with this more later." He walked toward the table to put down the wheel. His booted footsteps were loud on the floor. Unnaturally so, thundering in the silence.

He returned to stand in front of her.

She tipped back her head to look at him. His eyes were a shade or two lighter than when he'd won the bet. She saw keen interest there. Her heart ricocheted. It wasn't just from fear. Now it was the tendrils of genuine excitement. Maybe he was capable of giving her what she wanted.

"When you're ready, I want you on the spanking bench."

His voice... God. The timbre was deep and resonant with command. Despite his tenderness, he was a Dom who expected to be obeyed. She shivered at the realization. "Yes, Sir."

Previous Doms had tied her to St. Andrew's crosses, so the newness of this contraption left her uncertain.

"Your head will be toward the far wall, and I want your knees on either side. You'll rest your torso on the top plank."

Appreciating his very specific instructions, she took his hand. As she did, something glittered beneath the light. For the first time she really noticed the ring he wore. At first she assumed it was from the college he attended, but it was unlike anything she'd ever seen. The top was shaped like an owl, with piercing green eyes.

"Everything all right?"

"Your ring...it's unusual."

"I'll tell you about it sometime."

As she nodded, she climbed into place.

"So beautiful. Exquisite," he murmured when she lowered herself onto her stomach. "But stick your rear end out a little farther."

Embarrassment sent spirals of heat through her as she wiggled into position.

"You're sexy as hell, woman. I love having you in this position."

Over her panties, he rubbed between her legs. No other Dom had done this. Her scenes had been perfunctory, not… this. Pleasure made her clit ache.

"Are you getting wet for me?"

"Yes." She moaned.

He pushed the material aside, and his calloused skin abraded her tender flesh, rough against smooth, making her delirious.

"Could you come for me, sweet Shelby?"

Lost, she squeezed her eyes closed. It was as if he knew her body better than she did.

"I think you could. How long would it take you? Sixty seconds? Thirty?" Then he moved his hand away.

Involuntarily she cried out and pushed herself backward, begging for more.

"That's what I was hoping for." He skimmed a palm down her buttock.

Instead of soothing her, his touch kept her aflame.

"Would you like to be tied?"

Since she already knew that staying in place would be a challenge, she nodded. "Yes, Sir."

When he left her, the skin at the small of her back cooled. It was then that she realized he'd kept a hand on her the entire time he played with her pussy.

A few seconds later, he wrapped one of the fabric strips around her right ankle, outside her boot, then secured her to one of the hooks.

Without being prompted, she tested the bond.

He'd adjusted the length of the strap so that she'd have a little slack. After he secured her left ankle, he crouched next to her. He tucked errant strands of hair behind her ear. "Are you doing okay?"

"A little nervous." Especially now that the scene was going to get more real.

"Concentrate on your breathing." He skimmed his fingers down her bare arm, reassuring her. "In and out."

Her first few breaths were shaky.

"Another. Deeper."

On her exhalation, she relaxed a little, letting the spanking bench take more of her weight.

"That's it. Exactly right."

His approval went to her head, making her senses sing.

"How about your wrists? Would you like them tied?"

"I think so."

"Until you're absolutely certain, we'll leave them loose."

She turned her head to the side so she could study him. He was so large, uncompromising. But his eyes were dark, inviting trust.

"Because we're new to each other, I'm taking your hesitation as a no. If you change your mind, all you need to do is ask."

As best as she could, she nodded her understanding.

"And a blindfold?"

That might help her shut out the world so she could give herself over to the experience more fully. "Yes. Please, Sir."

Before he collected one, he shocked her by moving behind her to play with her pussy again. It took a single stroke on her sensitive clit to shove her toward the precipice again. She moaned.

"Should I make you wait?"

Her mind slogged through a sensual fog.

She could barely think, let alone speak. Her thoughts were a tangled mess from his deliberate and teasing onslaught.

He was masterful. He read her body language perfectly,

and each brush, every stroke was calculated to arouse. There would be no hiding from him.

"Tell me what you want."

"I want…"

He cupped her pussy.

"Please, Sir. Give me an orgasm."

"One. And a million more."

She closed her eyes and turned herself over to him. Trevor teased, then gently pinched, circled, and pressed.

This experience was completely new, arousal as part of their playtime. Her other Doms had been perfunctory. But this… She was in the position he wanted, with her ankles secured, and he was focused on bringing her pleasure.

As he brought her closer and closer to a climax, embarrassment was shoved aside by the primal beat of her desire.

Nothing existed but Trevor and his determination.

He fisted her underwear and wedged the material higher, lifting her, searing her clit. Then he slipped a finger inside her heated pussy.

"Oh, God!" Sights and sounds swirled through her mind. Captured by him, she floundered.

He found her G-spot and pressed against it.

She screamed as the orgasm tore through her.

Shelby bucked, desperate for more and equally as desperate to escape and curl into herself so she could recover.

But Trevor wasn't done with her. Instead, he continued his relentless onslaught.

"I"—she gasped—"can't!"

"Let's see."

She'd never been capable of coming more than once a night. But when he sucked on her clit, she went rigid, then collapsed, eyes wide open, unable to speak.

Seconds later, grinning, he crouched next to her. "Yeah."

He pressed a finger against his lips and captured some of her essence. "Evidently you're capable of giving me what I demand."

He touched her mouth, and she tasted herself on him.

"Lick it off me."

She did. Once again, he was so matter of fact that she experienced pleasure, solely because he enjoyed it. She'd had no idea that being with a Dom could be so perfect.

"You said yes to a blindfold, but I'm exercising my Dominant's prerogative and refusing. I like seeing your eyes, watching them go hazy. And I don't want you hiding your reactions when I use the flogger on you."

She was hungry for it in a way that stunned her.

"We'll start with a couple of hundred strokes."

"Hundred?" She sought his gaze, hoping he was joking.

But his jaw was set in a firm line. "I won't disappoint you," he promised.

Cool air whispered from the overhead vents, chilling her overheated body.

"I'm going to start really slow. Let go of your fear. Surrender to the experience."

"Easy for you to say." Then, in a whisper, she added, "Sir."

"I've got you, Shelby. I promise." He rubbed her rear gently, then, over time, a little more vigorously.

Despite her efforts to stay still, she moved and squirmed against the horse. Even that small contact made her pussy wet all over again.

"That's what I'm looking for, what it's all about. Your arousal." He strode to the table to collect the flogger, and he returned with it in hand, moving it in an elegant figure-eight pattern.

"Are you ready?"

Searching somewhere deep for trust, she curled her right hand into a fist.

"I'm waiting for your answer."

"I'm ready, Sir."

The first soft leather throng danced on her skin, a whisper and promise.

"How's that?"

"It was…nothing." Barely there.

"Perfect."

He caught her other buttock in a similar caress.

This shouldn't be possible.

Master Trevor continued, on and on, with a trace more sensation as the minutes passed. As if she were getting a massage, she let go, surrendering her weight, giving herself to her Dom.

"You're at two hundred."

Was she? The only thing she knew was that it wasn't enough. "More, Sir."

"That's my girl."

He continued, and she breathed in time with each leathery kiss. Her body warmed again. Then it blazed as the flogger landed more frequently and the bites were deeper. She screamed, from pleasure, not pain.

Seconds later, it was over, and his mouth was on her pussy.

He pleasured her. Devoured her.

She cried out as an orgasm catapulted her over the edge.

When she opened her eyes, her Dom was there, crouched next to her, stroking her hair.

She blinked him into focus, drowned in his deep blue eyes, and inhaled his masculinity, the intoxication of a sultry Southern night. "Hey."

"Hey, yourself." He unfastened the ankle closest to her.

"Was that really more than two hundred?"

"Three. Maybe four."

"I didn't think I could do that." And crave more.

"This is only the beginning. Over the next week, you'll get to find out how much more you can take."

The confidence in his words should have made her shudder. Instead, anticipation rushed through her.

Shelby was so relaxed that she didn't move while he released her other bond. When he was done, she tried to lift her head.

"Stay there."

As if she could move.

"This shade of red suits you." He rubbed her buttocks. "I'll ensure you're decorated with it every day."

She shivered.

Across the room, Trevor started to repack his bag. Fascinated by his efficient motions, she watched his every move.

When he was finished, he returned to help her up from the spanking bench. As if knowing how the world was shifting around her, he held on to her until she was steady on her feet, before fastening her bra back into place.

Trevor slipped the bolo tie over her head, then tightened it until the conch once again rested at the hollow of her throat. "I'd like you to wear a collar for the next week. A physical reminder of your agreement."

"I..." She curled her hand around the silver medallion.

"It's nothing permanent." He shrugged. "Symbolic."

"But important to you."

"To us both, I hope." He rearranged her hair, untucking it from beneath the tie. "It will be something you'll keep on until I remove it next Saturday."

Her heart raced. "Yes." She could do that for him.

"I have a room at the Maison Sterling tonight. I thought we'd stay there."

"Really?" Her budget had never allowed for that. She'd attended a going-away party for a colleague there. Even though others booked rooms so they could enjoy all the delights of the French Quarter, she drove home. Nothing about this evening—or this man—was ordinary.

"Shall we?"

Slowly she released her grip on the conch.

While she wiped down the spanking bench, he closed his bag. Now, more than ever, she wanted to try some of the other implements. Would a week be enough?

She exited the room in front of him, but he walked beside her as they descended the staircase, ignoring the scenes happening at Rue Sensuelle where Mistress Aviana had talked to her.

In the dungeon's main room, there was currently no waiting line for the bucking bronco. She brushed a hand over her chaps to smooth imaginary wrinkles from them.

As if sensing her intrigue, he stopped. "Earlier you said you didn't like being watched."

She glanced around. People were engaged in their own scenes or talking with friends. "I'll admit…"

Trevor leaned down so he could speak directly into her ear. "It's twenty, maybe thirty seconds at most."

Shelby scowled. "I doubt I could make it that long!"

"You didn't think you could take two hundred lashes from my flogger either."

Excitement and nerves warred in her, pummeling her with adrenaline. She glanced at the contraption, then the ride's operator.

He doffed his hat, then used it to beckon her toward him.

As was becoming a custom, she glanced toward Trevor, seeking…something. Approval? Encouragement?

His eyes were dark with interest. "It's a night of firsts."

"Do you want me to do it?"

The operator flipped on a switch, and the bronco made a slow, nonthreatening circle.

"I will never coerce you into anything."

"But…"

"You'll look hotter than hell. All that wriggling." He adjusted his cowboy hat. "Jiggling."

She rolled her eyes as she laughed. "Why doesn't that response surprise me?"

"I'm a helpless man, captive to your spell, sexy Shelby."

The earnest tone in his voice, the lack of a teasing spark, was the final encouragement she needed. Others might look at her, but Trevor, her Dom for the next seven days, was the only man she was aware of. All night, he'd showed his appreciation for her, chased away her embarrassment. "I'm in."

"Slaying your fears."

It was easier with him by her side.

Her steps faltered a little as she neared the bucking bronco. The closer she drew, the larger it loomed.

"Remember it's supposed to be fun," Trevor said.

But now she knew why they were a mainstay in bars. This would be much easier if she'd been drinking.

After placing his bag on the floor, Trevor wrapped his hands around her waist. He enveloped her in his strength and heat, and suddenly she wanted him to touch her entire body.

"Ready?"

When she nodded, he effortlessly lifted her and swung her into the saddle.

For that moment, while he looked at her, the world around them ceased to exist.

"Thank you," she managed.

The operator offered a pink leather glove, and Trevor accepted it, holding it while she slipped it on.

Once it was secure, she grabbed hold of the rope in front of her.

"Tuck your hand under it. You'll have a better grip."

"How do you know how to do this?"

"Misbegotten youth." He grinned.

She frowned, unsure whether to believe him.

"I'll tell you the story sometime."

"About ready there?" the operator asked.

Trevor ignored the man. "You'll use your free arm to counterbalance. You've been to a rodeo?"

"No."

"Seen clips?"

"Once or twice."

"There's a reason cowboys are waving an arm around. It's not for show."

"It's so they don't end up beneath a bull?"

He nodded. "Arm in the air."

Feeling self-conscious and a little ridiculous, she did as he instructed.

"That's it." He placed a palm on her buttocks and scooted her forward. "As close to the neck as possible."

Calling a piece of bent metal a neck seemed like a stretch.

"You'll want to squeeze your inner legs as hard as you can against the sides. That's the key. Work to counterbalance the bucking motions, and use your thighs."

"I'm beginning to understand more why you like this."

"I confessed. It's the gyrations. Damn." He brushed a finger across her lips. Even though he'd washed his hands after their time together, she was sure she could smell her heat on him.

Now she had something else to think about—him.

"You ready?"

"I'm not sure I'll ever be."

He stepped back and folded his arms and waited for her to tell the operator to start the machine.

The bronco turned in a small circle. She grinned at Trevor as she passed him. This was easy enough. Then the mechanical horse bucked.

"Stay forward!" Trevor called. "Squeeze those thighs like you mean it."

The bronco kicked, and she went flying in the air and landed back down with a hard plop that made her wince.

"Keep going! Fifteen seconds!" Trevor shouted.

"Really?"

The thing twirled around and around, sending her hair flying. Her vest parted. Since she was only wearing a demicup bra beneath, she was bordering on a wardrobe malfunction. And no doubt, she *was* jiggling. Breathless and exhilarated, she laughed.

"Twenty!"

The bronco pitched forward, the head almost all the way down to the crash pad, catapulting her into the air.

She landed on her butt, a little breathless.

Before she could find her feet, Trevor was there, helping her up, brushing strands of hair from her face. "You okay?"

"That was amazing!"

He high-fived her. "Officially clocked at twenty-seven seconds. You're in third place!"

"Seriously?" She studied the scoreboard before looking at him. He wore a huge, proud grin. "I had an excellent instructor."

Together they laughed, and he drew her against him. She could stay there forever, safe and warm.

"Did you enjoy it?"

"More than I thought I would."

"So did I."

"That's saying something."

"Oh. Most definitely."

When she pulled away a little, he adjusted her vest, covering her erect nipples.

Another couple walked toward the bronco, and Trevor

scooted her out of the way. Already, she didn't want to think about leaving him.

"Everything okay?"

"Yes." Trying to hide her sudden moroseness, she wrinkled her nose, pretending to be in deep thought. "Planning my strategy for next time. I need to move my free arm more." Though he frowned a little, he didn't question her small fib.

They made their way to the lobby area for her to claim her bag. "I need about five minutes to change."

"I'll be waiting."

Inside the locker room, she dropped her bag onto a long wooden bench and then lowered herself beside it.

Nothing in her experience could have prepared her for Trevor. With his kindness wrapped in steel strength, he'd started to chip away at the defenses she'd erected around her emotions.

"Hey."

Shaking her head, she looked up at Hannah Gill, one of the friends she'd come here with.

Hannah's eyebrows were furrowed. "Are you leaving?"

"I…uhm. Yes. With Master Trevor."

"Fiona told me he wanted you."

Shelby blew out a short breath. "I suddenly think I understand how you felt at that one event." When Master Mason had outbid everyone else at the charity slave auction to have a chance to claim Hannah for a weekend.

Without an invitation, Hannah sat beside her on the bench. "At least I knew what I was getting into." She grinned. "Well. As much as I could have. I made the choice in advance."

"Right?" Who could have guessed that Hannah would fall in love with the man or that they'd end up filming pilot episodes for their own home improvement television show.

Mason was clear that he wanted to be planning a wedding too.

"You know that Fiona and I are both here for you. We'll rescue you so fast he will have no idea what happened if you call either one of us."

"She is a badass." And she definitely looked after her friends.

Over drinks at happy hour, Shelby had heard all about Fiona flying to Texas to spend time with Hannah after she'd left Mason. Almost from the start, he'd wanted a commitment from her, but the idea of uprooting her carefully constructed—and safe—life had freaked her out.

"On the other hand, Shel, you could end up having a great time."

Maybe she could still influence Trevor to help out David.

"Mason tells me that Trevor's house is wonderful. Right on Lake Catherine." She shrugged. "Maybe it can be like a mini-getaway. You need one, right?"

"I'd been thinking more along the lines of the Bahamas or something."

"But something about being here makes you seem more relaxed already."

She blinked. "Am I that transparent?"

"You're glowing. Okay, you seem a little overwhelmed. Not in a bad way, though. More like what the holy hell is happening here, and how do I make sure it doesn't stop?"

For the first time, Shelby laughed.

"My advice? As long as you're willing, relax and seize every moment of pleasure that you can. You are willing, right? Fiona said you were."

"Nervous. But yes."

"In that case, carpe the hell out of it. You may never get this kind of chance again. If it doesn't work out, no harm, no foul. Call us. We'll dissect it at happy hour. But if you have fun, you'll have great memories when you finally settle down with someone boring. Maybe you can replay it when you're having vanilla, *oh baby, that was soooo good* sex with some other guy." Hannah exaggerated every syllable and infused them with a deadly dull tone. "And regardless, we still want all the details." She tossed back her blonde hair. "Either way, you've got friends and happy hour."

Before leaving, Hannah squeezed Shelby's hand. "Mason will be wondering what happened to me."

A few moments later, the locker room door slammed open. "Shelby!"

She jumped up. Trevor's uncompromising voice shot shivers through her.

"Three minutes, or I'm coming in!"

Grinning hugely, Hannah popped her head back inside. "I think he means it. You might want to hurry." Waggling her fingers, she disappeared.

Because she could no longer think straight, Shelby struggled to remove the boots and chaps.

His voice alone was enough to turn her insides into a river of need.

She worked her way back into her tight jeans, then slipped back into her boots. Time had to be up.

Then she shrugged out of her vest and folded it nicely before putting it in the bag.

And then...

He was there. Near her, hands on his hips. So large. Imposing.

My Dominant.

Breath trapped in her lungs, she looked up at him. Her nipples hardened, and her clit throbbed. From fear? *How fucked-up would that be?* Or maybe her reaction was caused by the warm approval in his eyes that stood as such a contradiction to his unyielding posture.

"Our car is waiting."

"Master Trevor!" Trinity, the club's hostess, burst into the locker room. As always, she was in a tight-fitting catsuit. And tonight, instead of her hair being a sleek pink bob, it was wild, spiky. Her violet eyes sparked with protective flares. "You can't be in here!"

"My sub and I are leaving."

"Out," she insisted.

Shelby grabbed a T-shirt, pulled it on, then picked up her bag. "Ready, Sir."

"Mistress Aviana will be speaking with you," Trinity warned.

"Thank you for looking out for Shelby." His voice was polite and polished. And his smile dazzled.

"You can stuff the charm, Master Trevor. It won't work on me. Club rules exist to protect our submissives."

"Which I appreciate. I'll accept whatever punishment Aviana deems necessary." He tipped his hat. "Evening, Trinity."

How was the woman immune from him? Shelby was smitten. She'd forgive him anything. "Not much of a rule follower, are you?" she asked after they made it past Trinity.

"When they suit me."

"Do we really have a car waiting?"

He opened the doorway at the top of the stairs that led to the exit. "Indeed. Even though the hotel is close, I wasn't sure those boots of yours were actually made for walking."

Even if she hadn't agreed to have sex with him, there was no doubt his smile would charm her out of her panties in less than an hour.

Outside, the cloying air of a New Orleans summer night wrapped around her, drenching her skin.

A driver stood next to a sedan that was emblazoned with

the Maison Sterling logo. As they approached, the woman nodded toward Trevor, then opened the back door.

Trevor took Shelby's bag while she slid across the leather seat. Cool air streamed from the overhead vents, like tiny whispers from heaven. "This is seriously deluxe," she said when he scooted in beside her. "Thank you."

Because unruly Saturday evening crowds spilled from sidewalks into the streets and numerous pedicabs wove through traffic, it took forever for them to pull in front of the majestic brick hotel with its wrought-iron balconies.

Her door was opened by a tall woman wearing the chain's livery, and Master Trevor placed a hand on her back, guiding her beneath the historic building's signature green awning.

She pushed through the revolving glass door and entered the lobby that spoke of elegance from years gone by. A few chairs were occupied, and farther away, jazz notes from a live band drifted into the air.

"We could stay and listen, if you'd like. They have a pizza and beer buffet for guests."

"Or?"

"We could go straight upstairs to the room."

Anticipation surged through her, and she nodded. "I'd rather do that. If that's okay with you?"

"Either way is fine." He drew her toward the elevator and pressed the button. "But my preference is to have you alone as soon as possible."

His words made her senses swim.

There were other people in the elevator, so he remained silent during the ride up, but the way he kept his gaze on her was a promise.

Within a minute, they arrived at his room, and he opened the door to reveal an enormous suite. The far wall had a bank of floor-to-ceiling windows, and the curtains were wide open, showing he had one of the sought-after balconies.

Because they were at the front of the building, they overlooked the French Quarter. Enchanted, she placed her bag to one side, then crossed the room. "This is amazing."

He came up behind her. Close. So close she inhaled his scent—power and determined heat.

"I could order a bottle of wine. Champagne, even, if you want to sit outside for a while."

She turned, bumping into him.

He cupped his hands around her shoulders, steadying her, shooting her pulse into a flurry.

"I thought we might… I mean I'd rather…"

While she sorted through her thoughts, trying to put them into words, he waited.

She'd never had an experience like this, with a man who was Dominant but was seeming to let her set the pace. He'd risked a lot of money to spend time with her, which meant she was at little risk for rejection right now. Still, though, she was apprehensive. She wet her lips before confessing, "I'd like to have sex."

CHAPTER 4

His soft smile was slow, containing a hint of predatory triumph.

Shelby swallowed deeply, not knowing what to expect.

"There's nothing I'd like more." He swept off his cowboy hat, tossed it onto a small table near the window, then claimed her mouth.

His kiss was anything but gentle. He was possessive, as if he meant it when he'd claimed her for himself.

Trevor was completely in charge of the pace, making her realize he'd allowed her to think she was in control a moment ago. She never had been. He hadn't merely been waiting for her to ask him to make love to her; he'd been seducing her.

With a groan, he pulled her tighter against him, and the hard, angular planes of his body were strikingly masculine, contrasting with her soft, feminine curves. He tasted of sweet persistence, and when he plunged deeper, demanding surrender, she was helpless to resist.

With agonizing slowness that was still too fast for her, he ended the kiss. The world tilted beneath her, and she grabbed hold of his shirt for stability. Once again, he was there, keeping her steady. Against her belly, his cock was hard.

When she was able to look up at him, he released her for a few seconds while he closed the privacy blinds. It shielded them from view, she imagined, but allowed some ambient light to filter in.

"At the club, I undressed you." He pulled over a chair and sat. "This time, I'd like you to remove your clothes while I watch."

No one had demanded this from her before. She guessed he wouldn't appreciate her suggesting they turn off the lights and jump beneath the covers instead.

She started to loosen the bolo, but he raised a hand.

"Leave it, please."

Of course. He had mentioned a collar.

Shelby tugged off her T-shirt. Beneath his gaze, her nipples puckered.

"Your breasts are magnificent."

Her ex had told her they were small and suggested she get implants once he was finally making the big bucks. The approval in Trevor's eyes told her she was perfect to him, making her confidence soar.

She bent to remove her boots, and although she wobbled, he didn't make a move to help. "Are you liking this, Sir?"

He grinned. "Immensely."

Next, Shelby unfastened her jeans, then worked them down her thighs and finally, off.

For a moment, she stood there before removing the demicup bra and her panties. It took all her self-discipline not to try to cover herself or say something to distract him.

"I'm greedy enough to want you naked all the time."

Then, he moved so fast, had her in front of him, then

facedown over his lap. Breath whooshed out as she pushed her hands toward the floor.

"Your ass is hot." He kneaded her flesh before teasing her cunt.

The room spun, making her grab on to his calf for stability.

Within seconds, he had her on the verge of an orgasm. Instead of letting her come, he took hold of her waist and set her back on her feet.

"Sir!"

"All in good time, Shelby."

She clamped her mouth shut and curled her toes into the expensive carpeting. Her clit throbbed. Demand chased through her, as if his firm touch was a drug she craved. Master Trevor was frustrating. Utterly... Dominant. She reminded herself she'd wanted that.

Fantasy and reality were nowhere close to each other.

Frustration crawled through her as she waited for his next move or instruction. When he didn't say a word, she clenched her hands at her sides.

Damn it.

A minute or so later, sexual desire no longer clawed at her. Instead, it receded enough for her to clear her thoughts. It was there, though, coiled, waiting for him to summon it, with either a command or a look.

"That's it," he said when she exhaled. "Patience."

She frowned ferociously, and all that did was make him glance at his watch.

He wouldn't be outmaneuvered.

That knowledge frustrated her and, shockingly, gave her comfort.

Shelby closed her eyes and counted backward from ten, a technique she used to refocus herself at work.

When she looked at him again, he was studying her, his

hands steepled. She shivered, realizing he'd never taken his gaze off her. "I think I'm not supposed to get frustrated, or something," she said.

"Whatever you feel is fine. I was prepared for anything when I denied you a climax."

"Would anything work?"

"I'm not easily swayed."

But he hadn't said no.

Finally, realizing she was holding on to her earlier frustration, she loosened her fists and allowed her shoulders to drop a little.

"Yes, precious sub. That's it." He stood.

If she'd moved through her emotions faster, would he have reacted quicker? On the other hand, her own work taught her that it took time for people to process new information and make peace with decisions.

He crossed the room to his bag and removed two pairs of soft cuffs.

The arousal reawakened ferociously.

His steps purposeful, he walked toward her. He tossed one set onto the mattress, then continued toward her. "Turn your back to me, and place your hands behind you."

Though the words were demanding, his tone was anything but. Rather, it was seduction and promise, making her want to comply.

His motions were sure as he fastened her wrists together. The truth was, he could have immobilized her with just the power of his words.

Then he lifted her from the floor and carried her to the bed and sat her on the edge. "Make your way to the middle, please."

Secured as she was, she was going to be a spectacle.

Instead of complaining, she pursed her lips as she tried to

figure out how to comply. There was no way to do this without wrecking the duvet.

Shaking his head, he reached out and pushed her onto her back. She squealed from the surprise. Then she realized that, in this position, she couldn't use her feet as leverage.

"Get on with it."

Holy hell, he'd been Dominant, and she loved it. Tightening her abdominal muscles, she wriggled about.

"This is fucking sexier than I thought it would be."

"You've got a mean streak, Master Trevor."

"Until you, I didn't. I have to confess that I may lose sleep dreaming up ways of making you move like this."

She contracted each buttock in turn and rotated her shoulders to inch back a little.

Shelby had to angle her body in order to pull each foot off the floor. "You could help me."

"I could."

But he didn't budge.

She sighed. With a sigh, she continued her crablike awkward motions to scoot across the bed. "With you, it really is all about the jiggling, isn't it?"

"Yeah." He shrugged. "When it comes down to it, I'm a simple man, Shelby."

That wasn't true in the least. But that he appreciated her curves made her giddy.

When she was in place, she tucked her shoulders back and propelled herself backward to land with a small *plop*.

"Very appealing." He sat on the bed and fastened the second set of cuffs around her ankles.

"I'm not sure how we're going to have sex like this."

"Let me worry about that." After standing, he tossed his wallet onto the nearby table, then pulled out a condom.

Hungrily, she turned her head to the side in order to watch his every move.

Facing her, Trevor unfastened his belt buckle. Then, as if wanting to torment her, he opted not to lower his zipper. Instead, he began unbuttoning his shirt, starting at the bottom.

God above, she wanted him to hurry.

She caught a glimpse of his honed abs and broad chest, then his well-defined biceps. He was gorgeous. Breathtaking. How was it possible that she was going to spend the next week with him?

He sat to toe off his boots and socks; then he stood and dropped his jeans.

Beneath the denim, he was commando. His large cock was already erect. She moaned.

"I want you, Shelby."

Yes. "Yes."

After rolling the condom into place, he placed one knee on the bed and used a hand to lift her legs.

What the hell was he thinking?

He positioned himself beneath her, pressing his shoulders against the backs of her thighs.

"This will never work, Sir." Had he forgotten her ankles were bound?

"Keep your legs high and relax your knees."

The position was impossible.

Rather than arguing with her, Trevor pressed forward. The strength of his shoulders parted her legs and gave him complete control. She was helpless as he teased her pussy with his index finger.

She gasped, becoming instantly wet for him.

"Don't fight me," he urged as he sucked her clit into his mouth.

"God! I can't." She thrashed her head back and forth. "I can't!" She was on the cusp of a climax. To get there, she had to lift her hips. Or she needed to escape him. But he'd cleverly fastened her hands beneath her and bound her ankles. She was completely at his mercy, and he showed none as he teased, licking, sucking, gently biting, then plunging his tongue into her. "Master Trevor!"

"Are you going to come, Shelby?"

"Yes!" If he'd allow it.

He continued on, parting her nether lips, then flicking his tongue back and forth across her engorged clit.

She was seconds away…

And then he stopped. With a wicked, wicked grin, he lifted his head before using a couple of fingers to play with her.

"Sir, you're…" She was lost, on the edge again.

"I'm…?"

Shelby couldn't remember what she'd been going to say. Masterful? Amazing? Sensational?

He flicked a fingernail across her most tender flesh.

"Oh!" The sensation was part pain, part pleasure.

He turned his hand palm-side up then slid two fingers inside her. He pried her apart, stretching her. Then he finger-fucked her, starting with slow, measured strokes. "I want you to be ready."

She was. So much so. No man had ever engaged in this much foreplay. It blew her mind, shredded any emotional doubts as to whether this was a good idea or not. Even in the short amount of time they'd been together, the experience of what was possible had enriched her. She wouldn't settle ever again, wouldn't allow any man to make her feel less than sexy or worthy.

"Let yourself go." Trevor moved his hand faster, delving in deeper, forcing his fingers apart even farther.

She was splintering.

His thrusts overwhelmed her.

"That's it."

Shelby ached to place her arms around him and hang on. Yet her bonds made her helpless, which in turn allowed her the freedom to give herself over to him.

He slowed, sought, then found her G-spot. Relentlessly, he pressed against it.

She bucked against him, desperate for escape, completion.

But he wasn't finished. He closed his mouth on her pussy.

"I've got to…"

"Take it."

As best she could, she leveraged herself off his shoulders, crying the whole time—from relief as much as desperation—offering him greater access to her cunt. He accepted, his heated tongue circling her needy little clit.

He pulled away and gave her pussy a loving smack. The entire universe exploded behind her eyes, and she screamed as the orgasm ripped through her, leaving a path of incinerated stars behind it.

"Yeah," he murmured. "That is what I was looking for."

She blinked the room back into focus. While she was lost, he'd somehow untangled their bodies and curled himself next to her, tucking her into the safety of his arms.

He hadn't released her bonds, and his erection pressed against her buttocks.

Trevor stroked her hair and was saying something she couldn't quite make out, but the growl of possession in his rough, masculine voice touched the deepest part of her femininity.

"How are you doing? Okay?"

She might have drifted off, but it was only for a few seconds. "Yes." *At least I think so.*

"Does anything hurt? Do you need me to unfasten your cuffs?" Even though she shook her head, he rolled her onto her back and checked for himself, spending a couple of minutes rubbing her wrists and ankles.

"You're spoiling me."

"Not at all." He grinned. "I'm being self-serving. Making sure you're good to continue."

Softly, she returned his smile. "I am. Very much."

"Your pussy?"

"That spank was…" She licked her lower lip. "Divine."

"Now I'm going to fuck you, Shelby."

It wasn't a question; it was a certainty. *Finally.* She wanted to be his.

"Tell me you want it."

His eyes were dark, and for a moment she had the ridiculous thought that he could see into her and know her deepest fantasies. "Please. Fuck me, Master Trevor."

Goddamn.

Her words, husky and pleading, rocked through him. Since he generally only played with experienced submissives, he'd never been with a woman like Shelby. Watching her metamorphosis this evening enchanted him.

At first she'd been nervous, but curious, when he said he wanted her as part of the wager. He wasn't sure he'd have been as bold if he'd realized she was all but new to the scene. But then he'd have missed the pleasure of her awakening, seeing her buttocks blossom with streaks of red from the strands of his flogger. Mostly, he'd have missed the expression in her crystalline eyes. The whole world was revealed in the green depths. At the club, there'd been a hesitant trust. And now, there was hunger that matched his own.

He skimmed his fingers over her left nipple. The tiny nub tightened, and with a gasp, she arched her back toward him.

Obligingly he lowered his head, capturing her breast between his palms so she couldn't get away while he sucked on her.

"That's…" She turned her head to one side. "It's…"

He waited.

"Can I ask…" She moaned. "I mean…"

"Sexy woman." He lifted away to look at her. "Talk to me."

"Will you do it harder?"

He sucked with more intensity; then he bit gently, making her cry out. Right away, he laved the injury with his tongue, circling and soothing, and he inhaled the sharpness of her arousal. Such a fucking turn-on.

Trevor replaced his mouth with his thumb and forefinger, and he tightened his grip, in a way that had to be painful for her before he moved on to her other nipple. She cried his name over and over, lifting her hips in a vain attempt to rub her pussy against his skin.

By the time he finished, she was begging for completion, and so was his dick. He wasn't accustomed to delaying his gratification this long. But he'd do it another hour if he needed to. An hour? Hell, he'd do it all night. Anything to give her the evening she deserved. Her pure, innocent response was a gift he'd do anything to repay.

"My nipples are so throbby."

"If you've changed your mind, we can play with clamps some evening. See if you might like them."

She sucked in a sharp breath.

"Not tonight, then." At his words, she softly exhaled. All of her actions were revealing, and he intended to become a student of them. "I've got other things in mind. Like spanking your pussy."

As much as she could, she clamped her thighs together.

Adorable. And completely ineffective. "Open yourself to me."

"Uhm…"

"Not sure where you got the idea that was a suggestion." He kept his tone light but uncompromising. She had a safe word, and one for slow down. Judging by the haze that seeped across her eyes, the order both terrified and excited her.

While holding her gaze captive, Trevor dipped a finger between her legs and entered her to draw out some of her essence. He used that dampness to repeatedly slide across her vulva in rhythmic motions. "I'm going to do what I said, so place the bottoms of your feet together and allow your knees to part."

"What if I don't want to?"

"Do you not? Really?" He carefully used his thumbnail on her clit, and she panted in perfect response. "Or are you stalling? Being obstinate? Perhaps you've got a touch of well-deserved apprehension." Using two fingers from his free hand, Trevor spread her pussy lips. "Think it will make me a little more tender in the way I touch you?"

She whimpered.

"Won't happen." He shook his head. "I don't respond to goading, nor do I compromise. If it's a limit or not something you think you can do right now, use a safe word."

"Apprehension," she confessed. "I liked it earlier. But that was, you know…"

"While I was playing with you. Like I am now." He pulled back his hand and delivered a sharp smack. She screamed, and it trailed off into a plea as he licked away the sting.

"Oh! That is so…"

"If you want more, offer your pretty pussy to me."

This time, she placed her feet together, and he tapped her knees, indicating she should allow them to fall open.

Wrinkling her nose, she complied. "I'm still nervous."

"Isn't that part of the thrill? The crash of adrenaline is a high all by itself."

She shifted her weight from one buttock to the other. "It's going to hurt, though."

"Of course it will."

Shelby swallowed deeply before confessing, "You're frightening me a little."

"Good."

With a soft curse, she buried her head in the duvet.

"How many shall I give you?"

"Do your worst, Sir!"

He laughed. "That kind of bravery is a bit foolish."

Surprising him, she looked back at him. "The truth is, I trust you. It will hurt. Maybe like a bitch, but you're going to make it worth my while. So I'm going to go with that."

Primal male instinct had urged him to take that wild chance, just for the opportunity to have her. Even then, he'd had no clue how fucking good it would be with her.

Trevor spent minutes arousing her, eating her, driving her to the point she thrashed beneath his touch and her muscles were supple. Only when she was out of her head and wild with desire did he dampen his fingers and smack her pussy half a dozen times in rapid, sharp succession.

Beneath his hand, she bucked as she sobbed. Then he turned on the small bullet vibrator and lightly touched her clit.

His responsive little sub went rigid, and her eyes opened wide. "Sir!"

"It's okay to come." He finger-fucked her while he held the toy against her. In mere seconds, she cried his name and climaxed all over his hand.

"I..." Tears seeped from the corners of her eyes. "That was..." She struggled for words as he switched off the toy. *"Fuck, Sir."*

"Good?" he guessed with a smile.

"Amazing is more like it." She blinked, and she lifted a shoulder, as if trying to free one of her hands so she could touch him.

Her praise fed him. He'd do anything to live up to the pure trust radiating from her eyes. "It was for me also." His cock wept precum and throbbed with insistent demand. He didn't remember ever staying hard this long before.

"You mean that? You enjoyed that?"

"Without a doubt. Watching your reactions gets me off." He traced the outline of the concha at her throat. "And this is far from finished."

Her mouth parted as he knelt over her.

"Are you going to unfasten me?"

"Not your wrists." He lifted her legs and buttocks from the mattress and then grabbed two pillows, plumped them, then resettled her on them.

"You want to try doing this the same way you..." Red streaks flashed up her cheeks.

"Used the vibrator? Ate you out?"

"Ah. Yes. That."

Her embarrassment made him grin. By the end of the week, she'd be beyond that. "It may not be the most comfortable, but it's certainly possible if you relax. I want to be deep inside you."

"Sir! But, that's—I mean. You're massive."

"Is that a compliment or a complaint?" At this moment, he couldn't be sure.

"Honestly? It's a fear."

"I'll be sure you're ready." He lifted her ankles and placed them on one of his shoulders. The image of her—long dark hair spilled across the white duvet in wild sexual disarray, nipples hard, apprehension, carved from jade daggers in her eyes, and her mouth open slightly, cunt scant inches from his fingers—would stoke the fires of his fantasies for years to come.

Trevor dampened a finger and played with her, raising her arousal before sliding it inside her. When she relaxed enough for him to slip in and out more easily, he added a second finger, then a third, spreading them out, preparing the way. "Let go."

She clamped her lips together.

"I promise I'll never hurt you."

As he continued, her breathing became more rapid, and she began to writhe as she moaned. Even though she might be nervous, her body responded to him. The sound of her, the scent of her—there was nothing more perfect. "Gorgeous."

"Sir, I'm ready."

So was he. Slowly he withdrew his fingers from her. After releasing the ankle cuffs, he stroked his dick to full hardness before raising her legs and placing each of her calves on either side of his head.

She swallowed hard.

"Keep trusting me."

"I'm trying."

He curled his hands around her waist. "I'm going to move you a little and help while you place your knees on my shoulders." Trevor lifted her and held her while she used her leg muscles to scoot her body into the position he wanted. "You're doing great."

Damn. He liked the sight of her, spread and vulnerable for him.

She adjusted positions as he guided his cockhead toward her entrance.

"Oh."

"Tell me if it's too much, and we can go slower."

"No. I want you."

Her soft, dreamy words nearly snapped his control. He wanted to be buried inside her, but she needed time.

At little at a time, he eased forward and gave her time to adjust before pulling out a little, then sliding in again, a little deeper.

As he did, her body relaxed by slow measures, and she no longer exerted as much force against his shoulders. "We're getting there."

He continued on until his dick was completely inside her. *Fuck.* So damn hot. So damn good.

"Nice."

Nice wasn't a term he'd use.

Trevor stayed where he was until she began to circle her hips, silently asking for more.

For a few seconds, twenty at the most, he allowed her to set the pace, until his body's demands became impossible to deny. He withdrew a little, then made repeated small thrusts forward, impaling her with each.

On his shoulders, her muscles relaxed in silent invitation.

"Take me, Sir."

It was permission. To fuck her like wanted. To make her his.

And he accepted the invitation, pulling all the way out to plunge all the way back in, hard. Fast.

He released her waist and placed one of his palms flat on the mattress and captured her chin with her other, holding her captive so he could drink in her responses.

Her eyes were glossy, and her gaze was hungrily feasted on him. Using the little strength she had in her abs and backs of her thighs, she lifted her body a little, offering even more of herself.

Pride washed through him.

This beautiful creature who'd been hurt before was giving

him a powerful gift. Her emotional as well as physical submission. It was as heady as it was humbling.

"Master Trevor, I can't wait. I'm going to come."

"Do." He claimed her mouth, kissing her as she came, the taste of her still on his tongue.

Shelby's tight internal muscles clamped down on his dick, and his body tightened. He ripped his mouth away from hers and gritted his teeth as his own climax demanded release.

With her body cradling his, he ejaculated in long, hot spurts. For a moment, he was lost. She'd given him so damn much tonight, and it was a fucking game changer. He'd never known that a woman's complete surrender could pack such an emotional wallop.

Aware that his weight was resting too much on her, he shook his head and used his palms to push himself up.

Her eyes were closed. He was relieved by that. He didn't want her to catch a glimpse of whatever the hell was racing through him.

He'd had sex his entire adult life without it meaning a damn thing.

But this? Her? "How are you doing?"

"I'm tired." She blinked a couple of times and smiled at him. "Otherwise, I'm…" She hesitated. "Satisfied. Although I think I might be a bit sore tomorrow. Maybe for a week."

He'd see she got a bath in some soothing salts. There was no way he could last several days without making love to her again.

Trevor allowed his cock to slide from her feminine heat. Before disposing of the condom, he rolled her onto her side. "Let's get you out of these cuffs." He released the clip holding the pair together, then unfastened each in turn. Then he rubbed the circulation back into them. "Lie on your stomach for a minute so I can massage your shoulders."

"You're a full-service Dom."

"Something like that." He pulled away the pillows and helped her change positions. He'd intended to only work on her shoulders, but he continued downward, making soothing circles on her skin.

"That's nice." Her voice was muffled, and she didn't move.

"Would you like a shower?"

"I should, but I'd rather rest." She curled her legs toward her.

He stroked her hair before crossing to the bathroom. When he returned, she was sleeping.

Trevor had always enjoyed showing his subs aftercare, but he'd never done it like this. He fetched a warm, wet cloth and used it to soothe between her legs while she murmured little sounds of approval.

Then he crawled onto the bed and somehow managed to get them both beneath the covers.

"This is nice." Though she was almost unconscious, she curled herself against him, her head on his biceps.

Trevor always slept alone. But with Shelby, he was breaking all of his self-imposed rules.

She shifted, and her buttocks brushed his cock, making him erect again.

So he didn't take her again, he held her tight, resting his thumb on the mother-of-pearl concha at her throat. Trevor couldn't wait to get his collar on her.

What the hell would he do if he never wanted to take it back off?

CHAPTER 5

Startled but not knowing what had disturbed her, Shelby blinked herself awake. Light filtered into the room…the unfamiliar room.

She turned onto her side and saw a cowboy hat.

Pulse galloping, she pushed herself up onto her elbows. Her vest, bra, and jeans were stacked in a tidy pile on the table next to the hat—Trevor's cowboy hat. *Master* Trevor's.

She dropped back down as memories flooded her.

Master Trevor asking David to wager her. David losing, and her temporary Dominant delving into her secrets before tying her and flogging her at the Quarter.

And then…

Bringing her back to the hotel and fucking her hard. With more intensity than anything she'd ever experienced.

She closed her eyes.

Her pussy was a bit sore, and she recalled him toying with her, spanking her there, burying his massive cock inside her.

After that…

Various recollections teased her. A warm cloth between her legs. Being naked, wrapped tight in his arms. A collage of the sexy things they'd done danced through her mind, leaving a searing trail behind.

But the accompanying emotions wrapped her in gossamer. Nerves. Fear. Apprehension. Trust. *Completion.* A sense of something so right that it didn't have words.

Ever since her horrible divorce, she hadn't dated much. She hadn't had sex, let alone spent the night with anyone. Except for with her girlfriends, her life had been superficial. She'd told herself that was better than being hurt again. Yet now that she was here with him, she realized how deeply she missed sharing little intimacies.

She gripped the covers tightly and reminded herself she wasn't in a relationship with Trevor. This was a seven-day arrangement, nothing more. At the end of it, she'd go back to her ordinary life. It wouldn't be smart to allow herself to consider anything more.

His deep, rumbly tones reached her, and she glanced around the room. She didn't see him, which meant he was likely outside. Had his conversation awakened her?

Trevor spoke again, and the cadence was enough to weave a spell over her. That had to be what happened last night. By the careful use of his voice—urging, implacable, suggestive—the man could compel her to do almost anything.

Desperate to find some sort of normalcy, she gathered a sheet around her and darted toward the bathroom.

Every part of her body protested. Her shoulders ached. The backs of her thighs had a dull burn. At the club, she'd been in a strange position on the spanking bench. Then he'd used cuffs on her, forcing her upper body into a bowed shape, and when he'd pressed his huge cock into her, the weight of his torso had stretched her thighs. The position had allowed him to go deep, but she'd need more yoga classes to keep up with him.

She eyed the gigantic bathtub. That would be luxurious. But she didn't know what his plans were. And she was a sub for the next week. Whatever that meant to him. It couldn't be all sex and bondage. Could it?

On a hook, there was a robe embroidered with the hotel's logo. Gratefully she slipped into the oversize fluffiness and wrapped the belt around her twice before tying it.

Because she didn't have an overnight bag, she settled for finger-combing her hair, using a toothbrush provided by the hotel, then scrubbing her face with a makeup-removing towelette.

Not that it helped much.

Her eyes were wide. Her mouth seemed swollen from his kisses. Her hair still had tangles, as if she'd had sex.

As she was turning, the overhead light refracted off the bolo tie.

He'd asked her to keep it on until he could replace it with a temporary collar. The truth was, even without its weight, she had no doubts he was her Dominant.

When she returned to the room, he still wasn't there. A single word snagged her attention. *Caroline.*

Shelby froze. Last night, they'd talked at length about her life, but he'd shared next to none about his. Surely he wouldn't have asked for a week with her if he had another woman. Sub?

Nervous, and more uncertain than ever, she opened the balcony door.

A phone pressed against his ear, Trevor looked up, gave her a quick, welcoming smile, and waved her out.

Not a girlfriend, then, she guessed. Unless it was an open relationship. But even then, there was no way any woman would be happy with the way he'd fucked her last night.

Heat and humidity wrapped around her, urging her back inside. She told herself the lure of a pot of coffee in a French press, along with a plate of fruit and pastries, was too irresistible. Especially since she'd burned so much energy last night. The truth was a little less palatable. She wanted to know who Caroline was.

For a moment Shelby hesitated, considering his privacy as well as the fact that she wasn't dressed. But since there was another couple also dining outdoors, both in pajamas, she shoved away her inhibitions and took a seat across from her Dom.

He poured her a cup of coffee and slid it toward her.

How had he managed to order room service and get everything outside? She was generally a light sleeper. Then again, last night was anything but ordinary.

The coffee was hot and strong, and in Louisiana fashion, tasted of chicory. Since it wasn't her favorite, she added a dollop of cream.

After a second, much more satisfying sip, she sat back.

Good manners dictated that she pretend to be uninterested in his call. Or at the very least, that she wasn't eavesdropping.

"Right," Trevor said, nodding. "Set it up for Thursday. Afternoon is best. Anything else?"

Shamelessly, she looked at the man she was committed to spending the next six days with.

Today he wore a white dress shirt, with the cuffs rolled back. The top two buttons were open. Instead of jeans, he wore lightweight gray slacks and casual shoes. If it was possible, his arms appeared even bigger, his muscles more cut than they had yesterday. Or maybe it was just that she knew what he looked like, how perfect, as if he'd been chiseled from marble.

For the first time, though, she realized how different their lives were. From David, she knew Master Trevor was a millionaire. Well, at least a millionaire, if rumors were to be believed.

On Sunday mornings, she liked to laze around, read a book, think about her day before getting up and doing something fun, like brunch with a friend. Mimosas were always part of the deal.

But he'd dressed as if it were Monday. He smelled of juniper and spice, and his hair was damp, with a stray lock curling over his forehead. If her guess was right, he'd showered. And he was settled in for his phone call.

As if sensing her interest, he met her gaze. He held up his forefinger, signaling he was almost finished.

She picked up a croissant and tugged off a corner. The buttery goodness melted on her tongue. So far, the experience with Master Trevor had been much better than she anticipated.

One tiny piece at a time, Shelby finished the croissant and was considering a second when he ended the call.

"Morning, precious sub."

Precious. It wasn't the first time he'd called her that, and it didn't sound like a casual endearment. It was soft and intimate, heavy with meaning. Her tummy fluttered. With a few words or a pointed glance, he possessed the power to upend her world. She couldn't be falling for him, just couldn't. "Sir." The whisper was all she could manage. To cover her nerves, she swiped her hands together to brush off any crumbs.

"Eat up," he encouraged. "We have a long day. And I have plans for you."

Her appetite vanished. Instead, she took another sip of coffee.

"Did you sleep okay?"

She glanced at the continental breakfast, then back at him. "I think you know the answer to that."

He grinned. How was it possible he'd slept fewer hours than she had but was completely polished?

"And your body? How is it feeling?"

Like it needs the trip to the Bahamas that I've been promising myself. All of a sudden she remembered him rubbing her back before she went to sleep. How many submissives were fortunate enough to have their Doms take such good care of them? "I'll be honest, I'm a little stiff. Muscles I'd forgotten about have reminded me of their existence. While you look as if you've already taken on the world." And won.

"I tend not to have good boundaries between work and my real life." He shrugged. "It's a failing. My mentor warned me about that."

"Your mentor." She traced the cup's handle. "Is that who you were talking to?"

"No. Caroline is my executive assistant, has been for almost ten years. Strictly a business relationship. Since I prefer to work from my home office, we rarely see each other, but she's indispensable."

"And you work on weekends?"

"Time is fluid. Things shift. I like to be poised to act. I ensure Caroline has plenty of time off, and she's well compensated for her efforts."

"It occurred to me that I don't know anything about you."

"I'm an open book. I'm not involved in a relationship. I don't have a submissive. No exes or children for you to worry about. Does that satisfy you?"

"It's not really any of my business." But she was eager to hear every detail.

"You'll be sharing my home for what's left of the week. That makes it your business."

"I…" She stopped when she realized she wasn't sure what to say. "Thank you."

"What else can I tell you?"

"I'm curious about your mentor."

For less than a second—so fast she might have imagined it—something dark frosted his eyes. Pain, maybe? But then as if aware he was revealing too much, he sat back, and his expression was as calm as it had been a few minutes before.

"I had no father." He shrugged. "Or, I did until responsibilities became too much after my twin sisters were born. At age ten, I became the man of the family, and I had to find ways to help my mom earn money."

She winced at the pain in the words, and the parts of the story he'd obviously left out. "That's harsh." The first time she saw him, he was ultrarich, and she assumed he'd been born into wealth.

"Doesn't matter, does it? We play the hand we're dealt."

A clever reference to the night before?

"And I was fortunate enough to meet Wayne Dixon. And he hired me to do yard work."

She didn't make a habit of reading business news, but even she recognized the name. "You mean the financier?"

"You've heard of him?"

"Anyone who grew up in this area knows his reputation. There's a bridge named after him."

"Turns out he liked the scrappy kid on a secondhand bike. Reminded him of his own youth."

There was probably more to the story than that, but he wasn't inviting any further conversation. "So that's your mentor?" she asked. "Wayne Dixon?"

"Yes."

Trevor had connections she had never imagined.

"Is there anything else you need to know?"

"I'm sure there are a million women who would want to marry you."

"Maybe a slight exaggeration. Surely it's only in the tens of thousands." He quirked his mouth in a quick grin that made him a dozen times less formidable. "Are you wondering why I'm still single, and no exes?"

"That's kind of personal, isn't it? You don't have to tell me."

"At first, I was focused on making a success out of the chances that Wayne offered me. I wanted to get my kid sisters through school, pay off my mom's mortgage. God knows she deserved it. And then…" He steepled his fingers and regarded her. "It's a serious thing. Marriage. Children. I won't do to my family what my father did to us. Frankly? I have a low bullshit tolerance. I'm not looking for someone who is interested in my money. I live a very simple life, away from the city with its distractions. A lot of women aren't suited to that. And I've been told I'm too intense, that I'm too committed to my work and my family."

She frowned.

"That's brought up another question for you."

Did she have the courage to ask this? Because she was afraid she'd drop the coffee, she put it down instead. "I wanted to ask you the same question you asked me last night. Why? Why did you accept the bet? Why did you ask for me?"

"*Why you?* For a dozen reasons. Because you were badly behaved, unable to stay still, casting impatient glances at Master David. You seemed to be begging for a good spanking. Hoping to find a Dominant who can handle you. One who is strong enough to give you what you really want."

"That's not true."

"No? Really?"

A voice of doubt whispered just the opposite. Had she been hoping to catch Master Trevor's attention?

"The only thing is, you need to trust yourself more. It's all right to admit what you want and to seek it out."

His statement hit too close to her heart. She was enjoying their time together, his sensual demands, the way he was inexorably pushing against her self-imposed boundaries, but she wouldn't tell him that. Nor would she consider what the realization meant to her. To escape the discomfort of what he'd said, along with her strong emotional reaction to it, she straightened her spine.

"You were a bit of a mystery." He leaned in closer. "I thought at first you had a lot of experience, but you're an innocent. To someone as jaded as me, it's appealing. And then I had a taste of you."

Breathless, she waited.

"You're damn hot." His words had a growl of masculine satisfaction that heated from the inside. "Once we were alone in our hotel room, you didn't hold anything back from me. When I started to fuck you, there was no pretense. You let me know what you wanted, didn't shy away from the exploration. You trusted me. That's fucking gold right there." He adjusted one of his shirtsleeves. "Because you're remarkable. That's why."

She blushed at his sincerity. No one had ever looked at her that way before.

His phone chimed. "Excuse me."

"Of course." While he checked the message, she unfurled her hands. She hadn't realized her nails had dug crescents into her palms.

"How long will it take you to get ready?" he asked, looking up, with the device in hand. "We have an appointment with Mademoiselle Giselle."

"Who?"

"She owns a shop nearby, and she is willing to meet us within the hour if that suits you. It's where we're going to purchase your collar."

Though he'd told her he wanted her to wear his collar, the fact that he'd taken immediate action caught her off guard.

"Can you be ready to go in forty-five minutes?"

"Yes, Sir." She gulped, her old life wobbling precariously beneath her. "That will be fine."

∼

"Are you sure this is the right place?" Shelby followed him inside the small shop on Royal Street. The front door was wide open, and chilled air beckoned tourists inside. There were stand-up coolers filled with water, soda, coffee, energy drinks, even wine and beer. Colorful dresses hung from racks. Shoes, ridiculously high heels as well as casual sandals, were displayed on top of neat, stacked rows of boxes. Carnival masks decorated all the walls, hanging next to pictures of trumpet players and New Orleans's numerous landmarks. Near the register was an assortment of items she'd expect to find—bracelets, pralines individually packed in plastic wrap, positive sayings on cards that could be tucked into a wallet or purse. But she didn't see anything that resembled collars. On their short stroll, she'd been imagining they'd stop in front of an unobtrusive door, much like the Quarter's entrance. She'd expected a quiet space, maybe even something that was a little freaky. This, however, was much the same as any other store she'd walked into.

"I assure you, it is."

"Ah! Trevor!"

With a smile, he turned toward the woman who emerged through a threshold that was disguised by strands and strands of dancing silver circles.

"Mademoiselle." He gave a slight bow before kissing the woman's cheeks. "Beautiful as always."

"Scoundrel." Her mysterious and dark eyes twinkled. "Sit a spell and tell me more."

With a chuckle, he placed his fingers against Shelby's spine. "May I present Shelby Salazar?"

"Darling Shelby. *Enchanté*. I wanted to meet the woman responsible for dragging me from my bed."

Trevor exerted a slight amount of pressure against Shelby's back, urging her forward. Regardless, she would have taken a step toward Mademoiselle Giselle. The woman was enthralling, with an inviting and irresistible energy.

Even by Shelby's standards, Mademoiselle was slight and petite. Her silver hair was caught at her nape by a sparkling barrette, and still the strands brushed the backs of her knees. Her sleeveless purple dress reached the floor but didn't hide the fact that she was barefoot.

"Aren't you lovely?" Mademoiselle Giselle's smile was genuine, and her voice held a hint of an accent, perhaps from many years before. Her dozens of bracelets clinking together, Mademoiselle took Shelby's hands and squeezed them with surprising strength. "Welcome to our world."

She looked to Trevor. "Our world?"

"Mademoiselle is referring to the lifestyle. The relationship dynamic."

Shelby sensed there was something more to it, but before she could press, he spoke again.

"Thank you for inviting us."

"It's more about Shelby than you, no matter how irresistible you are." She released Shelby's hands but held her gaze. "He's never asked me to open at this hour."

"You're not a morning person?" Which made two of them.

"I appreciate the mysteries of the night. People are less... guarded."

"Mademoiselle reads tea leaves."

She waved a hand, making her bracelets jangle. "That's just part of the act. I know things. The ritual, the ceremony of it. Boiling the water. Waiting. It sets the scene, enabling seekers to shed their inhibitions. I allow them to choose a teapot and the cup. That very process provides a window into their soul.

While I watch, I study their aura, see who they really are, not the shell they show the world. The leaves are revealing, but what I do is invite people to seek their own truth."

"Don't believe her. Mademoiselle has skills. She's good and accurate."

Shelby turned toward him, eyes wide. "You've had a reading?"

"On occasion."

"Enough chitchat. This isn't why you came."

Shelby was intrigued. "Do you accept appointments?" It might be something fun for the next ladies' night out.

"Of course."

"I'd like to see you."

The older woman's smile was knowing, as if she was anticipating that Shelby would say that.

She followed Mademoiselle through the tinkling silver curtain, past a set of stairs, then through an open door. Shelby missed a step as she entered another world, one with half a dozen mirrors—some wall mounted and others cheval, tipped at various angles. Crystals dripped from a stunning three-level chandelier. The floor was interesting, wooden planks, but in the middle were white hexagonal tiles, inset with black ones to create a large owl. The most shocking part was the bird's piercing eyes, crafted from green gemstones that reflected the overhead light in a hundred directions.

She flicked a glance toward Trevor's hand and the ring he wore, the one he'd promised to tell her about. His owl was a startling match to the one on Mademoiselle's floor. Too close to be a coincidence.

Part of her felt as if she'd been swept up into something she didn't understand.

"What do you think of Mademoiselle's private shop?" Trevor asked, breaking into her reverie.

"It's spectacular."

Trevor strode across the room to stand next to her. "Isn't it?"

Numerous cases artfully displayed collars and sensual high-end toys, crafted from stone, wood, steel, even glass. Among them were tall sets of wooden drawers, with some standing open. Lingerie spilled out in creative waves of hot primary colors offset by demure pastels with an occasional peek of something alluring in black lace.

But most eye-catching were the stunning gilt-framed portraits of a ballerina through the years. She was shown in various positions, and many had a subtle nod toward BDSM. In one she was blindfolded. In another, her arms were above her head, emphasizing a delicate collar around her throat. Shelby turned around, studying each. One showed the woman en pointe, her ankles tied together with ribbons from her pink ballet slippers. The pose spoke of pain and discipline, but her face was relaxed in what appeared to be transcendent obedience. Shelby's breath caught at the agony and the beauty captured by the artists. Then she looked at Mademoiselle Giselle. "It's you, isn't it? All of them." In the first, she couldn't be any older than eighteen or nineteen. One was obviously recent, but it was every bit as stunning as the rest—perhaps more so from the intensity in her eyes and the wisdom in her face.

"Very observant." She smiled.

"You're stunning, Mademoiselle."

"Thank you."

"You were a ballerina?"

"She still is," Trevor said. "Owns a local theater, and she dances in at least one production a year."

The other woman tipped her head to the side, exposing the long, graceful curve of her neck. "It keeps me young."

"A lot of people would disagree with that," Trevor said. "That hard work has to take a toll."

"Perhaps because they haven't been seduced by the beauty that lies just beyond the pain? It makes it worth the effort."

Shelby wondered if Mademoiselle was only speaking of ballet. Or was she hinting at something deeper? A life philosophy? Dreams? Risks? BDSM?

With a tiny key, the proprietress unlocked the cases that displayed the collars, then nodded toward Trevor. "I'll give you the privacy you require."

"Thank you."

Mademoiselle closed the door silently behind her.

"Are you kidding?" Shelby blinked. "She's leaving us alone in the shop?"

"Mademoiselle understands this is a decision that doesn't require her input." He drew her toward the case. "What captures your interest?"

With him standing so close—drinking in his scent, heat radiating from his body, and the knowledge of what this meant—her knees weakened. *None of them.* "I have no idea."

"Something delicate?" He walked to the far side of the counter and removed several velvet-lined trays. "Or more sturdy?"

Trevor picked up one that was part necklace, part choker. It had a black oval stone on the front, perhaps onyx.

She ran her fingers over it. It was light enough that she might not notice it while she was wearing it. But rather than it being jewelry, it had an actual lock on the back.

After setting it down, he selected one that was substantial, sturdy stainless steel with a square-shaped ring on the front. She'd seen a similar one at the club, and the Dom had a leash attached to it.

Forgetting to breathe, she looked at him.

"It makes you nervous?"

"Yes." She cleared her throat. Because her answer had been embarrassingly squeaky, she tried again. "A little."

"Perhaps that makes it the perfect one."

He pulled out another. This had long, artistic links, and the front was a stylish O-ring. Most people wouldn't recognize it as fetish wear, she realized.

"We'll skip the leather ones as I want to leave it on you for the duration of our time together." He chose several more and then lined up each next to the other, in a precise row. All of the collars were all different, in terms of size, functionality, beauty. "What else would you like me to add?"

She scanned the choices. The next case over had some that were nestled in pink satin. The light caught one, and she moved closer. The silver collar was less discreet than some, but delicate in comparison to the large one he'd selected. It had a raised, intricate floral and vine pattern. It was both functional and beautiful.

"Art nouveau." He studied it more closely. "And crafted from high-grade silver. Excellent taste." He laid it on top of the glass. "Any others that catch your eye?"

She shook her head. Now that she'd seen this, nothing else appealed. "No." Then because it was so appropriate in this setting, she added, "Sir."

"In that case, shall we make a decision?"

Under his guidance, she tried on all of the collars. When he fastened her selection in place, her heart thumped.

"It's perfect, isn't it?" He held a mirror in front of her.

Shelby ran her index finger across the metal's surface, tracing the dips and lines of the vine, lingering on a small flower. "Yes. It's exquisite." Even if he didn't like it, she might purchase it herself. It would be a sexy reminder of this moment, but also, something she'd feel sexy wearing when she visited the Quarter in future.

"So it's the one?"

"If it's okay with you, Sir." She met his dark, mysterious eyes.

"Nothing would make me happier."

He put down the mirror to select a small heart-shaped lock. "I'll remove this next Saturday."

"Yes," she whispered. Shelby tried to add Sir, but the word died in her throat as he moved behind her.

"Please lift your hair for me."

When she did so, he asked, "Ready?"

Fortunately he didn't wait for the answer she couldn't form.

The soft click of the lock closing echoed in the small room.

"You may drop your hair." He took her shoulders and turned her to face him. "An absolutely stunning choice. It suits you and your personality."

"Do you…" She cleared her throat then tried again. "Do you like it?" Was her voice as doubtful as it sounded?

"I approve of anything that marks you as mine." He fisted her hair to hold her in place, then captured her mouth and devoured her with a breath-stealing kiss. His passion shouldn't surprise her, but in a place that was only semiprivate, it did. The man—Dom—took what he wanted and demanded her submission.

When he released her, her lips were swollen, and her legs trembled. She grabbed on to his biceps for balance. But that wasn't necessary. He clamped his hands on her waist, offering silent, strong support.

"But yes. I do."

Yes? She shook her head. "What?"

"In answer to your question." He smiled. "Of all of the offerings in this shop, this particular collar"—he traced her skin just beneath it—"is my favorite. The craftsmanship is superb. And it is stunning on you."

"Ah!" Mademoiselle swept into the room. "I've had that piece for some time. It's a personal favorite of mine." Her eyes danced. "It's been waiting for you."

Shelby blinked.

"I trust my intuition. I purchased it and waited for the buyer to appear." She accepted Trevor's credit card. "Would you like a box?"

"No."

"Actually—" Shelby glanced toward Trevor. This was temporary, not permanent. *Right?* "That would be nice. Please."

His nod was sharp.

"Agitation tells us a lot, Trevor," Mademoiselle observed as she turned away to choose a lacquered wooden box. "It's the distance between where we are and where we would like to be. It's a new sensation. Oui? Unwelcome, perhaps. Different, at any rate."

"Tea leaves tell you that?" Gruffness made Trevor's voice rough.

"None needed." The woman faced them again and placed the receipt and box into a beautiful black handle bag with the store's name in raised gold lettering. "I'll see you again, Shelby." Mademoiselle's words were a statement, not a question. "You'll have things to sort through. But ultimately only you can know your heart. No one else's thoughts or opinions will matter. Trust yourself."

She accepted the business card that Mademoiselle slid across the counter. "Thank you."

After a few pleasantries, Trevor excused them.

"That was…interesting," she said when they exited through the main store and back onto the street. When they'd wandered down an hour ago, the French Quarter had been relatively empty, but now cars were bumper-to-bumper, and pedestrians streamed into shops. A few were already sipping hurricanes from tall glasses.

"Always. Coffee? Brunch, perhaps? You didn't eat much this morning, and you will need extra energy when I get you to my house this afternoon."

Heat that had nothing to do with the Southern sun surged through her, and the weight of his collar settled on her, part promise, part possession.

CHAPTER 6

"You won't be needing those."

At the implacable command in Trevor's voice, Shelby froze. Holding a handful of panties, she turned to find him filling the doorway to her bedroom. Somehow, he seemed even bigger than he had earlier, overwhelming her small home.

On the drive to her home, they'd discussed plans for the upcoming week. He'd encouraged her not to rearrange her schedule and informed her she could drive one of his cars back and forth to work.

There were a couple of clients she wanted to see, but there were others she intended to transfer to her colleagues. Hannah had been right. Shelby did need a little break, and the upcoming week was the perfect opportunity.

But until he'd issued his gruff statement, she hadn't considered he'd have requirements for the way she dressed.

With a few strides, he devoured the distance between them to scoop up the lingerie and dump it back the drawer. "Tell me why you think it would be okay to cover yourself in that way?"

This was all too real. She was falling into the abyss of surrealness. Since last night, she'd been swept up in an alternate universe, and at times, she didn't know how to behave.

After leaving Mademoiselle's shop, they'd eaten brunch at the hotel before riding the elevator back to his room. Following his instructions, she'd packed his belongings and stowed his hat in a box. Then he'd followed her home.

For some odd reason, she thought he might wait outside while she grabbed her clothes and toiletries.

"I'm waiting for an answer."

She cleared her throat. "I was thinking… Maybe when I go to work?"

"We can discuss that. So for now, grab a couple of pairs. Would you like me to choose for you?"

"No." She shook her head, and her collar moved. The metal rubbed her collarbone in a reminder of what she'd agreed to.

"Black is always good."

She fished out her favorites that met her requirements.

"Good. Do you have something you can swim in?"

She should be lucky that he wouldn't make her skinny dip. Shelby crouched to open her bottom drawer and pulled out one that would cover everything.

Relentless, he folded his arms across his chest. "Any two-piece suits?"

For a moment, she considered fibbing. She owned three but hadn't worn any of them in years. Somehow, he would no doubt figure out if she lied to him and go through her belongings himself. Caught, she sighed. "Yes."

"Let's see them."

She moved things around, but since he was so close, overwhelming her, she extracted a red one and then another covered in pink polka dots.

"A bikini, perhaps?"

Damn him.

She reached all the way to the back to pull out a skimpy little stringy thing that she'd bought on a trip but never had the courage to wear.

"Perfect."

"I should have known you'd say that."

"Or anticipated my desires and met them without being asked?"

Pulse thundering, she looked up. He appeared much as he had last night at the club, hard and uncompromising. His voice had an edge that made it clear he wasn't a man for playing games. A shiver jogged through her.

She selected a couple of outfits for work.

"Now for the time at my house. You'll need a few things you can be comfortable in. Shorts?"

"Second drawer."

Of course he chose the smallest ones.

"Dresses?"

"In the closet." She pointed to the far side of the room.

"May I?"

No man had ever gone through her clothes. "Of course."

She stood and followed him. Not for the first time, she wished she were better organized. Skirts hung next to work slacks and blazers, with blouses and long-sleeved shirts sprinkled between. In order to find what he was looking for, he'd likely need to sort through everything.

He thumbed through the hangers. "These will suffice." He pulled out a couple of sundresses and handed them to her.

"I have several more."

"You can choose one that you'd like to wear on the way to my place. Unless you'd prefer shorts? With the breeze off the lake, you might find them more practical."

"Agreed."

He selected several T-shirts from a shelf and instructed

her to put them in her overnight bag. "I believe we're finished here."

"Wait." She scowled. He'd obviously never seen her get ready for a trip. "That's not enough clothes for an entire week."

"While we're at home, you won't be needing anything."

Shelby tried to swallow, but her mouth was too dry.

"You'll want to change before we head out."

Since her jeans were all-but stuck to her, that was a good idea. "I'll, er, just meet you in the living room?"

In unspoken response, he raised an eyebrow.

Why did undressing in front of him now seem so much more intimate than what they'd already shared? Perhaps because this was her space, and she hadn't allowed any other man in it.

With an overblown sigh, she unfastened her pants.

"Shelby, Shelby. I appreciate how difficult some of my requests might be."

Requests? On what planet did he consider his words to be an option?

"Hear me, and hear me well, my precious, struggling submissive." He eased back her chin. "You can always refuse or negotiate, or even terminate our agreement. But if you are going to comply, please consider your actions. And ask yourself if you are behaving with the grace I expect from you."

Horrified by his gentle rebuke, she reeled.

"I expect—demand—to be with a sub who communicates with me, even if it's just to express discomfort."

The cold steeliness in his eyes enslaved her.

"If you are going to obey my directives, do so in a way that proves you are happy to wear my collar."

No other person had ever been this unyielding with her. Trevor didn't just want her body; he wanted everything she had to give. "I'm sorry."

"Your apology is accepted and appreciated." His thumb still beneath her chin, he traced a finger across her lips. "Thank you."

Expecting a kiss, she leaned toward him.

But he lowered his hand and stepped back from her. "You were changing into a pair of shorts."

First he reprimanded her. Then comforted her. And now he was reinforcing what he'd said. He made her mind swirl.

This time, even though embarrassment still scalded her cheeks, she sat on the edge of the bed to remove her boots and socks. Aware of his scrutiny, she stood. With her gaze downcast, she lowered the zipper before working the damp denim over her hips, then down her thighs.

"Watching you is my new favorite pastime."

His words rang true, giving her confidence.

Quickly she snatched up the shorts and did a small jig to squeeze into them.

"You look wonderful," he said when she finally straightened in front of him. "You'd be even hotter if we hemmed them." He took her wrist and moved her around so he could study her rear end. "An inch or so would do it."

Her mouth dropped open. Did he mean it? "I wouldn't be allowed in public!"

"Exactly." His lascivious grin lit his eyes and did ridiculous things to her insides.

He cupped her shoulders and drew her toward him. Not knowing what to expect, she remained rooted in place, looking up at him.

Slowly, agonizingly slowly, he brushed his lips across hers.

Fire seared her.

At that moment, she realized that her connection with him was unlike anything she'd experienced with anyone else. Even with Joe, their relationship—even their marriage—had been superficial. She'd kept parts of herself locked away. But Trevor seemed to see into her.

When she was ready to give him anything, he released her, sending a maelstrom of confusion through her.

"Anything else you need before we leave? Otherwise, you'll be tied up here for a while."

She shook her head to refocus on the moment. *That*, she was certain he meant.

"Shelby?"

For a second, she considered a bra, but since he hadn't let her wear one this morning, she already knew his answer. "Pajamas."

"Did I allow you to wear them last night?"

"I thought maybe that was different. You know, because I fell asleep after…"

"After I was finished eating you out and fucking your sexy body?"

Memories danced through her brain, making her hot.

"I won't want anything between us in the bed."

"I generally sleep in a negligee of some type."

"As tempting as that sounds…no. If you get cold, snuggle up to me. I'll give you everything you need for the next week."

She shouldn't believe that, but she did. "Ah, well. Then. Just toiletries. And shoes."

"Remember sandals for the boat. Something that won't be slippery when wet."

Were they still talking about footwear?

"Whatever you can gather in two minutes or less. The sight of your curves in those shorts has tested the last ounce of my patience."

∼

"This is where you live? It's…" Though they were technically still in New Orleans, the city was miles behind them, and they were traversing a road that seemed to divide Lake Catherine and Lake Pontchartrain.

He slid her a glance but waited for her to go on.

"It's spectacular. I never knew the view was so beautiful." The road curved slightly. "Or that there'd be water on both sides of us."

"Have you been out here before?"

"This area specifically? No. One summer when I was a kid, my dad and stepmom rented a place somewhere close to here. They invited me to spend a couple of days with them. I remember going on a boat, having to share a room with her kids, and they didn't like me. I don't remember much except for the fact I was traumatized and wanted to go home. And since my mom went on vacation to Paris with her new husband and his kids, that wasn't an option."

"Sounds painful."

"I got through. Mostly by escaping in books, pretending I was living someone else's life and not my own."

"Is that why you became a mediator?"

"I hated the way I was a weapon between them."

"And you wanted to spare others that kind of pain?"

She shifted a little. "That's almost too easy of an answer."

"Truth is always a little more complicated, isn't it?"

"It's probably more about conflict, to be honest." She knew he'd persist until she gave in. So she might as well keep it light and get it over with. "There was arguing. Years and years of it. Horrible fights, thrown dishes, broken knick-knacks, destroyed furniture. I'd hide under my bed with my hands over my ears."

"God, Shelby. I'm sorry."

"Then…" Maybe because she knew the relationship with

Trevor would end, she decided it was safe to expose her secrets. "There's my own divorce."

"Oh?" He slid a glance that was inquiring but also pointed.

We had our future mapped out. Well, until he fell in love with a colleague where he was interning." She tried to keep her voice light, which was difficult because his betrayal still stung. "The firm represented him at no charge, and David took me on as a client. He did the best he could, but I ended up with a lot of the debt."

"How's that?"

"I worked while Joe went to school, and I had a decent job. We were supposed to pay off the credit cards and auto loans as he started earning the big bucks. Of course, none of that was in writing. When we went to court, he said he had changed his mind about going into law and that he was going to continue with his studies. So he realistically didn't have any huge, immediate earning potential." She clamped her mouth shut. "At least I didn't have to pay spousal support. So there's that."

"And where is he now?"

"Trial lawyer, in Atlanta. Moved out of state with his third wife."

"You are well rid of him."

For years she'd told herself that. It had gotten to the point she almost believed it. But she was still chipping away at the financial and emotional debt he'd left behind. "You're right." She was grateful they didn't have kids together. At least that was one place she'd been firm. Maybe deep down, she hadn't been as confident in the relationship as she wanted to believe.

"That's your specialty, if that's the word? Divorce?"

"I've done some corporate work. But yes. I guess you can say that. Most of my cases involve families." And she did her best to help couples navigate the tricky emotional waters so their kids felt more secure than she had. Some days were more difficult than others.

"Does it have an impact on you?"

He slid a glance her way, and she turned slightly in her seat to study him. "In what way?"

He shrugged. "It can't be easy."

"I spend my days seeing relationships at their worst. They don't come to me until everything has fallen apart, irrevocably. Most of them have put in real time, going to counseling, giving it two, three, four chances. They've done everything they can to save their marriage. Happily ever after turns out to be a lot more work than some people imagined it would. Sometimes they get fixed on the romance and the wedding—fancy gowns, an event to remember. And there's not a lot of planning for what happens when things get tough, when there are money issues, or differences of opinion in raising children. I've seen acrimony, even hatred. There's one particular couple that stands out. They were in their eighties."

"Eighties?"

"Yeah. She said she'd given him the best years of her life, but she wanted to experience some joy before dying." She looked out the window. "That one was sad."

He didn't respond for a long time.

"Sorry. That was more than you needed to hear."

"No. I'm glad you told me."

The time, the silence grew, and she let it.

"Almost there."

She shook herself from her thoughts. Homes on stilts began to dot the landscape.

He continued past a number of streets, making his way to a place where the pavement made a big curve, then a left-hand turn. "I'm at the end, and I own the last two lots."

"For privacy?"

His grin was quick and wicked. "You'll have all the freedom you need to scream when I torture you."

Mouth wide, she dug her fingernails into the armrest.

"I'm kidding, Shelby."

God.

"The dungeon is soundproof. So your screams really are not a concern at all."

Dungeon? "You…?"

"I do. And it is."

Shelby couldn't breathe.

He followed the road as it forked to the right. "That's it, up there." He pointed ahead and to the right.

His enormous white home stood on pilings that appeared to be fifteen or twenty feet high. Each side had what appeared to be garages, and a large concrete area was between them, complete with a bar, hanging swing, and a large colorful sign that read GONE FISHING.

Once he'd stopped, he pushed a remote control, and a gate slid open. Seconds later, he parked on the concrete in front of the garage door, then turned off the SUV's engine.

"Let's get you settled."

After what he'd said, she was no longer certain this was such a good idea.

He pulled the keys from the ignition.

Trying to be brave, she opened the door and was almost immediately plowed backward by a great big black bear.

"Down, boy!"

The monstrous thing licked her face, then dropped back down to the ground. "What is that?"

"It's a Bruno."

She frowned, studying the four-footed, wagging, drooling, dancing animal. "What's a Bruno?"

At her mention of his name, the dog froze, looked at her

through large, beautiful eyes, then extended his front paws and dropped his head between them.

"No one is exactly sure what a Bruno is. I should have warned you he might show up. He's nosy that way." Trevor rounded the front of the vehicle. "Bruno is a bad-mannered vagabond. He showed up one day. We have no idea where he came from. Everyone thought he belonged to someone else. And it took about a year for us to figure out that he has no owner." He shrugged. "Which means we all adopted him. He indiscriminately sleeps around. Well, except for Mrs. Trudeau's home. She took him to the vet to get fixed, and he has never forgiven her. Turns out Bruno holds grudges. Who knew?"

She couldn't help but laugh.

"He keeps an eye on the neighborhood. Saved a four-year-old from a nasty encounter with an alligator. Caught a bunch of kids trying to break into one of the homes when the owners were away. As you can see, he checks out all the newcomers. So he earns his keep, and he shows up for dinner wherever someone's having a barbecue."

She studied the canine, trying to figure out what breed he was. "He doesn't look like any dog I've ever seen."

"Us either. Appears to have some Great Dane in him. Or mastiff, maybe? Some people think he might be part Great Pyrenees. But then there's his coloring. And the shape of his head. Sort of like a pizza box."

That sort of went along with her observation that his paws were the size of dinner plates. "When he"—*accosted*—"greeted me, I thought he was a bear."

"We've considered that too."

Bruno sat, his massive tongue lolling to one side, and extended his paw, which she accepted. "Well, it's nice to meet you, Bruno."

"You've received the official welcome to the neighborhood."

In the distance, a boat engine rumbled. Bruno whined once, then abruptly stood, barking nonstop. Before she realized what was happening, he'd dashed through to the back of the yard, where she lost sight of him.

"We're yesterday's news." Trevor grinned.

She'd never been more grateful for a distraction. This suddenly, somehow, seemed more normal, as if she was a guest, rather than a sexual submissive for the next week.

He opened the back of the SUV and grabbed her bag.

She followed him up the dozens of steps to the porch. "Your home is beautiful." There were four columns. In addition to being architecturally interesting, they appeared to support a second-level balcony.

"Mason built it."

Mason was Hannah's fiancé. "Seriously?"

"Check out his company's website. You'll see pictures of the entire process."

On the porch, she crossed to the railing to take in the panorama. There was no way she could have imagined anything like this. "Lake Catherine?"

Trevor joined her. "The front of the house overlooks Lake Pontchartrain."

"Really?" She turned to rest her elbows behind her while she looked up at him, and she had to shield her eyes from the sun. "I was honestly a bit surprised when I realized you didn't live in one of the more exclusive neighborhoods on the lake."

"Because?"

"I guess…" She squirmed. There was no good way to say this. "Assumptions." She'd mediated two divorces for wealthy couples with lakefront property. Wanting to retain the exclusive address was one of the biggest sticking points in the dissolution of each marriage. It was about more than just the money—living on a particular street was a status symbol. Maybe she'd underestimated Trevor. "You're able to live anywhere you wish. Right?"

"I'm financially comfortable, if that's what you're asking."

Since he'd made a twenty-five-thousand-dollar wager for a week with her, there was no doubt about that. "Sorry. I wasn't trying to be offensive, but I keep stepping in it, don't I?"

"This is where I want to be. For me, it's a lifestyle choice. I'm close enough to the city for meetings, and far enough away to be in another world. There's peace and seclusion. On a clear night, you can count the stars. Nature is everywhere."

In the distance a dog barked.

"And where else has a Bruno?"

She smiled, seeing the picture he painted. "Another assumption. From the sign." She pointed. "You mean it when you say you've gone fishing."

"Born with a pole in my hand. It's the only thing I remember my dad teaching me to do. Really, my only memory of him." His voice was as easy as his shrug. "We counted on our catch to feed us. I'd sell excess to earn money. That was before I started mowing lawns, hustling to make a dime."

"Which is where you met Wayne?"

"It's a long story."

Once again, he hedged when it came to his past.

"Shall we?" He walked across the deck to enter a code on the keypad affixed to the house; then he opened the French door and encouraged her to proceed him inside.

They entered into a stunning, wide open space, with gorgeous wooden floors, unlike anything she'd ever seen. The great room was filled with cozy leather furniture, a large television, a gas fireplace, and uncovered windows that overlooked the lake.

Quickly he sealed out the stifling humidity. "My office is to the right."

"Is it off-limits?"

When he didn't immediately answer, she turned to look at him.

"No one has ever asked."

She was beyond curious. Would it be as pristine as the rest of the home? Or would he have branded it with his indelible mark? "May I see it."

"Be my guest." He shrugged.

Before he could change his mind, she acted, throwing open the double doors and entering.

He had massive windows with an endless view. His desk was sleek and modern. Unsurprisingly, it was uncluttered. His college diploma hung on one wall, and various snapshots were featured in a collage-like display. "Your family?" Rather than waiting for an answer, she moved in closer.

Two women, with a strong family resemblance, beamed from one of the photos, dressed in formal wear. "Your sisters?" She glanced back at him.

"The twins. Yes." Trevor was lounging against the doorjamb, arms folded. "They were at a friend's wedding."

In another was a woman, with Trevor on one side and the girls on the other. "Your mom, I'm guessing?"

"You'd be correct. On Mother's Day. It's a tradition. We take a new picture every year, and I replace that one."

"That's lovely." She smiled. "The picture in the middle—if I'm not mistaken, that's you with Wayne Dixon."

"Correct again."

She studied the image a little more closely before pivoting to face him. "He's wearing the same ring you are."

"Keen powers of observation, Ms. Salazar. Maybe you should have been a private detective."

"Part of being a mediator is attention to detail, keeping track of all the various threads." When he didn't speak, she went on. "I noticed an identical one at Mademoiselle Giselle's, when we were shopping for my collar. You promised an explanation."

"I did." He pushed his shoulder away from the doorjamb but remained in the threshold.

"Is there a reason you're being secretive?" How complex was his life?

Without answering, he continued to look at her.

"There is, isn't there?" In a couple of her divorce cases, husbands had belonged to secret societies. She was no expert, but she understood that the groups had symbols, perhaps on a belt buckle or a ring, some way of alerting others that they were part of some kind of fraternal order. The owl, though, wasn't something she was familiar with. "A society of some kind."

"You enjoy puzzles."

"I do. Should I do an internet search?"

"No doubt you will, no matter what I say." He grinned, and funny things happened to her insides.

All of his mannerisms, from stern dominance to his tender care, and now his quick smile, melted all of her resistance.

"When you do, look up the Zeta Society."

Shelby forced herself to focus on what he said, rather than her reaction to him. "I've never heard of it."

His response was deadpan. "It's because it's a secret."

"Touché." She laughed.

"You'll have questions, and I'll do my best to answer them."

"There will be things you can't tell me."

He nodded. "Of course."

"Are there a lot of members?"

"Worldwide? More than you might imagine."

Worldwide? How was it possible she'd never heard of them?

"Finished here? If so, I'll show you the rest of the house."

She took another last glance around, and, just like she'd been outside, she was captivated by the view. "I'm not sure how you get any work done here to be honest. I'm not sure I would."

In a few steps, he was behind her. "I used to live in the city, with its more frantic pace. I had a small house out here, rustic, no air conditioner, only a fireplace for heat. One bedroom, one bathroom. It wasn't much more than a fishing camp, and I'd come up here every chance I got. Weekends, holidays. I never wanted to leave. John Thoroughgood, a friend of Mason's, started searching for a piece of property for me. It took a couple of years to find the right one. Mostly because I wanted more than one lot."

"Do you go out on the water every day?"

"There are winter days when the north wind is blowing when I'll be honest, I'd rather be in front of the fireplace watching repeats of bass fishing competitions."

"I can only imagine."

"Shall we?"

She followed him from the room, and he closed the doors with a definitive click. Letting her know she needed permission to enter the hallowed space?

"If you need it, the bathroom is over there." He pointed to a spot beyond his office.

She walked through to the kitchen with its decorator-inspired oversize island, quartz countertops, six-top burner, built-in espresso machine, and white glass-fronted cabinets. "This..." Shelby had no words. Even though she didn't love to cook, she would happily prepare three meals a day here.

"I hope you'll be comfortable here."

Comfortable? This definitely qualified as the getaway that Shelby needed.

"The refrigerator is kept stocked by the housekeeper. She comes and prepares meals twice a week. But if there's anything you need, we can either drive to town or boat to the marina."

Beyond the dining room, a second set of French doors beckoned. As if hypnotized, she walked toward them.

"Go on out and have a look," he encouraged, joining her to open the lock.

Once they were outside, she sighed. "Wow. Is this still Lake Pontchartrain?"

"This is Lake Catherine."

"So you have a different view from every side of the house." For as far as she could see, there was water and boats. "I think I get it." This place was more wild and free than areas closer to the city. "Living here, it comes with risks, though, doesn't it?"

"No doubt. Storms off the Gulf. Hurricanes. The house is built to all the latest specifications and then some. Still, you could say it tempts fate. You'd be right." He smiled. "Even if it's destroyed tomorrow, I'll have the memory of every single sunrise and sunset, though."

She walked to the edge of the deck. From here, ripples from the pool and hot tub below beckoned in invitation. His courtyard was mostly concrete with large chairs and colorful umbrellas. Plumeria and oleander formed a hedge around the perimeter, offering privacy as well as beauty. She glanced over her shoulder to see him. The sun silhouetted his broad frame, nearly making her forget what she was going to ask. She took a breath to clear away the toe-curling excitement that chased through her whenever he was near. "That… Is all of this yours?"

He nodded.

To re-center herself, she turned back toward the lake.

The pier's planks extended forever, with a couple of chairs bolted to the wood, presumably for fishing. At the end, there was a structure that contained a pontoon and another boat, cradled in a sling. "It's like you live in a vacation wonderland."

"You could say that," he agreed as he joined her. "I've never looked at it in quite that way."

For a few minutes, they stood next to each other and watched a boat pass by, dragging a large inflatable flamingo behind it. A couple of kids were riding on top, and their laughter and screams rippled across the distance.

"You can try that too while you're here."

"You have one of those?"

"Mine's a dragon."

She faced him. "Yours is a…dragon?" Then she blinked. "Are we still talking about inflatables?"

"Well…" A wicked, slow smile sauntered across his lips, sending her thoughts into a freefall. "You might have to blow it up."

"Oh Jesus." She blushed furiously. How had their conversation taken such a dirty turn?

But Trevor's smile was irresistible, and so was seeing this teasing side of him, a new facet she never suspected existed. The security of being in his own place clearly brought it out in him. She wondered if she'd ever relaxed that much. Or had she spent her life on guard, protecting herself?

"The boathouse has kayaks also, if you're interested. You're free to indulge in all the amenities. In fact, I hope you do."

His offer was lovely and appreciated. "Thank you. I've

never tried that. I don't suppose you have one that seats two people, and theoretically, I could have a glass of wine while you do all the work?"

He grinned. "That could be arranged."

"Really?"

"Tonight, even."

"I can't tell whether or not you're serious."

"Most assuredly. And you're going to need the relaxation after what I have planned for you."

The now familiar tension left her breathless.

"Let's go back inside. I'll show you the upstairs."

Was that where his dungeon was?

When they were back inside, he picked up her bag, then led the way to the second level. "There are two bedrooms up here."

His master suite was enormous, dominated by a king-size bed that faced a set of sliding glass doors that led to a private deck overlooking one of the lakes. There was a peace here, in the views of nature and in the way the home was constructed to take advantage of them.

Along one wall, he had a coffee bar, with a small refrigerator and sink. Two chairs were nestled against a wall, with a table between them. He even had a desk with a computer and a divan.

The bathroom had a walk-in shower and soaker tub in a little alcove with its own window.

His suite contained everything she needed to be happy. "I'm not sure I ever want to leave." The moment she said the words, she wished she could take them back. She was being impetuous. "I didn't mean that literally." That wasn't the entire truth. Part of her already mourned the end of the week.

"Mason will be pleased the home has that affect on you. That was the intention."

She appreciated his easy smile.

"Your closet is here." He opened a door, and she entered.

"Seriously? This is bigger than my bedroom." There was a built-in set of drawers, and nothing on the shelves or hanging from the rods. Her few belongings would be lost in the vastness.

It took her a moment to realize he'd placed her bag on a shelf and was saying something. "I'm sorry?"

"Come with me."

She followed him into the spa-like bathroom that had numerous windows and unobstructed views. And since there were no neighbors, there was no reason to close the blinds. "I've never seen anything like it."

"Exposure to sunlight, as well as the stars. And always, the lake."

"The attention to detail is amazing."

"The designer added all these candles." He swept his arm wide. "I've never had the opportunity to use them. But you are more than welcome to make yourself at home."

If she soaked in the oversize tub surrounded by flickering candlelight, she might never want to go home.

"Towels are in this linen closet. You can use the sink on the right. And those drawers"—he pointed to a spot beneath the vanity—"are empty. And there's plenty of room in the cabinets."

Commingling her toiletries with his? The reminder of what was happening here sent an electrical impulse through her. "This will be perfect." Her voice was higher-pitched than usual, revealing her sudden tension.

"Would you like to see the guest room?"

She held her breath. Since they were almost out of places to see, she figured he'd turned that into his dungeon.

Down the hallway, he opened the door, and she exhaled

in a rush. There was a bed, a wardrobe, a cozy chair, and a large television. There was nothing extraordinary about it.

Had he been teasing when he said he had a dungeon?

She sighed as she shoved away her earlier fevered apprehensions.

Evidently unaware of her inner turmoil, he led the way back out and showed her the laundry room. "You won't have need of it, however. Since I mostly intend to keep you unclothed."

Every time she started to relax, he said something that was a terrible reminder that she was his submissive.

"Now, I'll leave you to settle in. Meet me downstairs." He checked his watch. "Say, ten minutes? Is that enough time?"

The floor shifted. It took every ounce of her control for her to whisper, "Yes, Sir," instead of objecting.

When he reached the staircase, he placed a hand on the banister and turned to look back at her. "Shelby?"

"Sir?"

"I want you naked." He paused. "And don't keep me waiting."

CHAPTER 7

What in the hell was wrong with him?

Even though he was downstairs, he was aware of her. Her fresh scent lingered on the air, and he imagined her moving around his bedroom and placing her belongings alongside his. *Intimacy.*

With a sharp pivot to shatter his reverie, he paced to the rear set of French doors and stared out. Ever since he could remember, vast expanses of water had soothed him, whether it was a lake or the ocean itself. He found answers in the depths. There was a steadiness to it, something he appreciated.

Today, it offered no solace for his soul.

Even though he'd been involved with numerous submissives over the years, nothing could have prepared him for the sight of sweet, trusting Shelby in his collar.

The gorgeous art nouveau collar suited her. The moment he closed that tiny lock on the back, something unwelcome had crashed into him. Possession.

Last night at the hotel, while she'd still been wearing the bolo tie, he'd been taunted by a thought—that he might not want to remove his sign of domination. And now he was pretty fucking sure he wouldn't be capable of releasing her tiny padlock.

Hell and back.

In frustration, Trevor scrubbed his hand across his face.

He wanted her under his protection.

He wanted her as his.

These unexpected and wholly foreign emotions tied him in knots. Mademoiselle's earlier words had struck an uncomfortable nerve. He was, indeed, agitated. It thrummed in him, like something live, as persistent as the turning of tides.

Upstairs, a door closed. He'd given her ten minutes, and he knew she wouldn't take even thirty seconds extra.

Though she would be ready, he would have been smart to give himself a little longer. He needed time to think things through.

For him, patience was not a virtue—it was a skill he'd been taught by his mentor. He didn't rush. He planned; then he executed.

Deviation was not an option. If he didn't stay strong, he might end up like his father.

The man—Trevor sneered at that word—had been in and out of his mother's life. He'd abandoned her when she was pregnant with Trevor. But then he'd come back when Trevor was around four and said he wanted to be a family. His mother, as desperate for love as she was the help, accepted Jerome back.

Their relationship existed several more years, with Jerome running around, quitting jobs, drinking too much. And then they had twins, born prematurely. A few months later, when one of the babies was running a fever, he drove to the store in the middle of the night to buy children's pain reliever and kept on going, never to be heard from again.

Seeing his mother shattered had forced Trevor to grow

up. At age ten, he became the man of the house. Even as a child, he vowed he'd do everything in his power to take away his mother's tears and ensure his little sisters had a roof over their heads.

He'd brought home fish and learned to cook them. When he had extra, he sold them. Eventually, he had enough for a rusty secondhand bicycle. Intrepid, he'd jumped on the torn leather seat and pedaled to an affluent area of town. He waited for the guard in the pure white-painted shack to make his rounds; then Trevor furiously biked his way through the entrance, hid behind some bushes for a while, then stashed his ride. Pretending he was the son of a neighbor, he offered to help homeowners with chores, cleaning garages, mowing yards, carrying in groceries, washing cars and boats.

Wayne Dixon had instantly seen through Trevor's bold charade. Instead of sending him scampering back to his own neighborhood, Wayne had invited him inside, and Mrs. Dixon had prepared him a hot meal. After Trevor had eaten his fill, Wayne had given Trevor a long list of chores. At the end of the day, he'd been paid well. He'd clutched the cash as if it were a lifeline—and it was. Each Saturday morning, Trevor pedaled ferociously back to their home.

The summer he turned fourteen, Wayne started taking Trevor to work. He was given a respectable salary, and he had to use his own money for haircuts, khakis, Oxford shirts, dress shoes, even a belt. He'd learned about budgeting, saving, then investing.

Wayne wasn't just wealthier than Trevor could imagine; he used his money to do good on a scope that had been unthinkable to Trevor. In addition to working on emerging medical issues all over the world, Wayne invested in worthwhile businesses, then served on their boards of directors, steering the companies toward profitability. Only then did he take back his investments, sometimes with little to no interest. Always, he invested that capital back into another company.

He helped Trevor win a scholarship to college. And after he had completed several semesters, Wayne put Trevor in charge of a couple of investments, had him serve on the boards, ensured he knew how to be strategic.

After business school, Trevor had become the man's partner. Now they were fast friends, and Wayne was still his mentor.

Because he carefully calculated the chances of success in everything he did, Trevor avoided long-term relationships. He had the same physical and emotional urges as any man, maybe more so, but he refused to let them rule him. He stayed in control and harnessed the powerful energy.

That was, until Shelby and her wide-eyed trust.

Last night he'd awakened with her tucked against him. In the ambient light, he watched her. As if aware of him, she'd made tiny, satisfied sounds and moved a little closer. He'd wrapped strands of her hair around his hand and lifted them to inhale the scent of her. Some sort of flower, perhaps. Maybe from her shampoo. But there was something else there as well. Belief in him. In a way no one else had—perhaps ever.

He'd seen her hesitation when she walked out onto the hotel's balcony while he was talking to Caroline. Instead of making up her mind that he was seeing someone and getting angry, Shelby showed curiosity and joined him.

Because of that, he'd become even more determined to give her whatever she desired. If she asked for the moon, he'd wrap it up and add a star for good measure.

So what the fuck *was* he doing here?

Shelby made it clear that she wasn't in the market for a relationship. A month ago, that would have suited him fine.

Today he wasn't so sure.

Though he didn't hear her, he sensed her presence in the way his awareness prickled.

Trevor turned to see her on the bottom stair, a hand tightly gripping the banister. "There you are." Her expressive eyes were wide, radiating her uncertainty. "Exquisite."

She remained rooted in place.

"Come here, sweet Shelby."

After descending the final step, she slowly walked toward him.

"You're uncomfortable with your nudity." Trevor appreciated her bravery.

"Uhm…" She tipped her chin up. "Yes, Sir."

"I appreciate you doing this for me." And she'd done it without fuss, showing she'd learned from earlier.

She stopped in front of him and repeatedly opened and closed her hands at her sides.

"Let's set some ground rules, shall we?"

"Actually…" Her voice was little more than a whisper as she went on. "That would be nice. I'm a little confused."

"It will be clear to you when we're in a scene. And if it's not, simply ask."

She nodded.

"In the future, when I ask you to join me naked, please kneel. You'll get better at it with practice. And the next time you're watching a poker game that your Dom is playing, you'll be perfectly behaved."

She opened her mouth as if to protest but then quickly—smartly—shut it again.

"Excellent. You're a quick study." He nodded toward the floor.

Shelby lowered herself in front of him. Could he get her to do this while he worked every day? She'd be a hell of a muse. "Knees a little farther apart, please."

While she adjusted her position, he walked around her, and she tracked his movement. "Keep your head still."

"Yes, Sir."

"Unless I countermand my order, keep your gaze downcast."

"That's difficult, Sir."

"Because you don't know what to expect?"

"I think so. Yes."

"You may find that having structure calms you. You now know what position I expect and when. All you need to do is wait. And since you fidget, keep your hands laced behind you."

"I fidget?"

He quirked a brow, and she laughed.

"I mean, I'll do better, Sir." She finally remembered to lower her gaze.

"Let's try this again. Return to the bedroom. Wait thirty seconds, then join me again." He stood in front of her and offered a hand up.

"Thank you, Sir."

Once she was steady, he released her.

She didn't look back as she silently crossed the room, her hips swaying in an enticingly feminine way.

Thirty seconds later, she returned. This time, she was less wobbly as she lowered herself to her knees. She scooted around a little before lacing her fingers behind her, and her grip was so tight that he wondered if she might cut off the circulation. After a few shallow breaths, she remembered to look down. "Well done." It was an exercise in self-control not to lift her up, crush her against him, then fuck her into oblivion. "Now, please return to my bedroom and choose one of my shirts. You will be wearing it."

With her mouth open, as if to speak, she glanced up.

"It makes no difference which one." He was eager to see which she would select.

She nodded before rising again. This time, maybe because she was thinking about his instructions rather than what she was doing, her motions were much more graceful. "You have one minute, Shelby."

He told himself to look at the window and feign disinterest. Instead, he watched until she disappeared.

Her selection surprised him. She'd chosen a T-shirt he'd removed the previous day. "Why that one?" he asked when she was on her knees in front of him.

Bright pink stained her cheeks. "You didn't give me any instructions. And…" She swallowed.

"And?"

"It smells like you."

Sweet Jesus.

Trevor cleared his throat to cover the fact that she'd left him speechless. Then he gave a sharp nod. "Now put it on."

"Should I stand?"

"No need." He remained where he was, crowding her space a little. It shocked him how much he liked it.

She was so petite that the hem dragged the floor. Which was good as it meant it would cover her ass. In the past, he hadn't minded if anyone caught a glimpse of one of his submissives. With her, it turned out that he cared a great deal. "We'll be going to the dungeon."

Her head snapped up. "But—"

Trevor raised his eyebrows in question.

"You really have one?"

"Of course." He'd said so, more than once.

"I thought, well, since…"

"Go on."

She gave a furious scowl. "Where? I thought when you

showed me the guest room that you'd been teasing, maybe trying to frighten me."

"Frighten you? I hope you'll love the space as much as I do." He crouched before her. "About the dungeon, I'm completely serious."

"So where is it? Do you have a secret room? Like behind a bookcase or something?"

He couldn't resist. "Novel idea."

"Oh Sir!" Her little sound was a partial laugh, but mostly a groan. "You didn't just say that. Let me guess. Puns are a part of your charm."

They hadn't been.

A heartbeat passed between them, where their gazes were locked, and they shared a smile.

Over the years, friends and colleagues had told him not to take things so seriously. But Shelby's refreshing innocence appealed to a part of him he didn't know existed.

"You're not going to tell me, are you?"

"It's beneath the house."

He adored watching her eyebrows furrow together as she tried to make sense out of something.

"Isn't that a garage?"

"I have one garage. And the other is your new playroom."

"So the shirt…because we're going outside."

"Precisely." He pushed to a standing position. "I'll follow you."

"So… I'm not sure what you want me to do."

"Your choice. You may crawl to the door. Or walk."

She unlaced her fingers then laced them again. "Does it matter what I do? I mean, am I being set up to make a wrong decision?"

"Not at all." He stepped back. "If I have an order or strong preference, I'll always inform you."

"I appreciate that."

It didn't surprise him that she decided to stand. Would she ever make the other choice? "Shelby?"

"Sir?"

"My toy bag is next to the door. Will you bring it to me?"

Her steps were short, as if she was taking as many as possible, stalling. When she offered it to him, she was trembling. "Are you scared? Excited, perhaps?"

"Uh... Yes."

Both, then. "Shall we?"

Outside, she descended the staircase, then stopped. "To the right," he instructed.

When she reached the entrance, he entered a code on the keypad, then turned the knob. "After you."

For a fraction of a second, she hesitated, then after squaring her shoulders, she pushed on the door. He reached around to flick on the light switch.

"Oh wow."

He closed and locked the door behind them, then picked up a remote control to lower the temperature on the air conditioner.

"This is amazing."

"Does that mean you approve?" The floor was reclaimed cypress, able to weather any flood the area might receive. While he had no windows, and the walls were painted black, he had plenty of options available for lighting.

"I..." Holding on to her shoulders self-protectively, she glanced around. "I don't know quite what to say. This is... Like your own personal Quarter."

Where nothing was off-limits.

He'd installed hooks in the ceiling, on sliders that he could lock into place. A St. Andrew's cross was attached to the far wall. Recently he'd added an adjustable spanking bench that he could bend a submissive over.

Drawers contained many of his necessities, while

leather whips and paddles hung from hooks in a tall cabinet near a long table where he could stage each of his implements.

So he could extend a scene for as long as he pleased, he had bottled water as well as a small sink. Against a wall was an oversize leather chair for snuggling. It also provided a comfortable place for him to sit in case he wanted a submissive at his feet or over his knee. "Is there any particular music you like to scene to?"

"Did you mean it when you said this place is soundproof?"

"One hundred percent."

"So, I admit it. That makes me nervous. Right now, I'm more scared than excited."

"Completely understandable." He nodded. "We'll ease into it." It was his job as a Dominant to ensure she was ready to begin when he was. "Come with me. I want you to unpack my bag and put everything away."

"Is that supposed to help?"

"Not at all. It's simply a task."

He took her hand and led her to the place he stored his equipment.

He stepped aside, and she partially unzipped the bag before losing her grip on the hasp. Trevor said nothing while she took a steadying breath and tried again.

This time, she managed to get it all the way open.

"Now lay out everything on the table. Group them in an order that makes sense to you."

With great consideration, she did so.

"Excellent." He fished a set of keys from his pocket and extended them toward her. "Unlock the drawers and the cabinets, then figure out where each thing goes."

She shot him a frown, and her eyes widened. "I'm sorry, Sir! Right away, Sir."

"Getting better all the time, subbie." Trevor turned his head to hide his smile.

It took her some time to unlock each drawer, and he rested his shoulders against the wall and watched her, enjoying the dance of various expressions across her face, including a couple of slight grimaces and, when she saw his assortment of butt plugs, sustained wide-eyed shock. Her repeated gasps made him wonder if she might hyperventilate, and he reveled in the thought.

When she opened the drawer filled with nipple clamps and weights, she froze. He was tempted to reassure her that he knew most of them were on her limits list. But he schooled himself and remained silent.

She turned her head to seek his gaze.

"Yes?"

"You already know that most of them are a hard no."

"I wouldn't dream of asking you to try them," he agreed. "For submissives with a lot of experience or who love nipple torture, they're sublime." It was his job as a Dominant to give each woman he played with whatever she desired. "At the club, you seemed somewhat interested in the tweezers. What's nice about those is that they are completely adjustable."

"Nice?"

"That's in the eye of the beholder, perhaps." Trevor went to her and pulled out a pair. He affixed one of the tweezers to the web between his thumb and first finger, then adjusted the tightness. "Tug on the chain."

Her eyebrows deeply furrowed, she did so. Shelby's eyes widened when the toy effortlessly slid off.

He repeated the process, this time making the grip a little tighter. She had to exert a little more pressure to remove them. "See? Not a single mark on my skin. Why don't you try it?"

She took a tiny, almost imperceptible, step back before finally extending her hand.

"I'm afraid I'm not one for martyrs." He grinned. "Do it to yourself."

"Are you a sadist? Like getting off on watching me do this to myself?"

"Now that you mention it…"

Their gazes met, and she smiled at him. It tore a chunk off the tension and simultaneously created intimacy.

Shelby accepted the set from him and placed the pinchers on the delicate skin and tightened them a little. "That's not so bad."

"Surprised?"

"A little." She pushed the tiny metal ring a little higher, increasing the tension. "The rubber tips on them make it so they don't bite as hard as I thought they might."

"And?"

"I'm interested in trying them."

He smiled. "Shall we?" Trevor loosened the clamp and tugged it away from her hand.

"When? *Now?*"

"Remove your shirt for me, Shelby."

Her breaths were beautifully labored as she took it off. In the air-conditioning, her creamy skin was dotted with goose bumps, and her nipples were hard. Gently he captured and teased them until she moaned and grabbed hold of his wrists for support.

"Trevor…"

His name had never sounded sweeter on anyone's lips.

He lowered his head to suck on one hard, making it even more erect.

"I had no idea I could like it this much."

This was among the many firsts he wanted to give her. "Ready?"

Wide-eyed, she watched as he elongated her nipple, then placed the clamp. He went slowly. It needed to be tight enough to stay in place, but he didn't want it to be overly uncomfortable. "Doing okay?" His gaze on her, he stroked her between the legs, wanting her to associate the pleasure with the tiny bite.

"Yesss."

Her little hiss brought him immense pleasure, and he grinned.

Trevor put the second clamp on her, then slipped a finger inside her damp pussy. For the next couple of minutes, he toyed with her, taking her to the brink of arousal but not pushing her over the edge. Instead, he eased out his finger.

Her knees weakened, and she caught herself.

"Not as bad as you once imagined?"

"Except for the part where you didn't give me an orgasm."

Her response pleased him. At the club, she'd been less forthcoming, stammering over some answers. This time, he hadn't had to coax anything out of her. It was progress. Maybe by the end of the week, all of her inhibitions would disappear.

He removed the clamps and sucked on each nipple for a few seconds to ease any pain, slight as it might be. Then he offered the chain to her. "You may put them back, then continue unpacking my bag."

She scowled. "This is different than being at the Quarter."

"It is." Things were more theatrical there. And a scene didn't necessarily reflect real life, where toys had to be cared for, where there was an orderly discipline. She had played with Tops, watched scenes, enjoyed her evening, then gone out for a meal with friends. Here, it was just the two of them, with hours to fill, with the reality of BDSM front and center in their lives.

Trevor liked watching her economical motions as she put the rest of his implements where they belonged.

Once she was done, she looked to him for further direction. *Yeah.* "Please select a pair of cuffs and a blindfold." He couldn't get enough of her.

The softness of the breath she released filled the air, seeming to bounce off the walls. With trembling hands, she followed his order.

Trevor nodded toward the table, and she laid them out. "We'll begin with the small flogger this evening." The familiarity would soothe her, he was certain. "Then when I think you're ready, we'll experiment with the dragon's tail."

Her eyes went wide, and her deep swallow betrayed her nervousness.

Trevor had never been with someone like her. So curious. So innocent.

He traced one of the vines etched on her collar. Again, a sense of protection walloped him. This wasn't possession; it was much deeper. Which made it more troubling. Possession, he knew what to do with. Tenderness was new, unchartered waters.

Because it was uncomfortable, he started to steel his emotions.

Yet she was looking at him, studying him, and he was lost. Trevor moved his finger higher to stroke the column of her throat.

Her breath caught. In that moment, neither of them breathed as something passed between them. A spark? Recognition? Whatever it was, it seared with an emotional connection that shouldn't yet be possible. But once again, he was thinking of his life and the possibility of having her in it.

That idea was beyond ridiculous, and he shook his head to clear it of uncharacteristic nonsense. Yet even as he dropped his hand and turned away, the thought persisted.

Trevor put some distance between them, positioning a small wooden platform in the middle of their play space. Then he went to the side to lower the overhead bar before facing her again.

Silently he crooked his finger, and she came to him, hands twisted together, but with little hesitation in her step. Nerves, yes. But most of all, trust. "Step up onto the box."

While she did so, he collected the cuffs.

Obediently she extended her arms, and he wrapped each of her wrists with the soft bonds before securing each to hooks in the bar. "I'll raise your hands above your head, but I want you to keep your feet flat." In the future, he might force her onto her tiptoes, but definitely not for her first experience.

With her eyes closed, she nodded.

Slowly he raised the bar until he had her where he wanted her. He returned to her, and the position was perfect. She was tall enough to look him in the eye, and she did so boldly.

Trevor crowded her, smelling the heat that rose from her naked body, loving the way she panted, and the thickness of her nipples, still swollen from his clamps. He'd like to fuck her here, like this, with her helpless to resist his most carnal demands.

Forcing himself to focus, he checked to be sure her shoulders were relaxed and that he could slip a finger beneath the cuffs.

Then before he could change his mind, he walked away. "Did you have any input on what we listen to?"

"Anything that will drown out my thoughts. Help me get lost."

He agreed. It had been a long damn time since he heard the sound of his own pulse during a scene.

"Rock? I like the energy of Journey. REO Speedwagon. Maybe Pink Floyd?"

"All excellent choices." Aware of her tracking his every move, he told his virtual assistant to play an assortment of greatest hits. "Volume at forty percent."

Within seconds, bass bounced off the walls, haunting and reassuring. He allowed the beats to rush through him and forced himself to focus on the moment and shove away unwelcome thoughts of a future he'd never before contemplated.

Once he was centered, he returned to stand behind her. After rubbing his palms together to warm them, he massaged her shoulders, then her buttocks, then the backs of her legs.

Even though the music pulsed, it didn't drown out her soft, satisfied purrs.

Trevor squeezed her buttocks, and she jerked forward, and her sighs became moans. He wanted to cover every inch of her beautiful skin with his flogger, marking her as his. "Are you ready for the blindfold?"

"I think so." She closed her eyes while he grabbed it and settled it in place.

"You'll have your safe word."

She nodded.

After he selected a small flogger, he stood in front of her and drank her in. With her arms spread wide above her, her nipples puckered, and the satin snuggling her face, there was an added dimension of sensuality that made his cock even harder. "We'll start easy; then I'm planning to add the clamps and use the dragon's tail on you."

Her body went rigid.

"Keep breathing, Shelby. You're safe with me."

She forced out a breath but kept her muscles locked.

Realizing that coaxing her to change her position wouldn't help, he decided to let the scene itself reassure her.

He skimmed a finger across her forehead, above the blindfold. Then he cupped the back of her head to hold her while he dropped a gentle kiss on her full lips.

"Oh... Yes."

He placed the thongs of his flogger on her shoulder, then drew the thick suede strips lower, over her chest, relishing the sight of her swaying in response.

He repeated the action with her other shoulder, soft, gentle, and her body relaxed. *This* was what it was about. Her surrender.

Trevor kept a hand on her as he circled behind her and danced the falls over her shoulder blades, down her back, across her buttocks. "Keep your legs apart for me, precious sub." He explored all of her—her calves, the backs of her legs, between her thighs. With rhythmic strokes, he covered her breasts and rib cage and the slight swell of her belly.

"This... Is..." Her words slurred.

He grinned.

Using the music to set the pace, he increased the power behind his strokes, making her skin pink. Her face flushed, and her head lolled to one side. Somewhere along the way, she'd fallen silent, maybe lost inside her head. "Are you still with me, Shelby?"

"Mmm."

He lowered the flogger, then trailed kisses over her right shoulder.

"Nice." Her words were a mixture of a purr and a sigh.

While he was always a considerate Dominant, the affection between them was unique.

Trevor left her only long enough to exchange the flogger for the dragon's tail, a short whip of types, with a single piece of leather at the end, fashioned into a shallow V. He also picked up the clamps they'd played with.

With his hands and his mouth, he tormented her breasts,

sucking her nipples. Her lips parted, with pleasure? From apprehension of what was to come? Maybe a mixture of the two? If he was doing this right, she would be lost in the overwhelming experience created by the simultaneous collision of multiple thoughts and sensations that resulted in sensory overload.

He placed each clamp, then thumbed the tiny circular bar a bit higher, tightening it so it didn't slip off while he was using the whip on her.

She danced a little in place, but she didn't try to pull away or use a safe word.

Trevor dampened a finger to play with her pussy and smiled when he discovered she was drenched in her own arousal.

"Oh, Trevor. *Sir.*"

The sound of his name, breathlessly broken into two syllables, thrilled him. This had gone far beyond an ordinary scene for him. Her physical and auditory responses were the ultimate high.

Once he had both tweezers adjusted, he began flicking her still-pink body—front, back, side—with tiny bites from the dragon's tail.

With each, she murmured, her words no longer intelligible.

The music around them rose to a crescendo, and he increased the intensity and randomness of his strokes to match it.

She whimpered and cried out. A sheen of sweat covered her body, and her long hair flowed down her back.

As the vocalist climbed toward his stunning conclusion, light glinted off her collar.

The song's final notes hung in the air, then crashed around them. He dropped the whip, sending it clattering to the floor, and he reached between her legs to finger-fuck her and to play with her clit while she screamed her orgasm.

The music trailed off into silence; then the only sounds were their ragged breaths and her soulful sobs.

He dispensed of the clamps and had her released from her cuffs and blindfold in mere seconds; then he scooped her up into his arms and carried her to the oversize chair. He sat with her in his lap, arms wrapped around her. Her luxurious hair fell around her face like a veil, and he brushed back the strands.

She was looking at him through hazy eyes, wide with wonder.

For the first time in his life, he experienced a moment that he never wanted to end. With the same sort of certainty and clarity that he'd called on to make a success of his life, he knew that he would do whatever it took to make Shelby his.

And it started with him claiming her mouth in a deep, hungry kiss where he gave rise to the feral nature that she'd suddenly awakened in him.

CHAPTER 8

I can't wait to suck on your clit.

Heat scalded Shelby's cheeks, and she flipped her phone over so that none of her colleagues could see Trevor's sexy words. Which was ridiculous. Even though she was seated at the conference table, the closest person was several feet away.

She'd known better than to sneak a peek.

More than anyone, he knew how to arouse her, and not just on a physical level. He appealed to her on a mental level as well. Telling her what he planned to do when she arrived home made her reel as his fantasy unwound in her mind.

And he was as good as his word.

How was it possible that her life had changed so much in such a short amount of time?

Saturday night, she'd gone out with friends, intending to watch some scenes. Instead, she was in the middle of her week as a submissive, and it all seemed so normal.

At his house on Sunday afternoon, he'd introduced her to

his dungeon. She'd endured the sweet torment of nipple clamps, along with the delicate bite from the dragon's tail. But the wonderment of her own surrender had taken her by surprise. Unlike a previous experience, she'd recognized she was safe, emotionally as well as physically.

After the scene ended, he cared for her with such exquisite tenderness that she relaxed completely.

His care and concern extended beyond their sexy times. In the mornings, before she left for work, he made her breakfast and poured strong coffee in a to-go cup. At least once a day, he messaged her to see how she was doing. When she took a lunch break, he called.

Even more heavenly, he took care of dinner as well.

All she had to do was embrace the role she'd accepted for the week.

Each afternoon, when she arrived home, she followed his instructions to strip once the door closed behind her. She lowered herself to her knees—much more gracefully than she once had—and waited for him. Invariably he gave her a few moments alone to leave the workday behind her.

Even though it had only been a few days, she looked forward to being with him. Everything they shared gave her a peace she hadn't known she was missing.

On the heels of that thought came another, less welcome one.

What was she going to do at the end of the week?

Shelby had always enjoyed her life. Her work was fulfilling, and she looked forward to spending time with her friends on the weekends. But still, there were times she craved companionship, and she hadn't been aware of just how much she wanted that until the past few days.

It was nice to have someone ask how her day was, and she liked the way they sat together on the dock at the end of their evening. Conversation ebbed and flowed, much like the water lapping against the pilings. Monday night, they'd taken out his two-person kayak and they'd listened as the summer evening came alive with the sounds of frogs. It was a memory she'd cherish—among dozens of others.

"Shelby?" Louise, the most senior member of the team, asked.

She shook her head to clear it, aware that her colleagues were looking at her expectantly. "I'm sorry?"

"Marlene is out next Wednesday. Can you cover her client?"

"Uhm..." She shuffled through the papers in front of her. It was so unlike her to lose focus. Looking at her phone during staff meetings definitely needed to be off-limits in the future. Once she checked her calendar and saw it was free of appointments, she nodded. "What time?"

"Ten."

Next week. She'd be back at home, living her regular life then. The realization shot a pang or sadness through her.

"I'll email you the file," Marlene said, reaching for her phone.

"Thanks." After calendaring the appointment, Shelby pushed away her errant feelings. What she was experiencing with Trevor wasn't reality. It was an inexplicable, fantastical week, but in a few days, it would end. No matter what it took, she needed to remember that.

"You'll be back on Friday?" Louise asked.

"Yes. I've got the Lemieux divorce."

"Let us know if you need help. Any other topics for discussion?" When Louise was met with silence, she smiled. "Good. We're adjourned. Early for once."

Shelby shuffled her papers back into a file folder, then dashed to her office to wrap up the final details so she could get back home to Trevor and their evening ahead with Fiona and Andrew.

The drive was another pleasure she'd miss when their time was up. As she left the city behind, the traffic thinned, and she caught the first view of water in the distance. As usual, the closer she drew to it, the more she relaxed.

Then, as she turned onto Trevor's street, her pulse sped up.

She never knew what to expect, but his bluntly sexual message had her on edge.

As she climbed from the car, a cacophony of barks rent the air. Bruno leaped over a neighbor's fence and headed for her at full speed.

In his enthusiasm, he had her momentarily pinned against the car, paws on her shoulders, in a type of an overgrown puppy hug.

"Are you okay down there?" Trevor shouted out.

She laughed. "Saying hello to the welcoming committee!"

Once he'd greeted her, Bruno bounded away.

Maybe she needed to adopt a dog of her own. Receiving this kind of reception every day would make going home much more enjoyable.

She climbed the stairs, and Trevor was waiting for her, arms folded over his black T-shirt. Her steps faltered as he swept his gaze over her, lingering on her lower body for a fleeting moment. Right now, she had no doubt she was his submissive. Whatever he wanted, she would give him.

Silently, he opened the door, and she preceded him inside.

Since he hadn't countermanded the orders he'd given her earlier in the week, she placed her bag on a nearby table and kicked off her sandals.

Making her a bit nervous, he closed the door, then stood there with his arms folded, watching, waiting.

Shelby unzipped her skirt, then wiggled out of it, leaving

it in a pile on the floor. Within seconds, the rest of her clothes followed.

Once she was naked, she knelt, then lowered her head.

He didn't keep her waiting long. "You didn't respond to my text message."

She hazarded a quick glance up at him.

He was grinning.

"It…uhm. Bad timing, Sir."

"Ah. And did you have any reaction?"

Embarrassment flooding her, she nodded.

"And how is your clit now?"

"Still a little sore from last night, Sir." Because he'd brushed it twice with strands from the flogger.

"Good. Then it will feel even worse after I get done with it in a few minutes."

She dug her fingernails into her palms as a distraction from his terrifying threat.

"Please come with me."

With a tiny frown, she rose and followed him to the living room where he took a seat on the couch.

"I want your clit level with my mouth."

"You…" She tipped her head to the side, trying to figure out how to follow his direction. "What?"

"I figured one of us should be comfortable."

And it obviously wasn't going to be her.

Trevor offered a hand, and she accepted it.

"You may want to start by standing on the cushions. One foot at a time."

She took a single awkward step up, and her heel sank into the squishy surface. More than a bit wobbly, she tightened her grip on him and lifted her other leg so that she was straddling him. Straddling him was one of the most awkward things she'd ever done. Once she released him, he placed his hands on her hips to steady her.

"Not all that difficult."

Easy for him to say. She had no sense of balance, and this was lewd and uncomfortable.

"Fucking sexy as hell. I can see all of you. It'll be even better when you bend your knees."

Was she brave enough to do that?

"Now, Shelby. Or I'll add extra time."

Instantly she followed his obscene order. "I'm afraid of toppling over."

"I won't let that happen."

It took her several seconds of digging in her toes and adjusting her position to find something that worked—at least somewhat.

"Press your thighs against the back of the couch."

Once she did, he released her. She wobbled frantically before tightening her leg muscles.

"Well done. Now I want you to part your pussy lips for me."

"I'm serious. I can't do it without falling over."

"You can. I've got you."

"But—"

"Shelby. Nothing I said was open for debate."

His tone, gruff and relentless, shot arousal through her. "Yes, Sir." With her hands shaking, as much from fear as anticipation, she spread herself wide.

"What did I say I was going to do to you?"

"Suck…" She gulped. "Suck my clit, Sir."

"Should I start by licking it?"

That wasn't actually a question, she knew.

"Come a little closer, sub. And tell me again what my text message said."

After bending her knees a little more, she responded. "You said you couldn't wait to suck my clit."

"Yeah." He slid a finger inside her already damp pussy.

"That's exactly right." Then he coated her with her own juices, making her slick, making her cry out her arousal.

Despite her earlier protests, she realized she was perfectly safe where she was. He had a hand around her waist, and her body weight against the couch back was keeping her supported.

"I love having your cunt in my face."

His filthy words seared her.

Without warning, he licked her clit. She shivered.

"Keep yourself spread."

He licked, then sucked, taking the needy, achy nub into his mouth.

"Oh Sir!" It was so deliciously awful, all pleasure wrapped in sensual pain that sent the world spinning.

He was relentless, driving her to an orgasm, then a second that happened so fast that she didn't know where one ended and the next began.

When she knew she couldn't survive another moment, he released the pressure slightly, soothing with tongue and his lips, allowing her to breathe before sucking on her even harder than before.

She was somewhere in a deep, black fog when his soothing voice reached her.

"Your responses are so damn perfect for me, Shelby. You can relax." He gently took her hands and moved them from her pussy.

It took her a few seconds to return to her body. She wasn't sure where she'd been, but stars were swimming behind her eyes, and he was holding her around the waist. "That…" Where was the word she wanted?

"Hmm?"

"Hurt."

"Which was why you came seven times, I'm sure."

Seven? After two, she'd no longer been capable of thinking.

He helped her to untangle their bodies; then he drew her into his lap and cradled her against him.

How was it possible that being naked in his arms while he was fully dressed seemed so natural?

Without a word, he stroked her hair and waited while she regained her breath.

"That was…" *Mind-blowing.* How did he keep doing that? Taking an everyday experience and turning it into something magical?

"Yeah. It was."

Even though she could pull away anytime, and would with any other man, she remained there, ear pressed to his chest, reassured by the steady thud of his heartbeat.

"My hand is itching to spank your gorgeous ass, but that will have to wait until after our guests leave."

Blinking, she pushed back from him. "I forgot!" Fiona and Andrew would be arriving soon.

"Go put on your swimming suit. I have dinner ready for you. Boat's already loaded with snacks, wine, beer, and water."

"You've thought of it all." She reluctantly eased herself from his lap.

For good measure he gave her right buttock a sharp smack, and she yelped.

"A taste to hold me until later."

Shelby snatched up her clothes in one hand before dashing toward the stairs.

Halfway up, he called out. "Shelby?"

Curling her fingers around the banister, she stopped and turned back to look at him.

He was still seated, and his eyes were steely. "And wear

something over it. Shorts and a T-shirt." A possessive growl sliced through his words.

She'd had half her rear exposed at the club last Saturday, and now he wanted her covered? Not that she would just wear the skimpy suit, but his tone shocked her, in a delicious way.

"I didn't hear your answer."

Fighting back a grin at his unexpected demand, she offered a small salute. "Yes, Sir."

Once she was upstairs, she gave in to the smile and spun in a small circle. At this moment, she was happier than she remembered being in years.

Then, aware of the clock ticking, she shook her head and hurried toward the closet to change.

Within two minutes, she rejoined him in the kitchen.

As she walked in, he dragged his gaze from her chest to her knees before nodding. "Chardonnay?"

"I'd love some."

He poured her a glass and offered it to her.

"Thank you." After raising it toward him, she took a sip of the crisp, fruity wine.

"Have a seat."

He'd already prepared a plate for her, with a baked chicken breast and side salad. "Really, I could get used to this."

"So could I."

The air thickened, preternaturally still.

She couldn't breathe, couldn't dare hope.

One of them had to shatter this sudden intimacy, and since her nerves were suddenly shattered, she took a second sip of wine before rolling back her shoulders and shimmying onto the barstool. "You're not eating?"

"I already did before getting the boat ready."

"Well then, double thank you."

As she carved off a slice of the chicken, he rinsed a plate. "It's difficult to watch you work while I'm being pampered."

He glanced over his shoulder. "Believe me, Shelby. This is exactly how I want things."

A small shudder went through her.

"Exactly how I want things." He picked up a dishcloth to wipe down the counters.

Was there anything sexier than a man in the kitchen?

Well. Yes, definitely when it came to him. No matter what he did, she was attracted to him.

"How's dinner?"

Shaken from her thoughts, she took a bite of the Cajun-spiced chicken. Her mouth watered at the explosion of taste. "Oh God, Trevor. This is amazing."

"You're an appreciative audience."

"I mean it. Sincerely. It's perfect. Just the right amount of cayenne. Hot, without being overly so."

"Even if you didn't like it, I doubt you'd say so." He turned around.

"You could be right. But in this case, it really is divine."

"I'm glad you're pleased." He wiped his hands before putting the cloth down and excusing himself to gather sunscreen and hats.

After a few more bites, she covered her plate and stored it in the refrigerator. Seconds later, excited barks rent the air. Bruno's early-warning system ensured no one arrived unannounced.

She went outside and jogged down the stairs to join Trevor, who was doing his best to restrain the mutt while Andrew parked the SUV.

"He's harmless," Trevor promised as Fiona tentatively cracked open her door. "Big. Enthusiastic, but harmless."

Fiona crouched a little and crooned to Bruno, who tipped his head to the side, as if considering her, then Andrew. After wagging his tail, seemingly satisfied, the dog raced away, no doubt to greet someone else.

"Yours?" Andrew asked.

"No. Too much of a free spirit to belong to anyone." Trevor shook his head. "He's the self-appointed neighborhood watchdog."

While the men shook hands, Shelby and Fiona hugged.

"So…" Fiona glanced around. "This place is freaking spectacular."

"Would you like to see it?"

"Totally."

She touched Trevor's arm lightly. "I'm going to show Fiona around before we leave. Is that okay?"

He placed his hand over hers and smiled, making her heart slide to her toes. No matter what he did, whether it was sexy or something more innocuous, she had a physical reaction.

While she led Fiona toward the steps, Andrew grabbed their bags from the back of the vehicle.

"Okay, okay," Fiona said once the front door was closed behind them. "Tell me everything. *Every*thing. And I mean it."

Shelby laughed. "What?"

"You're wearing a collar, for shit's sake. And it's gorgeous. I need details."

"It's…" Unconsciously Shelby traced one of the decorative lines on it. "Temporary."

"Mmm-hmm."

"No. Really. It is."

"Because Doms do that all the time."

She shrugged. "This one did."

"So, did he happen to have it, or what?"

"We went shopping. In the French Quarter. A little shop on Royal Street."

"Wait. Are you talking about Mademoiselle Giselle's place?"

"You know it?"

"Are you kidding me?" Fiona waved one hand wide. "She's a living legend. I've only been behind the curtain once, and the prices were staggering. But…" She lifted a hand as if to touch the collar but instantly pulled back. "It's beautiful."

And she would only be wearing it another couple of days.

Shoving that unwelcome thought aside, she forced a smile. "You've got to see the views."

They passed the couch, with the cushions in disarray. Why the hell hadn't she fixed them? Convinced that Fiona would know exactly what had been happening just minutes prior to her arrival, Shelby quickly walked toward the kitchen then to the window at the back of the house.

"This is amazing."

"Isn't it? Sunrises. Sunsets. The soothing play of light on the water. I can stare for hours."

"I'd never want to leave."

Shelby propped her hips against the window ledge so she could face her friend.

"You needed a break from the real world. This couldn't be more different from your place."

"Very true." Lake living was nothing like her suburban neighborhood. "I've never had a Bruno before."

"I'm not sure anyone has a Bruno." Fiona regarded her. "How has it been?"

"I don't know." She sought for words. "Amazing. Overwhelming at times."

"And?"

"Freeing. As if I can be myself." She pulled back her hair and twisted it into a knot. "Or the person I've imagined I might want to be."

"That's pretty awesome. So he's a good Dom?"

"*Fiona!* I don't kiss and tell." She slid a hand against her nape.

"Oh my God, you just turned about thirty different shades of pink! That's all the answer I needed."

Shelby blew out a breath. "Okay. So back to you. How are things with Andrew?"

"I'm sure the guys are waiting on us." She turned to leave, and Shelby scowled.

"Is there something wrong?"

"Everything's fine. I mean…" She shrugged. "I don't know. Maybe I'm restless. Bored?" She said the word as if it were a guess, rather than something she was sure of.

"Scared?"

"I'm not sure that's the right word. It could be. We moved fast, and I thought it was what I wanted. I was content for quite some time."

"And he wants things to be even more serious."

"Once he sees that collar on you… Don't misunderstand. I'm happy for you, and whatever works for you and Trevor is perfectly fine. But I know Andrew will want to talk about our relationship again on the way home. I'm just…"

Shelby waited. Fiona had secrets, ones she hadn't shared. She gave the impression of being a free spirit, and maybe she was. Perhaps Andrew weighed her down too much.

"I need time to think things through, decide what I really want."

"Ladies!" Trevor's voice boomed through the air.

"Time's up." Fiona's words were rushed together, and she smiled.

"Glad that conversation's over?"

"Yeah. It was getting deep there!"

They headed toward the door. "So, Mademoiselle Giselle reads tea leaves."

"Really?" Fiona glanced toward her. "Are you thinking about it?"

"Definitely. I'm not sure why. But yes. I'm thinking about making an appointment."

"Shall we do it next time we go out?"

"I was hoping you'd say that."

"Second warning!" Trevor shouted.

"Coming," she called back.

"Sounds very serious." Fiona giggled. "All Dominant-like."

"He's got that down to a science. Or an art. Whichever it is."

"Anyway, shall we invite Hannah?"

"Absolutely."

"I'll call her and then let you know."

As they hurried down the stairs to the dock, they agreed that Shelby would schedule the appointments toward the end of the month. Which was a good thing. It would give her something to look forward to after she went back to her regular life.

"Consider yourself lucky that you didn't get to the third warning," Trevor said, his husky, sexy voice sliding over her in a way that made her wish that maybe she should have dawdled.

He leaned over to kiss her cheek. "How long do we need to entertain?" he whispered in her ear.

She made a pretense of batting her eyelids.

"I can push them overboard."

That he wanted to be alone as much as she did made her already achy clit throb even harder. "We need to be good hosts."

"Counting the minutes until sunset."

"Me too."

After making sure neither Fiona nor Andrew were

watching, Trevor swatted her behind, and she had to swallow her instinctive yelp.

He whistled as he led the way to the pontoon.

After helping her aboard, Andrew assisted Fiona, then threw off the ropes at Trevor's direction.

Within seconds, the breeze ruffled around her, the coolness a welcome relief to the stifling heat and humidity.

She leaned back with her eyes half closed, savoring the moment.

When they were somewhere near the middle of the lake, Trevor stopped the boat. "Wine? Beer? Water?"

"IPA, if you have it," Andrew said.

"White wine?" Fiona asked.

"And for you, Shelby?"

"I'll stick with wine." Better than mixing alcohol, for sure.

Trevor pulled out two beers from a cooler and twisted off the metal caps. "Mind putting them in koozies?"

He offered her a couple emblazoned with the words LAKE LIFE FLOATS MY BOAT and decorated with anchors.

While she slid the bottles into the protective sleeves, he uncorked a bottle of her favorite chardonnay and filled wineglasses etched with a picture of his pontoon.

"That's classy."

"Nothing but the best for you, Shelby."

"Which beer is for Andrew?"

"The one on the left."

She took the beverages to their guests before returning to Trevor. "Anything I can do to help?"

"There are snacks in the refrigerator. If you want to grab the charcuterie board, I'll get plates and napkins."

The refrigerator looked more like an ice chest, but it opened at the front and had several shelves. She pulled out a beautiful display of meats, cheeses, olives, and nuts. "Did you put this together?" She set the wooden board on a table. "Or was it your housekeeper?"

"I'm offended. Haven't I proven myself adept in the kitchen?"

"A man after my heart." She froze. The moment the words were out, she wished she could shove them back in her brain and lock them up.

He looked at her. He wasn't smiling. And his eyes were dark, brooding almost. "Yeah. I am."

He couldn't possibly mean that in anything other than a teasing way. Desperate to break through the sudden tension caused by her unwitting words, she readjusted the board.

"Among other things."

Fortunately Andrew was pointing at something in the distance, and engaged in a conversation. They'd missed the entire exchange.

"I meant it when I said we could shove them overboard. Whose idea was it to invite people over during our week together?"

She couldn't help but grin at the frustration in his voice. "Yours, I'm sure. Had to be. *I'd* never do something like that."

"Couldn't have been."

The lighthearted banter was something new for her. It was intimate in a way she'd never experienced with another man. She liked it, even though it was a little unnerving.

"What is that over there?" Fiona asked, turning toward them.

"It's a marina with an excellent restaurant. We can try it sometime. Boat over, have dinner. Then cruise back."

"See?" Shelby teased. "I'm vindicated. You're the one extending invitations."

"Anything to get you back out here."

She wouldn't be difficult to convince. On the heels of that

realization came another—that it might be too difficult to see him again after she walked away.

"There's a pair of binoculars beneath the aft bench."

"Aft?" Andrew asked.

"The back of the boat. You're welcome to grab them if you want a better look at the shoreline."

While Andrew did, Trevor uncovered the food and laid out the silverware and plates.

Even though she was full, Shelby couldn't resist popping an olive in her mouth before taking a sip of wine.

Food and drink in hand, she took a seat next to Trevor, across from their friends.

"How often do you do this?" Andrew asked, leaning back.

"Not often enough." Trevor propped one ankle on his knee. "Too much effort for one person."

"I'd do it all the time if I had this place."

"Monday night, he took me out in a kayak. Completely different experience. Equally wonderful in its own way. Bonus points, Trevor did all the paddling while I took in the scenery and relaxation."

"That's my kind of workout." Fiona grinned as she toasted him. Then, more seriously, she went on. "I've always loved living in the city—the energy, the proximity to restaurants and entertainment—but all of a sudden, I understand the appeal of the water."

"It's not for everyone." Trevor shrugged. "I've had neighbors who've moved back. The isolation can be too much for some people. There are plenty of owners out here who we call Weekenders. They come down occasionally, and most often on holidays and vacations."

"So that means there are a lot of empty houses?"

"It does, yes."

Shelby traced a circle on the rim of her glass. "It's as if you have the world to yourself at times."

"Privacy can be good for certain things," Andrew mused.

"Indeed it can." Trevor stroked the length of Shelby's spine, from top to bottom.

Awareness of him as a man, as a Dominant, flooded her. His tone, his touch. He was a master of her body as well as her mind.

She exhaled when Fiona leaned forward to fill her plate with three different cheeses. If Trevor didn't take his hands off her soon—really soon—Shelby was going to end up joining him in pushing their guests off the back of the boat.

For the sake of her sanity, she inched away from him.

"I've heard that Mistress Aviana may be planning another theme night," Fiona said.

"Oh?" Since those were Shelby's favorite evenings at the Quarter, her interest was piqued. "Do tell."

"I don't know if it's true, or not, but some of the ideas sound totally fun."

"Such as?" Did she have to drag the words out of her friend?

"Jungle for one."

Trevor placed a hand on her knee. "Meaning short skirts, right? Maybe with a little knot near your hip bone? And a skimpy bra. Leather, maybe? Barely covering your—"

"You're liking your fantasy a little too much, Sir." Shelby side-eyed him.

"I can't wait to see who wears loincloths!" Fiona giggled. "But it sounds more fun than a speakeasy."

"Wait a second." Shelby lifted a hand. "I'm not sure about that. Maybe a flapper-era gown with lots of sparkles. Long gloves. And men in tuxedos and top hats."

"And a cane?" Trevor added.

A naughty little shiver chased through her.

"Gotta say I'm with Trevor," Andrew said. "Let's go jungle all the way."

Shelby shook her head at both men. "Why am I not surprised?"

Trevor eased his fingertips inside the waistband of her shorts.

Fiona continued. "The other thing she might be tossing around is fire and ice. That could be interesting."

The fire part was already happening inside Shelby.

"Red skimpy outfits, "Andrew supplied helpfully.

From there, easy conversation resumed, about work, mixed with some current events.

Despite her jokes with Trevor about wanting to be alone, it had been a long time since she'd relaxed and enjoyed herself this much. There was no pressure, just… For a second she explored her thoughts. Belonging, maybe. Until now, she hadn't really realized that she'd been searching for that. Because she'd been bounced between her parents, more pawn than anything, she'd always been a misfit.

"Anyone want a swim before it gets too dark?" Trevor's voice broke into her thoughts, making her realize she'd mentally drifted away from the conversation.

"Oh hell yes." Fiona was the first to stand and pull off her shirt. She dropped it on the carpeted floor.

"Let me just open up the aft gate. There's a swimming platform. Anyone need a life jacket or pool noodle?"

Fiona shook her head and looked at Andrew. "Are you coming in?"

"Only if I get one of those floatie things."

Trevor stood and lifted one of the seats to pull out several long, round, colorful strands that appeared to be made from some sort of foam.

"Thanks." Andrew bypassed the pink and yellow in favor of bright blue. "Is it okay if I put my beer on the deck?"

"Not a problem." Trevor pulled out a pile of towels and

placed them on a seat where they had some hope of staying dry.

Seconds after he opened the back gate, Fiona pinched her nose and jumped in. Andrew was a bit more tentative. He sat first and then took his time inching toward the water.

"Here's our chance." Trevor sat so close to her that their thighs touched. "Our guests are in the water and paying zero attention to us."

"I'm beginning to think you arranged it that way."

"Yeah." He placed a finger beneath her chin. "Maybe I did."

His eyes were dark and purposeful, and she hungered for him.

"You know I never stop thinking of you."

Or the wicked things he wanted to do to her body? The same things that consumed her mind.

He kissed her, gently at first. Then, after she heard her friends laughing, which meant they weren't paying attention to her, Shelby relaxed, and he thrust his tongue deeper into her mouth, demanding and impatient. And more, a promise of what still lay ahead for them.

Then water splashed over her, making her yelp and pull away.

Fiona giggled. "Get in here, Shel!"

Trevor growled in Shelby's ear. "I'm going to make damn sure Andrew makes her pay for interrupting that kiss."

Maybe it was a good thing she had. Trevor made her forget the world around them existed.

"Might as well since I'm already wet." She stood and tugged off her shirt.

"Whose idea was that damn swimsuit?"

"Yours, Sir." She smiled as she dropped the garment in his lap. "Definitely not mine."

Aware of his gaze riveted on her, she took her time

lowering the zipper on her shorts, then overexaggerated a shimmy as she worked the denim down her legs.

"Shelby. You're fucking killing me."

"Just dressing in the clothes my Dominant selected for me." Who was she? She'd never been the type of submissive who misbehaved to cause a reaction, but the threatening glint in his eyes delighted her. Even her husband hadn't been this protective of her. Of course, she now knew it was probably because he had another woman on the side. But still, not only was this new, it was a tiny bit exciting.

Once her shorts were around her ankles, she stepped out of them. "Do you like the suit, Sir?"

"Jesus. You're even sexier than I imagined."

Over the past few days, his appreciation had allowed her to become less self-conscious of her body, and she appreciated the newfound freedom.

"Never again letting you wear this when there are other people around."

"Are you growling, Sir?"

"Yeah. Maybe I am."

When Fiona splashed them again, Shelby laughed. "I'm looking forward to being alone with you later."

"Not half as much as I am, little sub. Not half as much as I am."

CHAPTER 9

Trevor stood in the bathroom entrance, a shoulder propped on the casing, watching Shelby lounge in the bathtub with her head tipped back. As he'd suggested previously, she'd lit the candles but hadn't turned on the overhead light. Steam wafted through the room, and for a long time, he savored the sight of her relaxing, damp tendrils of her hair curled against her cheeks and neck.

As if sensing him, she turned her head toward him. "Thank you for this. It really is the ultimate luxury."

"I'm glad to see you enjoy it. You're the only one who has."

She lifted her neck from the tub's rim. "You've never soaked in here?"

He raised a hand. "I swear I haven't."

"In that case, I think you should."

Indeed? Trevor quirked an eyebrow. "Should I?"

"Absolutely." She twirled her index finger round and round in the water. "Now, even."

He couldn't be certain in the seductive darkness, but her cheeks seemed to redden. Even after everything they'd shared, she could still be shy?

"There's room for both of us."

"I accept your invitation." Not needing to be asked twice, he kicked off his boat shoes and pulled off his shirt.

Shelby watched interestedly as he removed his shorts.

"You're already half-hard, Sir."

And her words finished him off.

With his cock leading the way, he walked toward her. "Ideas on how this will work?" Because the faucet was mounted on the wall near the middle of the tub, they could theoretically face each other, but he was interested in what she had in mind.

"I thought maybe you could fit behind me."

So he could wrap his arms around her and play with her gorgeous body? His dick became even harder. "Excellent suggestion."

She inched forward, and he stepped into the small space behind her. "You'll need to move up some more."

"How do I always forget how big your body is?"

Even though she gave him a little more room, he had to nudge her farther forward again. Water came dangerously close to splashing out onto the floor.

Once he was behind her, he drew her back into the V between his legs. "That's better."

"The fit is tighter than I expected."

And much more appealing than he could have imagined. "Lean back against me."

Shelby adjusted her position so she could rest her head on his chest, and he cradled her with the tenderness she deserved. "This was an excellent suggestion." He breathed her in as he stroked her hair. "Did you add bath salts or something?"

"Mmm-hmm." She sounded sleepy and content. "It's a combination of eucalyptus and spearmint. And you may also be smelling the candles."

"Nicer than my showers."

She stroked her hand across his knee. "Thank you for this evening. Having my friends here was fun, and I know you went to a lot of effort to make it special. I appreciate it."

At some point, maybe she'd realize how much he wanted to please her. For a few minutes, they breathed together, content to relax in each other's company without needing to talk.

"Do you mind if I add a little hot water?" she asked. "I'm getting a little chilled."

Her question surprised him. Most evenings, she headed for bed before now so she could get up early. "You're not in a hurry?"

"I forgot to mention, I'm off work tomorrow."

"Are you?" Nice surprise. "Does that mean you can stay up late?"

Shelby leaned forward to turn on the faucet while simultaneously draining the tub a few inches. "Actually, it does. Tonight. Tomorrow's another story. Friday, I have a really difficult case that I'm not looking forward to."

"That's the one you said you had to take?"

She nodded.

"Then we'll savor the rest of this evening and face the future when it arrives."

Warmth swirled around them, and steam once again drifted up. "That's better." When she was satisfied, she twisted the taps to stop the flow, then moved the lever back into the closed position before settling back against him. "How is your cock hard again?"

"Again?" He wrapped his arms around her. "You mean still."

She giggled.

"It's a constant when you're around." This time, when he gathered her closer, he slid a hand over one of her breasts and was rewarded by her nipple pebbling for him. "Can you reach the soap?"

Since he wouldn't let her go, she had to squirm and reach in order to grab hold of it.

He lathered the scented bar, then slid his hands over her breasts and ribs, then her belly.

"Oh Sir. What you do to me."

As if it had a mind of his own—which he was pretty sure it did when she was around—his dick pressed against her. The slight friction was enough to make him grit his teeth. No matter how many times he had her, he wanted her again. "I'm glad you'll be home tomorrow. I have an appointment in town, if you're interested in joining me."

"How am I supposed to talk to you when you're doing this to me?"

"This?" He skimmed across her nipples, then pinched them. "Or that?"

"Yes." She moaned. "That."

"The meeting might interest you."

"Anything—everything—with you intrigues me. I can't stop thinking about you and wondering what you're going to dream of next. It keeps me horny. Oh! *Jesus.* No. I didn't say that." She pressed her fingers to her mouth. "That was a thought. It wasn't supposed to come out of my mouth!"

He grinned. "Glad it did."

"I can't say that kind of stuff."

"No need to be concerned about my ego, Shelby. You're not going to make my head any bigger than it already is." He squeezed her breasts lightly.

"It's not that. It's…"

He stilled his hands.

"Oh God."

Against her ear, he spoke softly in a tone that he hoped reassured her. "You can talk to me."

"But I can't."

She tried to pull away, but he held her tighter—not enough to be uncomfortable, but in a way that let her know he was serious about the conversation. When she didn't go on, he prompted her. "I'm listening, and I've got all night if that's what it takes."

"Admitting my thoughts makes me feel vulnerable."

Her words were a gut shot. "Because you're afraid I'll use them against you?"

"Trevor…"

"I've got you, Shelby."

"No. I don't think you'll throw them back in my face." A shuddering sigh rocked her so hard that it resonated deep inside him. "That's not the kind of thing I want to tell any man. I might say it to my girlfriends, someone I've known a long time. People who won't judge." She paused, and even though he wanted to rush in and fill the void, fix this so she felt safe, he waited for her to go on. "Friends who won't think I'm weak."

"Weak? For what? Wanting me as much as I want you? *Woman.*" This time he growled, low and purposeful. "You are one of the strongest people I know. Bounced around as a kid. Taken advantage of by a fucking lying husband. And here you are. You own a house. Have a successful career making the world a better place. You've got meaningful friendships with people who are protective about you."

"Which is why you invited Fiona and Andrew over."

He continued to hold her, and she finally relaxed against him. What Trevor didn't tell her was that she had a Dominant who was determined to serve up all of her dreams. "It drives me wild that you are adventurous. I want to do anything—everything—with you also." He thumbed strands of damp hair from her neck.

"Do you mean that?"

"Yeah. I do. What you said doesn't feed my ego—"

She scoffed. "I'm calling BS on that, Master Trevor."

"Okay." Sweet, sassy, challenging Shelby Salazar twisted him in damn knots. "Fine. Maybe a little." Now she was forcing him to be vulnerable in return. "But it's more about trust and adventure. You want to explore our time together every bit as much as I do."

His heart thudded, and each pulse reminded him of a ticking clock. It was already Wednesday, and he only had her until Saturday morning. And he hadn't figured out how to get past her defenses to convince her to stay.

The fact that he wanted that shocked the fuck out of him. But there it was, and he hadn't been more certain of anything in his life.

"Do you see that?" She pointed to one of the windows, where the moon had appeared. "Your place really is amazing. I can't imagine noticing that in the city. I mean, obviously the moon rises every day, but my neighborhood has so many trees—magnolias, live oaks—that I never get a clear view of the sky. But out here, you can see everything."

"It's a little humbling."

"How vast the universe is? And how insignificant we are in the scope of things?"

"Maybe it's a reminder of which things really matter. Our connection to others, the good we can do."

"I like your version better than mine."

"About that appointment…"

"Tomorrow?"

"It's at David's law office."

She sat up and shoved herself away from him so fast that water crested the tub's edge and whooshed onto the floor in a giant wave. "What?"

He grinned, and she twisted around to face him, kneeling in front of him.

"What?" she repeated, a giant frown burrowing between her eyebrows. "Why?"

He nodded toward the soaked floor. "You created a tsunami."

"I asked you a question."

"So you did."

"Waiting for an answer."

He held back a grin, knowing she was mentally drumming her fingers. "We were working on teaching you to show patience, were we not?"

"Master Trevor." Her eyes flashed, an enchanting combination of adorable indignation and demand.

And in seconds, everything would change. "You want to know why?" He held up a hand. "I'll be honest. There's only one reason. It matters to you."

She raked back hair from her forehead.

"You were willing to put yourself on the line for him."

"It's about David, yes. But it's more about what he does," she corrected.

"Understood. And because he made a bold move as well, I'm interested in hearing more."

Her beautiful, slight shoulders trembled. "I...I don't know what to say."

"He's got thirty minutes of my time. Be warned, I'm not making any promises. I've just agreed to a meeting."

"Wait." She blinked. "This... You set this Sunday morning. You were talking to your assistant when I came out onto the balcony at the hotel."

"Yeah."

"But we'd only..."

Fucked? Scened?

It was so much more than that for him. They hadn't only fucked or scened. They'd made love, and he'd awakened with her trustingly cradled in his arms. "That's all I needed."

"I don't know what to say."

"There's nothing needed."

She blinked back tears. To see them sparkle like diamonds was worth anything to him. "Thank you."

"I mean it when I say there are no promises."

"There doesn't have to be. All he wanted was the opportunity to make a presentation."

"In this case, I decided I wanted to visit in person." It was easy to put together a slide show and revenue figures, adding narrative that slanted the facts or hid them entirely. In situations like this, nothing substituted for walking through the hallways, seeing the offices and clientele while making a needs assessment. Buildings told stories, and he was willing to listen. Despite his warnings to her, if he could be of assistance, if David was in a place that he would accept Trevor's guidance, he was determined to help. He approved of people giving of themselves to make the world a better place.

With far more confidence than he'd ever seen from her, Shelby moved toward him. Water splashed over the edge again, and he didn't give a damn. Seeing her prowling like this was its own beautiful reward.

He spread his legs, and she stopped in front of him. With her gaze riveted on his, she reached for his cock and closed her hand around him.

There was a gleam in her eyes, something he'd never seen before. A woman's hunger for her man. It aroused him.

On her knees, she leaned forward to lick the precum from his cockhead.

He groaned, and she sighed with satisfaction.

What she did to him…

Shelby licked and sucked. As he closed his eyes, he held her head to guide her movements, helping her pleasure him.

If this was the reward, he would spend his days dreaming up new ways to keep her happy.

Her movements, her soft whimpering approval, all drove his hunger. Although it would take a minute, maybe less, to spill inside her mouth, he wanted to pleasure her.

It took all of his self control to ease her away from his shaft.

"Mmm-nmm." She shook her head as she looked up at him.

"In the bed."

"You don't like this?"

"Oh. I do." Too damn much. "I want your body. All of it."

"All?" She pressed her lips together before speaking again. "I want to give it to you."

His cock leaped. "Shelby…"

"I know what I'm saying." Her breaths were short and shallow.

"You don't have to. This isn't about David. You owe me nothing."

"I realize that. This is something I'm ready for. I mean…"

There it was, that familiar, innocent blush.

"Not everything, everything. Right? Maybe an experiment."

"Meaning?" He wanted her to say the words. To be brave enough to ask.

"Are you really going to make me discuss this?"

He was still holding her head. Just a bit, he tightened his grip. "Yeah."

This time, her sigh was deeper, almost resigned. "There are parts of this whole BDSM thing that I don't like."

"The honesty." He paused. "Being vulnerable."

"Yes."

Trevor waited. She would capitulate, even if it was from the sheer force of his will.

"So… However you would suggest."

"Be specific, Shelby."

Her flush deepened, and a spark flashed in her eyes. No doubt she would give him all he demanded, but she wanted him to know she didn't like it. Still, her safe word was always a lifeline, and he admired that she didn't reach for it.

"I'm ready to try anal."

"Good girl." Though her words wobbled, and the last one was almost inaudible, she had taken the first bold step.

"I don't know what… I mean, how." She offered a helpless sigh. "But I'm willing."

"We'll start with a finger. Graduate to a plug."

Her shoulders shook, yet she didn't object.

It took them a few minutes longer than he liked to climb from the bathtub and mop the floor.

Finally he had her dry and naked on his bed.

He placed a small bottle of lube on his nightstand before instructing her to lie on her back. "Spread your legs."

From the air-conditioning her nipples were hard. Goose bumps chased across her arms. The ends of her hair were damp and starting to curl. She was utterly beautiful, and his. He'd never forget being her first.

"I want you to keep your legs apart." Not that he'd give her another option. He positioned the backs of her thighs on his shoulders, making escape all but impossible.

Though she complied, her body was rigid, meaning he had work to do.

He began with gentle restraint, licking her slit, toying with her clit, sliding a finger inside her.

As she began to relax, he increased the tempo, thrusting deeper into her, then eventually adding a second finger.

With his tongue, he laved her everywhere, moving down as far as her ass for quick seconds, then retreating the moment she went still. "Relax." Trevor fucked her with his hand, faster and faster until she thrust her pussy against him in age-old demand.

"Oh Sir!"

He kept up his own pace, filling her, retreating, licking.

As unobtrusively as he could, he grabbed the lube with his free hand and squeezed a dollop on her, drenching her.

Then he entered her with a third finger, and she screamed. "Trevor!"

"You can orgasm."

That exact moment, she gave herself over. Shelby grabbed the bedcovers and lifted her pelvis from the mattress.

As she thrust herself against him, he circled her tiniest opening. She froze, but he relentlessly drove her, licking her cunt harder, making her forget what he was doing.

As he thrust in and out of her pussy, he inserted a fingertip inside her anus and pulled back before she could protest. "Come for me, Shelby." He rolled his shoulders forward, spreading her wider. "Give it to me."

She closed her eyes and arched her back in surrender, and he continued to tongue her pussy as he slipped an entire finger inside her rear.

"Oh!" She cried out his name, then whispered it again and again, as her internal muscles clamped down on him and she climaxed all over his face.

After a final shudder, she collapsed.

With deliberate and slow motions, he withdrew his finger from her; then he kissed her belly before going into the bathroom to wash up. He returned to her with a damp washcloth and soothed her private parts before joining her in the bed and pulling her against him. "You survived your first anal experience."

"It was…"

He waited.

Even though her words were muffled by his chest, her word choice rocked him. "Amazing."

"Amazing?"

"Astounding."

Even better.

"I had no idea I'd like it so much." She lifted herself a couple of inches off his body. Her eyes were smoky with desire.

"Yeah? You'd do it again? Maybe with something bigger?"

"I'd consider it."

He fucking loved her newfound confidence. Her newfound confidence? Oh hell. It was so much more than that. He was falling in love with *her.*

When she lowered herself back down, he cradled her even tighter. The closer he edged to losing her, the more determined he became to hang on.

Shelby grasped her purse strap tighter as she and Trevor walked side by side down the sidewalk toward David's law offices. Even though she studied Trevor, she couldn't read his reaction behind his mirrored sunglasses. The only thing she saw was the reflection of her own wide-eyed curiosity.

This morning, they'd awakened early and had hot sex before showering together and dressing and deciding to eat breakfast in New Orleans. Their time together had been relaxed, a continuation of the intimacy from the night before.

On the drive into one of the less affluent parts of the city, he'd asked further questions about the types of cases David accepted. She'd been honest, that he took so many that he couldn't adequately represent everyone. He had a team of volunteers, but their resources were limited also. "I don't really know what drives him. But it's as if he has something he wants—maybe needs—to make up for."

Without saying a word, Trevor nodded.

There was still part of her that didn't believe he was doing this. Yet she was thrilled he was doing this...partly for her.

"This is it," she said, not that he hadn't noticed the dilapidated overhead sign with its rusted chain. At one time, the lettering had been proud, his name etched next to an image of a pair of balanced scales. Now, the name of his practice was chipped and faded from years of relentless storms and neglect. He had much more important places to spend the small amount of money he brought in.

Trevor reached for the doorknob and had to twist it twice to get it to release.

Still, he said nothing. Betrayed nothing.

Inside, there was a small waiting room with several nearby offices, the windows and doors covered by blinds with broken slats. Overhead fans circulated oppressively hot air. Phones rang in the distance, and several children squabbled at the play area in the far corner.

Trevor removed his aviator glasses and tucked them inside his sport coat. Even though it was the middle of summer, he still dressed professionally. Not so much that he looked out of place, but enough to show respect for what he was doing and how serious he was about it.

"I'll let David know we're here."

Trevor nodded while she pulled out her cell phone.

Instead of taking a seat, he wandered around, looking at the items on the walls. There were a few framed pictures of New Orleans and the Mississippi. Those had been purchased at local thrift stores. But there were other things that mattered to David. His clients' bill of rights—what each person could expect to receive. A listening ear. To speak with someone who knew the law. Adequate representation or a referral to someone who could provide that. In another frame, there was a note that thanked people for waiting if necessary and promising they, too, would receive the same kind of attention as everyone else. There was also a framed picture that Trevor studied more closely. It was of David receiving a community service award.

Her phone chimed with an incoming message. After receiving it, she walked over to join Trevor. "David is finishing up. Shouldn't take more than a minute or two."

Just then, his office door opened, and a youngster, maybe around three, barreled out, screaming as he ran.

"Christopher!" his mother called, making a mad dash after him but hampered by the baby in her arms.

Trevor stepped into action, blocking the youngster's path, scooping him from the floor. "Hey, guy." His voice was kind, inquiring. "What's up?"

The boy froze, mouth open.

"You're off somewhere in a hurry."

The harried mother, followed by David, stopped near them. "I'm sorry." She glanced around the waiting room at everyone staring. She was flushed, and Shelby knew it was probably as much from the embarrassment as it was from whatever brought her to the law offices in the first place.

Christopher was still staring at Trevor.

Shelby tipped her head to the side, looking at the man she'd woken up next to, the one who'd satisfied her on so many levels, and she wondered how little she knew about him.

"He has some…" The mother sighed. "Problems."

"Behaving like most little boys I know, aren't you, big

guy?" Then he looked at the mother with the full force of his attention and devastating smile. "Can I walk you to your vehicle?"

"I don't…" She blushed. "I take the bus."

"Let me call you a ride."

"No." The woman frantically shook her head and looked back at David. "I can't. No."

"I'll handle it," Shelby said, pulling out her phone to open a car service app. Most of the firm's clients didn't have their own transportation. No doubt Christopher's mother had a lot of pride, and maybe she also was afraid she'd be expected to pay for the car.

"No. No, please."

"It's okay." David patted the mother's shoulder.

"But—"

"Turns out I have a coupon for a free trip, tip included." Shelby told the white lie with a smile. "I just need your address."

The woman frowned, as if guessing the truth. "Really?" Just then, the baby started to make soft whimpers. "It's her feeding time."

"You've got your hands full." Shelby kept her voice as soothing as possible. "Let us do this for you."

"Accept the help," David urged the woman. "This once."

She bounced the baby and reluctantly gave Shelby her address. "Thank you. For everything."

Trevor pulled back a little to look at the child. "Are you going to be good for your mom?"

The boy nodded.

His ease with Christopher revealed an entirely new side of Trevor. She hadn't spent a lot of time thinking about having children, but watching Trevor with the young boy rocked an unfamiliar pang of maternal instinct through her.

Uncomfortable and a little disconcerted, she glanced away.

Surprising her, Trevor continued to hold Christopher until the driver arrived; then he went outside with the small family to help them into the vehicle.

"Didn't know he had it in him," David mused.

"He's…" What was the right word? "Remarkable."

David chatted with a man in the waiting area until Trevor arrived, still cool and composed, despite the full-on summer heat.

Together they walked to a small conference room, a place where volunteers occasionally manned phone banks.

"Quite the operation," Trevor mused.

"Not enough to meet the need."

It didn't escape her that David took a chair on one side of the table, leaving the position at the head available for Trevor.

Instead of accepting the unspoken invitation, Trevor sat next to her.

She wondered if it was possible to care for him any more than she already did.

"I've received the financials you sent over."

David slid a finger inside his collar, but he didn't apologize or look away.

"I'm interested in a five-year plan. Assuming we gave you a donation, what are the ways you could serve the community better?"

Shelby turned to look at Trevor. *A donation?* To her knowledge, that hadn't been under discussion. Wasn't David hoping for a loan?

David scowled, as if the question hit him unexpectedly too. "Hell, Lawton. I can't see past tomorrow."

"Let's be honest, shall we?" Trevor asked. "With the shitty

state of your checkbook, you're not going to be able to pay back a loan, no matter how low the interest."

"Lawton—"

"What you're doing here is important work. No doubt there's need. You're doing too much pro bono and low-cost work to restore the building. If it's a loan you want, maybe we can consider moving you to a smaller location."

David's shoulders slumped. The exchange between the two men was as fraught with tension as the poker game at The Quarter had been, and her stomach tightened.

"There aren't a lot of smaller places out here."

"I know." Trevor nodded. "I had a real estate professional check. So that would mean a different area of town."

"Which wouldn't be as accessible for his clients," Shelby added.

"True." David drummed his fingers on the tabletop.

"You own the building." Trevor made a statement rather than asking a question, Shelby noted. Clearly he'd done his homework before showing up.

"I've got a mortgage on it." David's complexion was chalky. Until now, she didn't know how bad things really were for him. "And my credit is not good enough to refinance."

"You've got a few options. I can find you private financing. We can also get Mason's company in here to do some remodeling. Possibly at cost. You could also clean up the second floor, build it out, rent some of it to businesses. Maybe consider private residences."

"Are you fucking saying you're willing to help?"

"You've won some important cases. The work you do here matters. And perhaps we can set you up as an actual nonprofit and try to secure some donations. Fundraisers, that type of thing. You can work on the important cases. And if you wish to spearhead the vision, I'm good with that. But we can also hire someone, a cross between a CEO and CFO to guide the future."

Shelby's heart fluttered.

"I don't know what to say."

"You'd better fucking start with yes; otherwise you've wasted a pile of my time." Trevor stood.

David pushed back from the table so fast his chair shot across the floor. "Thank you." He extended his hand, and Trevor shook it.

"I'll be in touch. If you'll excuse us?"

No one thought it was a question.

They were back in his truck and headed toward Lake Catherine when Shelby's pulse returned to normal. "That was…" *Oh Trevor.*

He took his gaze from the road to momentarily glance in her direction. Once again, his expression was cloaked by the sunglasses.

"That was beyond anyone's expectations."

"Thanks to you."

She shook her head. "I never asked you to do that."

"No. But once I knew you were involved, I wanted to find out more. I didn't think you'd offer your time and expertise unless it was worthwhile." He stopped for a red light. "I was correct."

For the rest of the drive, she went over the events again. It took a lot of self-discipline, but she managed to shove away the intrusive memories of Trevor interacting with Christopher and taking care of the small family.

Once they were back at his house and Bruno had adequately greeted them, Trevor preceded her up the stairs and inside.

He closed the door behind her then, whipped off his sunglasses. "Our time is limited, Shelby. I want you naked."

Trevor—Master Trevor—her Dominant, was once again in control.

Even though she should be accustomed to being the center of his attention, the power and intent in his blue eyes made her fingers shake as she dropped her purse to the floor and swept her blouse up over her head.

"I have a few things in mind for tonight."

"Oh? Do you?" She tried for breezy, but the tremble in voice betrayed her, and she sounded like a needy, uncertain submissive.

"But we have the afternoon first."

"Did you have something in mind, Sir?"

"Inserting a plug up your ass, sexy Shelby."

His words were naughty. Even a week ago, the consideration would have been unfathomable. But now, it was a tempting turn-on, and her insides tightened.

"What do you say to that?"

After last night's experience, she was willing. "Yes."

He smiled, a soft sensual approval that made her tummy flip-flop. Of course, it wasn't just that. It was everything else also. The way he treated her friends and David. Then there was the stressed mother with the young kids. Trevor Lawton was so much more than she'd ever imagined.

"In that case, finish undressing; then walk up the stairs and wait for me on the bathroom floor, on your hands and knees, your ass in the air."

All week, he'd been patient in helping her get past her apprehensions, so much so that she was now sometimes confident. This request, though, pushed her again. Having him slip a finger inside her while she was in the throes of ecstasy was different than waiting in a compromising position.

Like the implacable Dominant he was, he spread his legs apart and folded his arms. She'd agreed to his demand. And unless she changed her mind and safe worded out, he would be implacable. "Yes, Sir." Aware of him taking in every part of her, she finished undressing then walked toward the stairs.

"I'll give you a two-minute head start."

It was tempting to dash up the stairs to escape his scrutiny, but she took her time. At the top, though, she dashed for the bathroom.

With seconds to spare, she lowered herself into the position he'd ordered. She was tempted to face the door but guessed that wasn't what he would prefer. His strong footsteps echoed off the steps when she finally stopped dithering and raised her rear.

Then... There was silence.

It took all of her willpower not to glance over her shoulder but to wait on her Dominant.

"Sometimes I think you couldn't be any sexier, and then I'm proven wrong. You're a beautiful woman, Shelby. A stunning sub."

She expelled the breath burning in her chest. "Thank you, Sir."

"Stay where you are."

Was this a special form of his torture?

He didn't leave her for long, and when he returned, he crouched behind her. "Lower your forehead to the floor so you can reach back and spread your buttocks for me."

This shouldn't be so difficult. After all, she'd already given her ass to him. Shelby shook her head to stop the thought. She hadn't given it; he'd taken it. Offering it was far more unnerving.

"Shelby?"

"Yes..." she murmured. "Sir." Even though her balance was a little uncertain, she did as he said.

"Beautiful." He placed a finger against her.

His touch was firm and wet, and she surmised he'd used a fair amount of lube. Fortunately.

"Your hole is so tight."

Last night, he'd been licking her, playing with her pussy when he'd entered her tightest hole. But now, there was no distraction.

"Now, my good sub, bear down against me."

She screwed her eyes up tight against her innate embarrassment.

He smacked her right flank smartly.

With a yelp, she wiggled her ass, having no choice but to give him what he demanded.

"Very good. We're going to do this for a while."

Once he passed her initial resistance, she began to relax. He slid his finger in and out, deeper and deeper with each stroke.

Something cool and wet splashed onto her. More lube, no doubt. He was nothing if not a thoughtful lover.

When she was stretched and filled with the lubricant, he pulled out. She pressed her lips together to fight back an instinctive protest. She'd actually liked it.

"The plug is slim, no bigger than my finger. Latex, so it has a little give to it. You'll have no problem with it."

Easy for him to say.

"Give me more of your ass, Shelby."

With her eyes closed, she arched her back even farther, sticking her butt scandalously high in the air.

"Jesus," he whispered.

Every time she pushed past her comfort zone, his verbal reward was worth it. This time, he kissed the small of her back. He made it so easy for her to take risks she'd never been able to before.

"I'll go slow. Stay with me. You may be tempted to pull

away, and if that happens, move back toward me. It'll go faster that way."

The plug was nothing like his finger. It was more rigid, and it went in, it flared out, forcing her hole farther apart. She breathed harder and dug her fingernails into her palms. "Ugh!"

Even though he'd been clear in his instructions, she fought to escape, but her relentless Dominant captured her, inserted his forearm beneath her hip bones, and pulled her back toward him. Simultaneously he pressed deep in a single, forcible motion.

"*Fuck.* No! I can't do this."

"You're there." He stroked her spine. "You already did."

She stopped struggling. The plug snuggled in, and her anus closed around the slim stem. Now that it was inserted, she barely felt it. "It's in?"

"It is, indeed." He stood to wash his hands; then he used a washcloth to wipe the excess lube from her before helping her to stand. "It looks beautiful, by the way." He turned her to face him. "I like having you stuffed full for me."

She flexed her buttocks several times, adjusting to the sensation inside her.

He was quiet, obviously waiting for her to say something.

"It's not awful."

"Good. Now part your ass cheeks and go sit on the side of the bathtub."

Shelby gasped. "Are you…? You can't be serious."

"Deadly."

That set to his mouth, she recognized as pure determination. His will would prevail.

Filled with embarrassment, she did as he said. Because she was spread, the base of the plug was against the metal, forcing the plug a bit deeper. She moaned, and this time, it was from pleasure.

"Now, get dressed. We'll go somewhere fun for a late lunch." He turned to leave the bathroom but stopped in the doorway and looked back. "When we arrive at the restaurant, remember to part your ass in exactly this same way when you are seated."

With a happy whistle, he left, long before she could express her stunned outrage.

CHAPTER 10

Shelby turned on the cold water in the bathroom of her office building. The past six hours had been some of the most grueling of her career.

After expelling a breath to release the tension she'd fought not to show, she filled her cupped hand with the chilly water and splashed it onto her face.

Though mediation wasn't necessarily easy, this one had been difficult from the beginning. The Lemieux couple had been married for almost ten years, and Jocelyn had recently gotten pregnant. Percy had been overjoyed, until Jocelyn announced she wanted a divorce to be with her lover. Paternity tests had ensued, proving Percy was the father, and he was determined to raise his son. Jocelyn's gentleman friend had proposed to her and said he was happy to raise the boy as his own, infuriating Percy.

Dealing with Jocelyn and her emotions was like navigating treacherous seas. And Percy's grief and anger were a volatile cocktail.

Shelby called on all of her training to remain the detached, neutral party the couple needed. But there had been moments that tugged at her, reminding her of the way she, too, had been pulled on by her parents.

Worse, Shelby saw parts of her ex-husband's behavior in Jocelyn. Jocelyn wanted to be with someone else, and she could see nothing beyond that, not the hurt she was causing her husband or the devastation he felt at losing his child before it was even born.

As in most of the cases Shelby dealt with, there were always two sides. Percy could be self-absorbed, pursuing a political career at the expense of time with his wife. Jocelyn was alone and lonely much of the time, and her new man was enchanted with her.

It was just unfortunate a child was involved.

In the end, even though Shelby had compartmentalized her thoughts and feelings and done her job well, neither party was pleased. They'd barely been civil to each other. Percy had managed a cold thank-you toward her before leaving, but Jocelyn had given her a hard glare. At least that was one thing the Lemieuxs agreed on. Neither of them liked her.

She pressed her damp hands more fully against her face, willing away the dull headache that had been building for the past few hours.

When she glanced in the mirror again, the sparkle from one of the strands of ivy on her collar caught her eye. Staring at it, she took a deep breath. The thought of Trevor and his strength grounded her, helping put the world back in order.

Realizing the water was still running, she twisted the knob to stop the flow.

By the time she patted herself dry with a paper towel, she was able to return to the conference room to gather her belongings.

On her way out the front door, she waved to the receptionist.

"Judging by the looks on their faces when they left, I think you need a margarita and a beach after today."

The trip to the Bahamas she kept fantasizing about? For the first time in a few hours, Shelby managed a small smile. "Doesn't that sound like heaven?"

"I still think we should take a cruise for our office holiday party."

"We can dream, right?" Maybe they could figure out how to at least do a paddlewheel dinner cruise on the Mississippi River.

"Enjoy your weekend. You've earned it."

Outside, Louisiana's humidity drenched her, making ringlets of hair curl onto her cheek. After brushing the strands back, she climbed into the car and turned the key, only to have hot air blast from the vents.

Lowering the windows helped marginally, and while the air-conditioning struggled to push out anything cooler than hell's own heat, she fished her phone from her purse.

Unsurprisingly there were a few messages from Trevor.

I know this was a tough one. And I have complete confidence you did well.

With a small pang of appreciation, she scrolled to the second message.

Looking forward to seeing you.

Clutching the phone hard, she leaned against the seatback. She yearned for him. The week together had been magic, and already she was emotionally counting on him. And that led her into some very dangerous territory. This was a fling. Nothing more. No matter how difficult, she needed to remind herself of that.

Finally she became aware of the cool air washing over her skin, and she shoved off her melancholy to reply to Trevor's message.

*I'm on my way—*She paused, her finger hovering over the

keyboard. She was on her way…where?—*To your place? To your house? Home?*

Home?

The thought startled her so much that she shook her head.

For the second time in as many minutes, she'd allowed her vulnerable emotions to stray into dangerous territory. His place was not her home even though he'd done his best to make her comfortable.

Their time together, as hot and as naughty as it was, wasn't real. Shelby was too smart to allow herself to get swept up in the fantasy she'd been living.

Impatient with herself, she hit the backspace key until the letters vanished. Then she tried again.

I'll be there in about thirty minutes.

She reread her response before sending. It was perfect. Innocuous enough not to reveal what was going on inside her head and her heart.

His immediate response lit up her phone.

I've got you.

She turned up the volume on the radio to forcibly push away the thoughts that were winding their way back inside her brain despite her best efforts to keep them at bay.

Within the promised half hour, she pulled into his driveway.

As she climbed from the car, the usual explosion of barks rent the air as Bruno rushed toward her at a full gallop.

His greeting made her smile and helped push the immediacy of the day a little farther into the background.

Seconds later, he gave her a sloppy kiss before loping away.

Trevor was waiting outside on the deck. Without conscious thought, she fell into his arms. Trevor wrapped her close in the hug she desperately hungered for, even if she didn't want to be so needy.

For more than a minute, she stayed there, her head cradled against his chest as she breathed in his masculine scent.

"It was a long day for you." He tucked a wayward strand of hair behind her ear. "Bad one?"

"One of the worst."

"What do you need? To sit for a while? A glass of wine? To talk? To discuss something else entirely? A scene?"

"I'm not sure." Out here, the heat was relentless, zapping the little energy she had.

"We'll figure it out. Let's go inside," he suggested.

Once he closed the door behind them, she dropped her purse onto the floor. This was so familiar, and yet not at all. This was the last time she would be coming home from work to his house. Tomorrow she'd be going back to her own place and her regular life. Not that she knew how to define that anymore.

He studied her but didn't ask her to remove her clothes. Part of her appreciated it. A bigger part was confused. Maybe she did need it and the reassurance she found in the routine and his expectations. "I want..."

"Anything, Shelby."

"Make love to me?" Even as she asked the question, she realized how stupid she was being. The pep talk she'd been giving herself in the car, her resolutions, all fled the moment she was near him. In this moment, he could give her solace, and she wanted it.

"Not a scene, then?"

She shook her head.

Always the perfect, perfect man—lover—he captured her chin and gently kissed her before taking her hand and leading her up the stairs.

In the bedroom, he undressed her, taking his time opening each button on her blouse.

As she kicked off her pumps, she shrugged the silky shirt from her shoulders, and he placed it on the nightstand before unhooking her bra, then removing her skirt.

Shelby craved a connection that was as emotional as it was physical. She wanted to touch him, explore the rough, sexy planes of his body. Softly she placed her palm on his chest. "May I take off your clothes?"

"Anytime." His voice was gruff with restraint. "I mean that."

She lifted up onto her tiptoes to brush a gentle kiss across his lips, and he folded her in his arms. While still letting her lead, he captured her mouth in a way that was reassuring. Trevor Lawton was steady, more so than any man she'd ever known.

Her motions were awkward as she tugged his polo shirt up and off. Unlike him, she wasn't tidy. Instead, she dropped his clothing on the floor.

He helped her with the button at his waistband, but he kept his hands on her spine as she lowered the zipper and allowed his casual slacks to fall. She was grateful he helped with his shoes and stepping out of the pants.

Removing his tight boxer briefs was a challenge because of his enormous cock.

God, she wasn't sure she'd ever be accustomed to the sight of him when he was fully erect.

"Take me to bed, Shelby."

She swallowed her nerves and entwined her fingers with his. He made this so easy for her. "Uhm, sit on the edge of the bed?" Then she cleared her throat and tried again. "Please sit on the edge of the bed."

Trevor grinned. "Aye, my bold sub."

Once he was where she wanted him, she straddled him and rubbed her clit against his cock.

"Fuck."

Emboldened, she rubbed harder, enjoying the way his dick became even thicker, more engorged.

The faster she moved, the damper her pussy became.

"You're a damn sexy woman."

"It's you." He'd helped her find her inner confidence, and under his tutelage, she was flourishing.

His cock slid toward her entrance. With a guttural groan, he grabbed her around the waist and removed her from his lap while he reached toward the nightstand. "I promised we'd use condoms."

What was wrong with her? For the first time since her divorce, she hadn't given birth control a second thought. She had no desire to take unnecessary risks, especially when it came to pregnancy, but this man made her think of nothing else other than being joined intimately.

Unbidden, the image of him holding that young boy yesterday at David's office returned to play in her memory. There was no doubt he'd be a great father. "Have you ever wanted children?"

The small silver packet in hand, he looked at her.

Her timing couldn't be worse. Shockingly, though, his cock remained every bit as stiff as it had been.

"What makes you ask? Besides the fact I'm holding a condom."

"It's partially that, but… I don't know." She shook her head. "Actually that's not true. I think it has to do with the case I was just mediating." He knew it was about divorce and that there was a custody issue, but she hadn't told him anything else. "The wife is the one who initiated the proceeding."

"Go on."

Shelby sighed. "She's pregnant with her husband's baby, but she moved out and is living with another man."

"They're sure it's his?"

"That was one of the first questions everyone had. The paternity test was conclusive."

"And the husband is pissed?"

"It's more than that. Angry, yes. But devastated too. He wants to keep his family together. In this case we covered things that I've never seen before. I mean…" She brushed back her hair. "Every divorce is different with unique requirements. But this one has so many different angles. The husband wants to be in the delivery room, and she's opting to have the new man with her instead. So we had to work out that he was able to be at the hospital and able to see his son within an hour of birth."

"Fuck." Trevor winced. "I get why the whole thing was challenging. I'd fight hard for my offspring too."

"This was sad."

"Close to home for you?"

Being used as a pawn, yes. Being a spouse destroyed by betrayal, yes. "Parts of it were."

Staying with the conversation, he went on. "In answer to your earlier question. Yeah. I've thought about fatherhood. Never had a relationship that was long-term enough to seriously consider it. Having kids is a big obligation. And I'd want to be damn sure I was with the right woman before bringing them into the world. It would be a forever thing for me. I'd never abandon my children."

The pain of the past scraped across his vocal cords. She had her own issues with her parents, but they'd been part of her life, even if peripherally. "You were good with that little boy yesterday."

"Imagine it's not easy going anywhere with two kids."

"I know she appreciated your help."

"And yours. The way you handled the car situation was brilliant." He offered her the condom as he stroked himself, making his cock fully hard again.

Her motions were unsure as she unrolled the condom down his shaft, and he covered her hand with his to help her.

"I'll have you do that every time in the future."

It was undeniably sexy.

"Come here, Shelby." He helped her back onto his lap, facing him. "Ride me."

He licked his fingers and played with her pussy until she was drenched, wide open for him.

Even though she was on her knees and he was letting her set the pace, he cradled her hips, helping her keep her balance and rhythm as she slid up and down.

"I love watching you do this."

As urgency built, she rocked herself faster, and tilted herself forward so that his penetration was deeper. She wrapped her arms around his neck, offering all of herself to him.

Alpha male that he was, he accepted. Then, after nipping her shoulder, he closed his hands on her breasts. The slight pain rippled through her, turning her on even more.

"Give me your orgasm." His voice was low and gruff, filled with demand.

She was lost in his tenderness, his utter dominance.

Spiraling inside her head, she came, crying out and pitching forward as the powerful orgasm gripped her pussy.

As he always did, Trevor caught her. Holding her with simultaneous strength and reassurance. "I could make you come a hundred times a day for me."

Unable to catch her breath, she rested her forehead on his shoulder. For maybe thirty seconds, she gulped in air.

Eventually she realized that he was stroking her back and whispering endearments. That undid her. He was the man she'd always dreamed of being with. Strong and capable of devastating kindness.

But he'd been clear this was only for a week.

Blinking back the sudden tears that threatened to overwhelm her, she snuggled against him. Every moment with him was becoming more and more dangerous to her emotional state. After experiencing his tender lovemaking, being welcomed home and comforted by him, sleeping in the same bed, hanging out with friends, helping David... How was she supposed to endure her normal life?

As if sensing her inner turmoil, he wrapped his arms around her.

Shelby told herself to resist. But her body would not obey her mind's order. She wanted him, no matter the cost.

"Are you all right?"

"Yes." She gulped the knot in her throat so she could whisper the lie instead of confessing that she was starting to care for him so deeply that it was like staring into an abyss. "You were right earlier. It was a long day."

"Rest. Then we'll have dinner. How about we take the boat to the marina? Watch the sunset?"

That would get them out of the house and this terrifying, beautiful intimacy.

He helped her from his lap and onto her side. It was only then she realized he'd satisfied her without coming himself. She wasn't sure she'd ever been with a lover as generous as Trevor. "Uhm..."

He turned toward her.

"You didn't come."

"We have the rest of the night." He gave her a lazy grin before sliding his gaze down her body, making her nipples instantly harden. "And I have some wicked plans for you, Shelby. Wicked, wicked plans."

She gave him a small smile and hoped he didn't see through it to the apprehension beneath.

~

Half-asleep, looking forward to holding his sweet submissive before sharing a leisurely morning together and afternoon scene in his dungeon, Trevor reached for Shelby.

When he realized her side of the bed was empty, he cracked open an eye. It wasn't quite dawn, and the sheets were cool, meaning she'd been gone for some time.

He turned toward the bathroom, and it was dark.

With both eyes closed again, he listened intently for sounds of her moving around. Seconds later, hearing none, he sat up and threw back the covers.

He walked to her closet and flipped on the light. Everything was gone, and her drawers were empty. Similarly all of her toiletries had been scooped from the bathroom vanity.

Frustration and irritation flashed through him.

What the fuck? And how had he ignored her subtle warning signs? Yesterday, she'd arrived home from work, and her behavior had been different than ever before.

Their lovemaking was exquisite, and they'd followed that with drinks and dinner at the marina. Afterward they'd had a short scene. Though she'd orgasmed hard, her reactions had seemed guarded.

She'd slipped from the bed right away and taken a bath with the door closed. When she rejoined him, she curled up beneath the blankets near the edge of the mattress. He'd pulled her back toward him, and she'd kept her body stiff for long seconds before yielding with a sigh.

Sometime during the middle of the night, he'd awakened to find her back where she'd started.

In hindsight, he recognized that she'd been distant since

she arrived home. But instead of following her clues, he'd convinced himself that the divorce case she was working had taken its toll. But then there'd also been the questions about wanting children. Had she been hinting that she wanted some? Had he handled that wrong as well?

Trevor dragged his hand through his hair. How the hell was he suddenly navigating a field of landmines?

The scent of coffee wafted toward him.

Thank fuck.

At least she hadn't left.

He pulled on a pair of slacks and a T-shirt before jogging down the stairs.

Shelby was in the kitchen, wearing business clothes rather than something casual. Her hand was curled around a coffee cup, and her hips were propped against the countertop.

"Morning." Jesus. He'd never been this uncomfortable with a woman. Especially in his own house.

"I brewed coffee. Hope that's okay."

"After what we've shared over the past week, you need to ask that?" His words were abrupt, and his temper was growing shorter by the minute. "If you're not comfortable here now, you never will be."

She had the grace to flush.

Technically they had the rest of the day together, but he'd be damned if he'd hold her to it if she wanted to leave.

His back to her, Trevor poured himself a mug and took a swig, straight up.

Once he trusted himself to be civil, if not polite, he turned to face her, and that's when he noticed her bag sitting nearby on the floor.

"Trevor, I…"

He waited.

"Need to leave."

"Is there a reason?"

The heat that had flooded her cheeks receded, leaving her pale. "No. It's...Saturday, and..." Still holding her cup near her face as if to hide her expression, she shook her head. "There's no sense prolonging it, right? This way you can get back and have the rest of the day to yourself. To fish. Or whatever."

That wasn't what he wanted. "Shelby."

She didn't respond.

"Look..." He had no idea what to say next. From the time he was a child, Trevor had compartmentalized his emotions in order to focus on what he needed. Right now, he was struggling in a way he never had before. In the end, he settled for listening. "Talk to me."

"There's nothing to say. Really." Silence hung, stretched. "Thank you for an enjoyable week. I hope you found me worthy of your bet."

"Yeah. I did." He slammed his mug onto the counter, then advanced on her.

Because she was already backed against the counter, she had no easy escape. "And you, Shelby? Did you get everything you wanted? My full attention? A real BDSM experience? Or was this a casual, fun experience? A vacation from your regular life?" Trevor recognized he was being an asshole; he just couldn't help it. Her casual dismissal of him, of them, their week together, all of their experiences pissed him off. "Hmm? Or are you disappointed? If so, we still have the rest of the day. I can step up my game."

"Trevor." Her hand shook, and her coffee was precariously close to spilling. "No. This was wonderful. Everything I could imagine. Don't ruin it."

"Is that what I'm doing?" He took her cup from her and set it down, exerting magnificent control so that he didn't shatter the porcelain. "You've orgasmed for me. Dozens of times. Been vulnerable in my arms. Screamed. Cried out. You even begged, didn't you?"

At that, her expressive green eyes widened.

Trevor tucked a strand of hair behind her ear and leaned in a little closer, near enough to kiss. "You couldn't have been a more perfect partner. Your patience while waiting is now sublime. You can proudly take your place as a well-trained submissive." He traced one of the mesmerizing vines on her collar. "And you've worn this for the whole world to see."

"It was only for a week. We both agreed."

"So we did." He nodded tightly as he dropped his hand. And he took a step back. "You're not going to tell me what happened?"

"Nothing." But the word cracked with emotion, *with a fucking lie.* "Everything's fine."

He waited. But other than her eyes swimming with tears, she revealed nothing. He was torn between comforting her and taking her shoulders and demanding an answer. In the end, he did neither. "If that's what you want."

He'd never been more helpless.

"Yes. Please. I'm ready anytime."

"Give me ten minutes." He took twenty, because he needed to think through things in the shower.

He replayed their entire week, from the way she looked at him while she was on her knees at the Quarter to their experience in his dungeon, to laughter with Fiona and Andrew, and ending with last night. Hell if he could come up with anything that had gone wrong between them.

Once he was dressed, he met her in the living room. She was perched on the edge of the couch where he'd eaten her pussy Wednesday after she returned home from work. If she remembered that event, she showed no sign of it.

He walked to the front door. She'd already placed her bag

next to it. Yeah. She was definitely thinking of the future, not the past.

Because it was so early, there was little traffic on the roads. "Breakfast?" He slid her a sideways glance.

She didn't look at him. "Thanks. I'm not hungry."

Neither was he, and he hadn't expected her to say yes. He wanted to be polite, and having a little more time together would have been nice. Maybe he could have gotten some kind of answer from her. No doubt that was exactly what she hoped to avoid.

For the next half an hour, she checked social media and occupied herself playing a mindless game. When he parked in front of her house, she dropped her phone in her purse.

"Let me take off your collar."

Nodding, she unbuckled her seat belt. Then she turned her back to him as she lifted her hair.

Jesus. He didn't want to do this.

It took him a few seconds to release the heart-shaped lock. Once it sprang free, Shelby reached up to remove the collar.

Then she turned, the exquisite piece extended toward him.

"Keep it." Maybe it would help her remember their time together. It would for him. Which was why he didn't want it.

"It's yours. You paid for it."

When he didn't take it, she placed it on the console.

He opened his door.

"Thanks, but I can see myself in."

Gritting his teeth, he said nothing.

Shelby was already halfway up the path when he caught up with her.

She fumbled the key in the lock, which meant she was more bothered than she wanted to let on.

Finally she opened the door and slipped inside. "Thank you for seeing me home."

"Shelby—" Damn this. He should let it go, but he couldn't. "Why?" He hated the tension rubbing his vocal cords raw.

Gently, so, so insultingly gently, she closed the door. On him. On *them*.

Like a lovestruck idiot, he remained there, hand poised to knock, doing nothing but staring and wondering how the hell he was going to get through losing someone he'd never really had.

And if that was true? Why was his soul shredded?

CHAPTER 11

On the coffee table, Shelby's phone vibrated. She glanced over at the display. Fiona. Again.

Even though she'd blocked Trevor's number after he tried to reach her on three separate occasions, Shelby jolted each time the device rang, half hoping, half scared it would be him.

Instead of answering Fiona's incessant summons, Shelby turned the cell phone over and then turned up the volume on the television show she was streaming. Fortunately there were more than fifteen seasons of the medical drama to entertain her.

For two weeks, she'd cocooned herself at her home, leaving only for work and to pick up essentials. During that time, she'd taken more baths than she could count, and she'd cleaned out every closet and all her drawers.

Despite the fact that it was still summer, she'd taken up baking for the first time. Her freezer was filled with cakes and cookies—and that happened after giving platefuls to all of her neighbors and colleagues.

Even though she kept telling herself to build time and

distance from Trevor, she couldn't resist the compulsion to look at his social media accounts—sometimes more than once a day. And she didn't always limit herself to the most recent posts. Often she scrolled back through his photos. In some he was pictured with his family, wearing a big smile. Others with clients or Wayne Dixon were more professional. She'd seen so many of those expressions, and each was a reminder of him, which brought her sorrow and compounded her misery.

Because that wasn't enough torture, she'd also read everything ever written about the Zeta Society—not that it took very long. For an organization that had been around for over a hundred and fifty years, there was very little information about them.

The most in-depth article appeared in *Scandalicious* and included the names of the founding seven members. Sometime in the 1930s, members had been nicknamed Titans, and the name had stuck.

Reportedly the society owned a massive estate on the banks of the Mississippi River in Louisiana. Beyond that was a lot of conjecture, mostly from anonymous sources. Dues were said to be astronomical, and the wait-list to join was years long.

A reporter had sneaked into the yearly gathering where he confirmed there was a massive bonfire and a procession, held in grand New Orleans style.

After the exposé appeared, the reporter was fired. Now he wrote biographies about famous people. On one book cover, there was a man wearing a ring that matched Trevor's.

Her phone stopped ringing, and Shelby exhaled her relief. Since she returned home, she'd turned down several invitations to meet up with Fiona and Hannah for happy hour. When David texted, asking if she wanted to join him for a trip to the Quarter, she'd shot back an instantaneous refusal.

She was too fragile to risk seeing Trevor, especially if he was with someone new. God knew when she'd be ready for that. Never, maybe.

Even though the television was loud enough to wake the neighbors, it didn't drown out the thoughts of Trevor. In fact, nothing seemed to. Something would make her think of him, and then she would be consumed by the pain of her memories.

When he looked at her before she closed the door on him, he asked why. His voice had been hoarse and his expression stricken, making his blue eyes even more piercing.

Struggling to fight off her tears, she hadn't answered, mostly because she was a coward.

She didn't have the courage to tell him the truth, that she was more scared than she'd ever been. Sometime during the week, he'd become important to her. Maybe it had been because of his patience when they scened or the way he held her while they slept. For certain, resistance softened when he invited her along to visit David's law center. Seeing him interact with the rambunctious young boy and stressed-out young mother had given her a glimpse at the humanitarian she guessed him to be.

But it had been the next day—after she arrived at his home after mediating the Lemieux divorce—when she lost her heart to him.

Trevor wasn't just there for her—it was so much more powerful than that. He was kind and generous. Not only was she falling in love with him—she was starting to depend on him. And that was one thing she couldn't allow.

Scared of what was happening to her, she gathered her emotions close and locked them away.

A long-term relationship was not for her. Not only had she lived the devastation of being a pawn after her parents' divorce, but she'd endured the devastation of losing her own marriage. If her memories weren't enough to keep her focused, her work was. Every day, she dealt with the cruel reality of unhappily ever afters.

Why prolong things with Trevor?

So she could become even more attached? Hurt worse when it ended?

One thing Shelby was certain of—she wasn't strong enough to survive that.

The biggest problem was, time and distance hadn't helped heal her heart. In fact, even though it seemed ridiculous to her, the ache was worse now than the day she'd had him remove her collar before she said goodbye.

She readjusted a pillow behind her, then hit the back button to restart her television show. Fiona's interruption had brought thoughts of Trevor to the forefront once again. It was a constant struggle to keep them at bay.

Forcing herself to focus, she skipped the introduction.

Seconds later, her doorbell rang, followed by a pounding on her door. "Shelby! We know you're in there!" Fiona's voice was loud enough to be heard over the racket she was making. "Your car is in the driveway. Open up before I use your spare key."

Why had she ever told her friend where that was?

For a few seconds, Shelby contemplated what to do. Keep quiet and hope Fiona was bluffing? Open the door and shoo her away?

The pounding continued. "I mean it, Shel!"

She tipped back her head, trying to decide whether Fiona was a good friend or a terrible one. Not that it mattered. She was persistent.

Realizing the sooner she faced this, the faster she could get back to the television, Shelby stood—just in time for Fiona to make good on her threat and unlock the door.

She marched in, accompanied by Hannah. Both women

were dressed for a night out while she was wearing leggings and an oversize T-shirt.

"Did you forget?" Fiona asked.

"Forget?" Shelby blinked.

"We have appointments with Mademoiselle Giselle tonight, and we're having happy hour at the Maison Sterling."

The place she'd spent the night with Trevor. Once more, all thoughts circled back to him. "Uhm—"

"Don't say it." Fiona made a show of buttoning her lips. "Not a word. Don't even think it. We already came up with all the excuses you are going to try to use. So we've already done the work for you."

Hannah nodded.

"You're getting dressed. You're going to stop feeling sorry for yourself. You're going to have a good time, even if we have to force you into it."

"Look—" She grabbed a handful of hair and held it off her nape, but it didn't matter. Fiona had already dashed into Shelby's bedroom.

"We did call and message," Hannah said by way of apology. "Several times."

"I know."

Hannah reached out and took Shelby's hands. "Since I can't begin to guess what you're going through, I won't even try. But I'll tell you this. Your friends care about you deeply. Whatever happened, we love you."

Tears that she'd successfully kept at bay for days began to swim across Shelby's eyes.

"You can talk about it if you want. I promise you, Fiona is an excellent listener. She got me through when I freaked out about my relationship with Mason." She squeezed Shelby's hands "I'm not too bad myself. You can tell us anything, or you can spend the evening pretending everything is okay.

All of us need a break from reality so we can enjoy our lives."

"Jeans or a dress?" Fiona called out. "I'm not asking you, Shel. I want Hannah's opinion."

"Contrary to what you think, I can dress myself!"

"Uh-huh."

Rolling her eyes, she pulled out of Hannah's grip.

"Glad it's your turn and not mine." Hannah plopped onto the couch. "She's a force of nature. If you want to have any say-so in what you're wearing tonight, you'd better seize it. She's already picked out your hairstyle too."

"What the hell?"

"Messy bun. Means you did something with it, but putting it up won't take a lot of time." She made a show of checking her smart watch. "Reservations, you know."

"She's unstoppable."

"Like the tide. Only less predictable."

There was that.

Shelby hurried to join her friend.

Several outfits were strewn across the bed, everything from her tightest sundress to an elegant skirt and blouse, to a pair of jeans with a formfitting white T-shirt. There was, however, only one pair of shoes selected. Strappy high-heeled sandals. Not a bad choice. They'd go with anything.

"You've got less than ten minutes."

"Fine." Since her friends were both in jeans, she opted to join them.

"Get changed."

Since they scened together at the club, there didn't seem to be much point protesting the fact that Fiona was still in the room.

"Your closet looks magnificent. When I'm all up in my emotions, I eat. Ice cream. I'm not particular about the flavor as long as the fat and sugar content is off the charts. But you? Cleaning?"

"And baking."

Fiona tilted her head to one side. "Who are you? And what have you done with my friend?"

"In my defense, I didn't eat most of it."

"So you've got some left?"

"Cookies." She gnawed her lower lip. "And cake."

"We're taking some of your stash with us."

"Please do."

"It'll go good with ice cream. Put the ice cream on the cake and top the masterpiece with cookie pieces. Or wait, make a sandwich out of the cookies? Stir in some cake first?" Still talking, she grabbed Shelby's wrist and pulled her into the bathroom where she dropped the lid on the toilet. "Sit down."

"I can do my own makeup."

"We have a schedule, and I plan to keep us on it."

Caught up in the whirlwind that was Fiona, Shelby sighed. And really, she was grateful for her friends. She'd been morose, which was unlike her. Already she was more animated than she had been since she was at Trevor's home.

Fiona dabbed and plucked and swiped on mascara. Then she selected a bright red lipstick and twisted the tube up.

"No, no." Shelby shook her head. "No."

"Oh yes. If you'd have been ready to go when we got here, we wouldn't be in this situation right now. You may want to cooperate; otherwise we're going to have a hell of a mess to deal with. This is that twelve-hour stuff."

She was bested by Fiona's determination.

Seconds later, after carefully applying the color, Fiona stepped back and grinned. "Very bold. Sassy. I like it. Now your hair."

"We're in a hurry, remember?"

Ignoring her, Fiona dug through some of the plastic bins in the closet and found bobby pins and a hair tie. "Scooch around so I don't have to lean over you."

With only a few twists and tucks, then securing her masterpiece in place, Fiona stood back. She pursed her lips, then moved in again to pull out a few strands of hair to frame Shelby's face. "Voila! You look as if you spent hours on yourself. Let's move."

Now that Shelby's bedroom and bathroom were both disaster areas.

In the living room, Hannah stood. "Wow. All that in under ten minutes? Impressive. Of course, when Fiona is on a mission, she's unstoppable. As I well know."

Fiona zipped them into the city. From the backseat, Shelby closed her eyes a couple of times against the terror that came from seeing the risks her friend took. "Next time I'll drive."

"You could have picked us up."

"I know." She held up her hand. "If I'd answered my phone. Lesson learned."

Fiona met her gaze in the rearview mirror. "Good girl."

The three laughed at the intentional BDSM purr in Fiona's voice.

"We missed you at the Quarter the other night," Hannah said, turning in her seat.

She'd missed being there also. All night, she'd wondered what her friends were doing. Having dinner. Moving toward various equipment. And that thought had sent her reeling, remembering Trevor taking her upstairs to a private room and all the delicious things he'd introduced her to. "I wasn't feeling well." She shouldn't pursue this line of conversation any further. Even though it wasn't smart, she couldn't stop herself. "How was it?"

"Meaning? Was Trevor there?"

Shelby's pulse galloped.

Fiona braved the silence. "He was."

"He didn't scene." Hannah turned again to look at Shelby. "He spent the evening in the bar, not drinking. From what I saw, a couple of women approached him, but he turned them down."

She dug her fingernails into her palms. He had every right to play with as many women as he wanted, yet she was ridiculously happy that he hadn't.

"David joined him for a bit, and he says they talked about plans for the law offices."

So that was moving forward. That made her smile a little. At least something good had happened as a result of the wild, ridiculous bet.

"Mason also talked with Trevor, but he refused to tell me about their discussion. I'm positive he's doing it just to annoy me."

Shelby shook her head. "Surely not."

"Anyway, he left early."

Had he asked about her? Was he curious at all?

She should shove aside those questions, but the loss of him from her life left a hole in her heart so big that she was sure the world could see it.

"Are you ready to talk about it?" Fiona asked after she whipped around another car so fast that her vehicle rocked.

Maybe that would help. Since her friends were in relationships with BDSM dynamics, they would no doubt understand some of the things she experienced with Trevor —physically, and maybe emotionally as well. If nothing else, they'd listen without judgement. Keeping her emotions to herself wasn't helping her get better. "Over drinks?" That would buy her time to think about what she wanted to say. And after being Fiona's passenger, there was no doubt Shelby would need fortification.

For the rest of the drive, Hannah chatted about the reality show she and Mason were filming and plans for their upcoming wedding.

Fiona, however, despite being so bossy with Shelby, said very little about her own life.

When they pulled up in front of the Maison Sterling, adrenaline poured through her. Everything about the building, from the elegant green awning to its liveried doorman who doffed his top hat, reminded her of Trevor.

Inside, her loneliness became worse. Entering with him and being zipped up to his room, then later the next day walking through the lobby wearing his collar.

"Are you okay?" Hannah asked as they walked toward the bar, their heels loud on the polished marble floor.

"You're pale." Fiona's accusation seemed to echo off the historic walls. "Stop that. You're ruining my makeup!"

Fiona's ridiculousness made her laugh.

"That's better."

They found a table in the old-world bar, away from other patrons. The lights were dimmed, and a candle flickered on their table. Light jazz spilled from unseen speakers, contributing to a luxurious ambiance.

She sank into a soft leather chair, then picked up the happy hour menu. Not that she had any doubt what she was having.

Moments later, the server arrived with a crystal bowl filled with premium nuts. This place was among New Orleans' most expensive, but there was a reason for that. Not a single detail was ever overlooked.

"Are you ready to order, or do you need a few minutes?"

Since she knew the conversation ahead might be difficult, Shelby went straight for the most potent thing on the menu. "Cat Five." The hotel's renowned, lethal hurricane, was made from the sweetest juices and rum from Barbados.

"Floater on top?"

She frantically shook her head. There was enough alcohol in the drink without adding an extra shot.

"Margarita. Frozen. Extra salt on the rim," Fiona said, fishing a cashew from the crystal bowl.

"Same," Hannah agreed. "But light salt."

They made small talk until the beverages arrived. After the first sips, they all sat back in the chairs. Hannah and Fiona faced Shelby, saying nothing, just waiting. Beneath their scrutiny, she squirmed and leaned forward to play with her colorful paper straw.

"Okay. I'll start." It wasn't a surprise that Fiona took charge. "When we came out to the lake, you were wearing Trevor's collar. And you seemed happy."

"I was."

"And…" She sighed. "Don't make me drag it out of you."

"It was never supposed to be permanent." Every day, part of her missed its weight and reassurance. "I told you that."

"I've been to Mademoiselle Giselle's shop. All of her items are expensive. That was a lot of money for a one-week fling."

"I gave it back."

"What went wrong?" Hannah asked.

"Honestly? Nothing." This time she took a much longer drink. "I mean… God." She gave herself a minute to think. "We agreed to spend a week together. And I was really starting to fall for him."

"It seemed mutual," Fiona said. "You two worked as a couple on the boat. Andrew and I both noticed Trevor wanted to throw us overboard so he could have you to himself for a while."

"That obvious, huh?" Shelby smiled, and that relieved a million of her burdens.

"You think?" Fiona licked some of the caked-on salt from the rim and followed it with another nut.

"He's not just an excellent Dom; he's a good man."

"Now it makes total sense why you've been moping for two weeks."

Shelby glared at her friend.

"I know how complicated it can be," Hannah said. "Did he turn you down?"

"No. But he didn't offer anything more either. Like it was at its natural conclusion. And when I was leaving… He didn't seem pleased. I guess he thought I'd stay for the entire day, but it seemed pointless." She toyed with one of her loose strands of hair. "I didn't want another scene when I was already feeling emotionally vulnerable."

"You didn't want it to be over?"

Shelby sighed. "It needed to be, though. Before I got hurt any worse."

"So you two never discussed it?" Hannah asked. Then she leaned a little closer. "I'm not one to judge. After the weekend I spent with Mason, he wanted me to stay, make it permanent, move away from Austin, which also meant quitting my job. It was sudden…fast. Too fast. And I didn't really know how to ask for more time. Couldn't figure out how to make a long-distance relationship work. The drive would be nine hours or so. Or the constant flights. And not ever enough time together. But uprooting my life after forty-eight hours together seemed insane. So I left."

Shelby hadn't heard that much of Hannah's story before. She knew Mason had bid on her in a Quarter slave auction event, and she knew the two were together, but she hadn't known how rocky their beginning had been. "Trevor never said anything like that. I think maybe he assumed…" She pursed her lips. Assumed what? That they'd keep seeing each other? Date? "But it doesn't matter. The truth is once I started falling for him, I needed to get away."

"It's your stupid job," Fiona proclaimed, picking up her

glass and taking an enormous drink. "And your dumb fuck of an ex."

"Another round, ladies?"

Oh God. The server had overheard them? And she was too professional to reveal anything. "I think we're good," Shelby said. After all, they had dinner plans too.

"Don't worry," the woman said. "I have one of those too." She smiled. "Will this be on one ticket? Or would you like separate bills?"

"I'll take this one," Fiona said. "When I break up next week, one of them can pick up the bill."

"Yes, ma'am."

When they were alone again, Shelby turned to Fiona. "Are you serious?"

"No." She shook her head emphatically. "It was a joke."

But Shelby wondered. There'd been moments of tension at the lake, and this wasn't the first hint Fiona had given about there being trouble. Not that it was an entire surprise. She'd never had a relationship that lasted very long, and Andrew wanted to move to the next level, something the free-spirited Fiona might struggle with.

"And this is about you. I'm not letting you off the hook. You spend all day, every day immersed in divorce cases. Disaster after disaster. That would take a toll on anyone. And not all men are cheating jackasses like Joe."

"I know that." Or master manipulators like her parents.

She thought back to the stories Trevor told her about his upbringing. Needing to be the man of the family and help out financially at age ten. And again, that indelible memory of him with the child at the law center returned to play with her mind. And as he'd said, he wasn't the type of man to abandon his wife or children. Trevor Lawton was unlike anyone she'd met. And still, she was haunted by the betrayal of her former husband.

Logically she knew Fiona was right on all counts. Maybe spending all day immersed in ugly custody battles and acrimonious matrimonial dissolutions wasn't in her best interest.

"I'm also going out on a limb here." Fiona waved her straw as if it was a battle flag. "Hiding away isn't helping one little bit, is it?"

The server returned with the bill, saving her from answering.

Before they left to go to the restaurant, Fiona got in a parting shot. "Trevor seemed every bit as lonely as you are. Just for the record."

They left the car with the hotel's valet and walked to one of their favorite restaurants about three blocks away where they had another round of drinks to go with their enormous Creole sampler plate.

"Those tea leaves are going to be really interesting," Hannah said.

Fiona nodded. "Agreed."

A few minutes before nine, they entered the brightly lit shop. Even though it was Shelby's second visit and she knew what to expect, the storefront still seemed at odds with the other world that lay beyond the obvious.

"We're here to see Mademoiselle," Shelby told the woman in front of the cash register.

"She's expecting you." She waved toward the threshold. "Please. Go up the stairs."

Hannah and Fiona exchanged glances; then they followed Shelby through the curtain crafted from tinkling strands of silver circles.

Unlike last time, the door to the private shop was closed. As they ascended to the second level, the sounds from below faded, and their shoes echoed off the ancient wooden planks.

At the top, there was a yellow door with a large brass

knocker in the shape of a grotesque replica of the horned, winged gargoyle famously perched atop Notre Dame Cathedral. She took a breath and raised her hand toward the odd-shaped head, not quite sure how to best grab it, but the knob turned, and Mademoiselle stood in the opening.

Her smile was warm, and the hand she waved extended to all of them. Her numerous bracelets slid together in a momentary beautiful symphony. "Welcome." This evening, as expected, she was barefoot. Her long diaphanous gown was varying shades of green, mostly emerald, but with swatches of forest, fading to mint in the delicate pleats. "I've looked forward to this day."

She glanced at Shelby's throat. Then, seeming to notice the absence of the collar, Mademoiselle nodded before embracing Shelby. For maybe thirty seconds, she stayed where she was, grateful for the woman's intuitive understanding of the comfort she needed.

When she was stronger, Mademoiselle patted her shoulder reassuringly before releasing her.

She turned to her right. "You're Fiona." It wasn't a question. "Fierce, oui? Protector of all. It's my pleasure."

Fiona blinked. Shelby was stunned that her friend had no immediate comeback.

"And Hannah. Strong and creative. Perhaps more than you'd ever realized?"

"Uh… Uhm…"

"She is," Fiona supplied loyally.

"And a heart that is big," Mademoiselle continued, still addressing Hannah. "Perhaps a little guarded yet?"

"Do we even need the reading?" Hannah asked. "I feel as if I've already had it."

"Yet you have questions that linger." Again, Mademoiselle Giselle made a pronouncement. "S'il vous plaît." Mademoiselle stepped back to invite them in.

Her apartment was as unique as she was. Large antique pieces dominated the space, but it was wide open and bright. Fresh flowers adorned almost every surface.

They followed her into a kitchen with floor-to-ceiling white cabinets. The oversize industrial appliances hinted that she enjoyed entertaining. And on the marble countertop was a dizzying array of matching cups and saucers. There were also numerous teapots. Some were whimsical. Others were made from stout stoneware. Several were delicate porcelain. Behind them was an orderly row of tins, each labeled with the name of a different tea.

Mademoiselle silently crossed to the stove and turned on a burner to heat the kettle. "Who would like to be first?"

No one volunteered.

"I suggest Fiona, oui?"

Fiona pursed her lips together, surprising Shelby. Since Fiona was bold, up for anything, her hesitation was unusual.

"No need for nerves." Mademoiselle's voice soothed. "Begin by selecting a cup and saucer you like."

Now that she was given a task, Fiona seemed more confident. Her hand shook only slightly as she selected a bright blue cup with matching saucer.

"Perfect." Mademoiselle didn't seem surprised by the choice. "Now measure a teaspoon of tea."

Fiona reached for oolong and waited while Mademoiselle poured hot water on the loose leaves.

"There's an art to this." Mademoiselle placed the kettle on the stove, and again her bracelets tinkled. "You'll enjoy your tea and leave a little at the bottom of the cup. When we get to the reading, you will be looking for symbols, letters and such. Clear your mind and be open to whatever appears."

As Mademoiselle spoke, Fiona finished her beverage.

"Good. Good. Now consider what you want. Do you wish

to know some general things? Or is there something specific you desire guidance on?"

Fiona frowned in deep concentration.

"Take the handle in your left hand and silently ask your question. When you are ready, rotate your cup counterclockwise three times."

Transfixed, Shelby watched.

"Gently turn your cup upside down over your saucer. Then we'll leave it for about a minute while it drains."

Fiona exhaled and followed the instructions.

When Mademoiselle nodded, Fiona picked up the cup.

"As I mentioned, have a look to see what images might be there. Sometimes it's helpful to look at larger patterns first."

Shelby glanced over. Most of the leaves had drained onto the plate, but plenty remained. Some at the base of the cup, others clinging to the sides.

Fiona shook her head. "I don't see anything."

Before responding, Mademoiselle turned the burner on once more. "Allow the leaves to reveal themselves. It's helpful to have an open mind, especially around the question you were having."

Fiona met Shelby's gaze, and they exchanged shrugs.

"Some confusion is normal," Mademoiselle assured them. Though her back was to them, she'd spoken as if she'd seen the exchange.

Trevor had been right. Mademoiselle was good.

"Trees." Fiona stared into the depths of the cup. "An entire forest of them."

"And where are they located?" Mademoiselle turned down the burner before rejoining them.

Fiona scowled. "I'm not sure what you're asking."

"Anything close to the handle reflects the present. To its left can signal what is leaving your life; to the right can indicate what may be coming."

"I'm screwed." Fiona returned the cup to the saucer with a clatter. "They're everywhere."

"Ah. And to you, what does the forest represent?"

Shelby studied her usually unflappable friend. Fiona was frowning, and her hand shook.

"Not being able to see clearly?" Fiona guessed. "That old adage, can't see the trees for the forest. Or the other way around." She shrugged. "I have no idea."

"Also the unknown? Mysteries of the unconscious?" Mademoiselle's words were gentle. "Tell me about the bottom of the bowl. What's coming to pass eventually."

"This could be wishful thinking. But it could be a sun."

"May I?" Mademoiselle glanced at the leaves but didn't touch the cup. "The sun. Yes. And over here. Rotate the cup toward you. Perhaps that's an ankh? The Egyptian symbol?"

"I see it!" Fiona nodded.

"Sometimes it's a symbol of protection? We know how fiercely you take care of your loved ones." Mademoiselle paused, and everyone studied her. When she spoke again, her words were part curiosity, part steel. "Who does the same for you?"

Fiona shivered. "That's a little unsettling."

"Hmm." Mademoiselle's tiny response was noncommittal. "The question will return when the time is right. Is there anything else there for you?"

"I think I have what I needed." Fiona placed the cup on the table with a loud clatter.

"Your intuition can be trusted. More will reveal itself in due time." Mademoiselle rested her hand on top of Fiona's shoulder, then gently patted a couple of times. "All will be well."

As Fiona gave a brave smile before nodding, Shelby studied her. What had the reading stirred up? Thoughts about her relationship with Andrew? Or was it something else entirely? Though they'd been friends for years, Shelby knew little about her past or what made Fiona the strong, capable woman she was.

"Hannah?" Mademoiselle's soothing tone restored harmony to the surroundings and ensured that the evening continued the way it was supposed to.

"My turn, I guess." In a nervous gesture, Hannah pushed her brunette hair back before choosing her cup and saucer.

Once she'd finished her tea, she repeated the steps Fiona had taken. And after studying her cup for at least a minute, she shrugged. "This is more difficult than I thought it would be. Does anyone see anything?"

"This is about you tapping into your intuition. Divining what is meant for you."

"I'll try again." She looked at the leaves from several different angles. "Uhm. A circle."

"A ring?" Fiona asked.

Hannah gnawed on her lower lip. "Maybe. Mason's mother is getting married soon."

Hannah and Mason had been together for a while, and they were filming a home renovation show. Mason was clear to everyone that he wanted to marry Hannah, but she wanted to move more slowly than he did.

"What part of the cup is it in?" Mademoiselle asked.

"The bottom."

"And when is the wedding?"

"A couple of weeks."

"Hmm."

"What?" Hannah demanded.

"Symbols in the bottom of the bowl tend to be a little further in the future."

Fiona squealed. "So it could be your wedding!"

Hannah blushed, which was telling.

Shelby leaned in closer. "Are you getting closer to agreeing?"

"Uh…" Her flush deepened.

"You are!" Fiona exclaimed. "I'm so happy for you."

Hannah placed her cup back on its saucer.

"The leaves tell us many things." As always, Mademoiselle's voice calmed and reassured. "Possibilities. Probabilities, even. But not certainties. You always have free will. And the circle may represent something to you other than a ring. Friendship. Closure."

Hannah nodded. "Maybe from the crap in my past."

"Choose your path with confidence. Find your joy."

"Right now, I'm happier than I ever have been."

With a knowing smile, Mademoiselle once again returned to the stove to boil water.

Now that it was her turn, Shelby sympathized with her friends' struggle. Finding meaning in something that looked like random blobs of leaves and twigs was more difficult than it appeared.

"Perhaps a general impression?"

What she was going to say was ridiculous. "Clouds." Once she voiced it, it seemed accurate. "Storms."

"Where do you see that?"

"Near the top."

"Close to the handle? Far away?"

"Both sides."

"Oui." Mademoiselle nodded. "A reflection perhaps of where you are and what is in your immediate future."

Shelby's breath burned. She hated it. Mademoiselle was right. Storms raged inside Shelby's mind, in a mad conflict between her heart and mind.

"And the middle or bottom of the bowl? Are there more clouds?"

"No. Does that mean brighter days ahead?"

"Does it?" Mademoiselle asked. "As I mentioned to Hannah, the reading is subjective. You always have free will and more sway over your future than you might believe. Choices. Please. Feel free to see if there's anything else there for you."

Shelby rotated the cup so she could examine all the angles. "At the very bottom. An anchor, perhaps."

"Are you being weighed down by something?" Fiona asked.

"What are other possibilities?"

Shelby appreciated Mademoiselle's question. It was easy to fixate on one meaning.

"Stability?" Hannah guessed. "Like a boat can remain stable, even in the ocean, if it drops its anchor, right?"

"Perhaps it also speaks of water," Mademoiselle mused.

All of the guesses, along with her own intuition, represented her time with Trevor on the lake.

Shelby continued to stare into the depths of her cup. She recalled him being there for her after the Lemieux divorce case. It was more than that, she realized. He'd been there for her every day, ever since her introduction to scening with him. He cared for her physically as well as emotionally. He'd been her anchor against the storms raging around and through her.

"Taken together, the images tell a story, do they not?"

Oddly there were no leaves between the top of the bowl and the bottom. The space between the clouds and the anchor was clear.

The problem was, she had no idea how to get from where she was to where she wanted to go.

It was scary, an abyss. Even if she knew how to get there, she wasn't sure she even knew how to attempt the journey.

CHAPTER 12

"Is everything okay, Mr. Lawton?"

Cell phone pressed against his ear, Trevor frowned and paced the length of his front deck. The soft concern in his assistant's voice unnerved him. "Why wouldn't it be?"

"It's Sunday morning."

As usual, his day was filled with appointments.

"And it's barely five a.m." Caroline's reply was softer than it usually was.

Fuck. Was it?

He checked his watch. One minute after. Since he'd gone to the Quarter—and hadn't seen Shelby—he'd drowned his angst in work. Though he hadn't been aware of the time, the fact that the sky was still inky and dotted with stars should have reined in his phone-dialing impulses. "Sorry, Caro." How damn inconsiderate could he be? "It can wait until tomorrow."

"I'm awake now. Let me grab my pad." There was a ruffling in the background, followed by a masculine protest.

Caroline had company? What the…? He dragged a hand through his hair. How had he not realized she was in a relationship? They'd worked together so long that it sometimes seemed they shared a brain, yet he didn't know what was going on in her personal life?

"I'll be right back," she whispered. To him? Or to her visitor?

"Hurry," the male responded.

"Look, Caroline." Trevor exhaled his frustration. "I mean it. We don't need to do this now."

A tiny click echoed across the line. Caroline closing the bedroom door?

"I'm ready, Mr. Lawton. Powered up, stylus in hand."

Just because his life was in shambles—not sleeping, barely remembering to eat, pushing projects farther, faster than usual—didn't mean his assistant didn't deserve some time to herself. She deserved a break from him. In fact, everyone in his life did.

Ever since Shelby shut the door on him almost three weeks ago, his mind hadn't stopped spinning. What had gone wrong? And what the hell was so bad between them that she blocked his calls? At least he assumed that was what she'd done considering he instantly received her voice mail the moment he hit the Send button on his phone.

No matter which way he looked at it, he couldn't come up with anything that made sense.

"Mr. Lawton?"

"Yeah. I'm here." *Focus.* Which would be easier if he'd slept more than a handful of hours in the past few days. "About the Reshift project. Set up a meeting with Dan and Lewis for early next week."

"Assuming a video conference call?" The question was rushed yet hesitant.

"No. Bring them in."

"You're interested? Really? Not just as a personal favor?" Caroline's voice no longer held any traces of sleep.

Caroline had brought the project to him, and she'd apologized for using their relationship to circumvent his usual vetting process. He didn't mind. In the balance ledger of life, he owed her more than a few favors.

After a single glance, he'd been intrigued. Her brother and his partner had spent years figuring out how to recycle many different kinds of plastics into new products, from outdoor rugs to comfortable slippers, toys, even socks with outrageous sayings on them.

What excited him even more were their proposed uses for the five hundred billion coffee cups tossed in the trash each year. The thin plastic lining made them notoriously difficult to recycle, but Reshift had found a way to make new objects out of the waste, including office supplies like pencil holders and paperweights. His favorite use was flowerpots—from large sizes meant for outdoor use to much smaller ones that would hold a single flower.

He picked up a prototype that they'd sent to him. It was a stout cream-colored octagonal vase, complete with a multifaceted succulent growing from soil fertilized by coffee grounds. The creativity of the pair excited him. They might never become millionaires from their work, but they were doing good, and who knew what other brilliant ideas they would have? "I'm making no promises. But it's worth my time to have a deeper look." There were challenges to be sure. The recycling process was cumbersome, perhaps too much to ever be affordable. And collecting enough material could be a challenge. Then there was marketing and sales of the refashioned objects.

"They never thought…" Caroline fell silent. "I can't thank you enough."

"I'm glad you brought it to my attention. If nothing else, going through the process will help them refine their pitch, and I'll give them some business advice."

"They'll be thrilled. Really."

"I'll leave the arrangements to you. Calendar it when you finalize the details."

"Anything else, sir?"

A million things, just to keep thoughts of Shelby at bay. "Enjoy the rest of your day. If I call you again, ignore me."

"You know I'd never do that."

"That's an order, not a suggestion."

"Of course, Mr. Lawton." She laughed before ending the call.

Once he was alone again with his thoughts, he dropped the phone onto his desk, then put the vase back.

Since it was far too early to make any other calls, he opted to brew coffee and head outside, kill some time before he headed into the city. At ten, he was meeting with David and Mason, and this time Wayne Dixon was joining them.

Near the boathouse, Trevor flipped on the green underwater dock lights to attract fish.

The activity brought Bruno bounding across the yard and out onto wooden planks.

"Hey, boy."

The overgrown pup plopped down and pushed his huge head against Trevor's thigh, demanding attention.

He wasn't sure he'd ever been more grateful for an interruption.

Bruno stayed much longer than usual before some other noise attracted his attention. With a soft whimper, he took off, and the world fell silent except for the occasional leaping fish.

Having a pole in his hand always righted his world, but not today. He should have opted for a bike ride or a run, something that would burn off excess energy.

Eventually the sun peeked over the horizon, but even that made him think of Shelby and how much she'd enjoy seeing it. Especially if he brought her a cup of coffee or perhaps a mimosa. Wasn't that what Sundays were for?

Again, thoughts of Shelby returned, whether he wanted them or not.

Frustrated and lacking his usual patience, he strode to the light switch and turned it off before putting his pole away and yanking the boathouse door shut. He rammed the bolt home.

Unbidden, Mademoiselle Giselle's words about agitation that morning at her store returned to him.

"It's the distance between where we are and where we would like to be."

That definition had fit his life from the first moment he met Shelby.

No matter how many times he told himself to forget her, he couldn't. And that confounded him. Hell, it even pissed him off.

If Shelby were here, he'd suggest they eat breakfast in New Orleans before going to the law center. She'd be so damn happy to see the progress they were making.

Instead, he made a lonely breakfast for one, then headed for the shower.

Since he still had a couple of hours to spare, he spent time in his office going through a pile of proposals, none of which held his attention.

Much earlier than he needed to, he left, and he wasn't surprised to find David already there, along with Mason.

The renovation was slower than usual since the crew was only working at night and on the weekends. David refused to close the doors even for a day.

"Coffee's in the kitchen," David said. "Looks like you could use it."

"What? I showered."

"Still not sleeping?"

"It's overrated." And elusive as hell. Still, because he wanted it as much as he needed it, Trevor went and poured a cup.

He joined Mason and David at a desk where blueprints were spread out.

"That wall"—Mason pointed—"is going to be removed. We'll put in a structural beam, which will make this area bigger."

Which would allow the space to serve the community better. One Saturday a month, David wanted to do an open house of sorts. A number of lawyers would volunteer their time and accept walk-in clients. There would also be adequate room for tables and phones for the days when he allowed people to call in with legal questions.

Mason, too, was supplying his time at no charge. The home improvement network that was filming his show had even stopped by a couple of times to video the site.

Trevor hoped that when the episode aired, it would galvanize contributions.

While Mason was providing a timeline, the door opened, and Wayne strode in. Trevor greeted his mentor, then introduced him to David and Mason.

"It's a pleasure," Wayne said, shaking David's hand. "Impressive what you're doing here."

"Thank you. Honestly? None of it has been my doing. It's all thanks to Trevor."

"Not at all." Trevor shucked off the compliment. "You've put in the heart and hard work."

Wayne nodded before turning toward Mason. "And our local celebrity, I presume?"

"Hardly." Mason grinned. "I don't have a bridge named after me, unlike you."

"It's all about doing good. Like we are here."

Though both men were Titans, they hadn't met until now.

After they all grabbed a fresh cup of coffee, they headed into the conference room. Unlike most law offices with a sleek place to meet, this was dominated by a long metal table surrounded by folding chairs, some of which had rips in the fake leather upholstery, allowing stuffing to ooze out. Not very confidence inspiring.

Once the room was renovated, Trevor would arrange for a furniture delivery.

For now, it was serviceable.

"I have a proposal," Wayne began when everyone was seated.

Trevor had been looking forward to this day for a week.

Wayne studied David. "I'd like you to join my legal team."

He'd been reaching for his cup, but he dropped his hand to the tabletop, then glanced at Trevor.

"This is such an honor. I'm..." In shock, he shook his head. "There's no way I'm qualified to represent—"

"Hear me out." Wayne's tone said he wouldn't tolerate further interruptions. The man was accustomed to being in charge, and his time was precious.

Securing his interest had been one of Trevor's greatest coups.

"I know you want to be here," Wayne continued. "And you should be. But if you joined my team, you'd raise your profile significantly. You can litigate, I assume?"

"Of course!"

When he said nothing else, Wayne nodded. "Good. You won't need to give me a lot of time, but you'll need to have an office at Barney and Scheck."

"At...?"

One of the most prestigious firms in the state, if not the South. "Close your mouth," Trevor advised.

"We can get someone in here to help you manage things better. If your reputation improves, you'll bring in paying clients, which will enable you to afford to continue with your charitable efforts."

"I… Uhm." David cleared his throat. "I don't know what to say."

"You'll meet me tomorrow morning at their offices at eight." It wasn't a question. Wayne stood.

David followed suit and shook the man's hand.

"Dress for success," Wayne said. "Gentlemen." He nodded in a sharp way that included everyone, then strode from the room.

"The fuck just happened?" David asked, slumping into his chair.

Trevor rapped his knuckles on the table. "Sounded like opportunity knocking."

"I… Jesus. I can't believe it."

"You're doing a worthwhile thing. The rest of us are glad to be along for the ride."

Mason nodded. "The first of the offices will be ready by next weekend." His adviser, John Thoroughgood, had suggested David remodel the second and third floors and lease out the space. And Thoroughgood had agreed to be the first tenant, which would bring in immediate income. Yesterday, a mortgage broker had also expressed an interest in moving in as soon as possible.

"This is…" David shook his head. "I don't know. Beyond anything I could imagine. I owe Shelby one."

Though Trevor wanted to deny it, he couldn't. If he hadn't been intrigued by the badly behaved submissive kneeling next to David, Trevor wouldn't be here. Chances were, he would have never seen the file.

"Has she seen what you've accomplished?" Mason asked.

Trevor's breathing turned sluggish. He thirsted for information about her, even though he didn't want to.

"No. I need to invite her down. Maybe take her to dinner."

"How's she doing?" Trevor hated himself for asking.

"No idea. Haven't seen her. Call her and find out for yourself."

"Yeah." He raked a hand into his hair. For all the good it would do him.

"We're good to go on the Getting Hammered event?" David asked.

"A week from Friday," Mason confirmed. "Four o'clock." Each month, the historic preservation group that he belonged to hosted an informal happy hour gathering in a historic building that was being renovated. Beer, wine, and appetizers were served, and money was raised. Mason suggested opening up the law offices to the group as another way to increase David's profile and solicit donations at the same time.

Mason had sent out the invitations himself, and he'd included high-profile names on the guest list, including the mayor and the local congresswoman.

"Let me know if there's anything else you need from me," David said.

"Food and drink will be delivered by three."

"I'll make sure the last client is out of here before that."

Trevor wondered about that. If someone walked through the door at four, David would no doubt see them.

"I need to get home," Mason said, leading the way to the main room where he rolled up the blueprints. "Hannah and I are having lunch with my mom and Norman. Wedding details. Never ending."

"When are you going to start planning your own?" David asked.

"Keep hoping Hannah will agree to have me."

"You'll wear her down." David's voice oozed confidence. "Everything worthwhile takes time."

Why was everyone a damn philosopher?

David extended his hand. "Appreciate everything you've done, Lawton."

He was genuinely pleased to be part of this. Not only did it give him a way to channel his angst into something useful, but partnering with others was something he enjoyed. Far too much of his work was solitary.

"Get some rest. You look like shit."

"Thanks for that." Trevor scowled at David, but even Mason nodded. The realization that they were both right made the insult even worse.

On his way out the door, Trevor paused. David had been right earlier. All of this, including the renovation and David's new position at Barney and Scheck, was due to Shelby's loyalty to her friend and her willingness to put herself on the line.

Trevor just wished to hell that she had been by his side today to see all the good her bravery had created.

"You're on your way, right?" Fiona demanded.

Pacing the kitchen floor, Shelby sighed. Why had she answered the phone?

"Shel? Tell me you're in the car driving right now."

A couple of weeks ago, David had called to let her know how excited he was about the Getting Hammered event, and he said he wanted her in attendance. He was pleased by the changes at the building, and he wanted to share them with her. Several times since then, he emailed her with updates and pictures. Most recently, he informed her that he had rented out four of the upstairs offices.

"Shel?"

"To be honest, no. I'm not planning to come."

"Are you serious?" Outrage streaked across Fiona's voice. "You know how much this event means to David."

Shelby stared at the vellum invitation on the kitchen table. "Trevor might be there."

"Oh my God. So what? Everyone will be there, including me, Hannah, Mason."

When Shelby didn't respond, Fiona filled the silence. "Look. We are all part of the same social circle. You can't avoid him forever."

Rationally she knew that.

"You might as well get it out of the way."

The image of an anchor in the tea leaves floated through her mind. Fiona had guessed that it meant something—someone?—was weighing Shelby down. Hannah suggested perhaps it meant stability. It turned out that they were both right. Shelby's feelings for Trevor were keeping her from moving forward, and their week together had brought her a peace that she hadn't known she was missing.

After the reading at Mademoiselle's apartment, Shelby had given in to temptation and unblocked his number. Not that it mattered. He hadn't called or sent a single message.

Shelby told herself she should be grateful. But in the darkest hours of the night, she was forced to face the truth. She was devastated. The moment she found a little bit of courage, he'd stopped trying.

If she knew he was still interested in her, going tonight would be easier. But what if he was there with another woman?

"How about if I pick you up? That way you don't have to show up alone." Fiona suggested. "Say yes."

Fiona was right about one thing. Even if it wasn't tonight, Shelby would eventually see Trevor again, especially now that he was serving as an adviser to David. And she wasn't certain she wanted to avoid going to the Quarter for the rest of her life. Her self-enforced isolation was wearing her down. She needed to go out with her friends and start having fun again. "Okay."

"Okay?" Fiona echoed. "Really? You mean it?"

"I need half an hour to get ready." Already she was questioning her sanity.

"I'll be there."

Shelby hurried to her bedroom closet and sorted through the hangers until she found a short skirt and a black top that she liked to wear with it. Strappy sandals completed her outfit.

Critically she surveyed herself in the mirror. The skirt was tight around her hips, and the shirt hugged her breasts. The heels may not be the best choice for a building that was undergoing renovations, but self-confidence was more important to her than anything else right now.

In the bathroom, she swept her hair up into a messy bun, then applied eye shadow a little darker than usual, then swiped on a second and third coat of mascara. Finally, she highlighted her cheekbones with a brush of pink blush.

If Trevor was at the event, she wanted him to notice her.

Which was why she also opted for red lipstick.

She grabbed her purse and headed for the door just in time for Fiona to honk the car horn from the curb.

"Whoa, damn." Instead of dropping the gear shifter into Drive, Fiona stared at Shelby. "If I was into girls, I'd date you myself."

Shelby laughed, unsure how she'd gotten lucky enough to have Fiona as a friend. "Thanks. But let's go. I've already made us late."

As they neared town, the roads grew more congested. "I can't help notice you didn't mention Andrew's name earlier, when you were talking about who will be there this afternoon. Is he working or something?"

When Fiona turned up the volume on the radio instead of answering, Shelby turned in her seat. "What's going on?"

"We are…uhm…taking a break." Fiona's hands tightened on the steering wheel.

"Crap. I'm sorry I wasn't there for you." Shelby mentally kicked herself. She'd been so wrapped up in her own issues that she hadn't noticed her friend had ended her relationship. "Are you doing okay?"

"Damn tea leaves."

That, Shelby could relate to. "Those trees you saw?"

"You know, I wanted to do the reading for fun. I thought it would be a kick. You know, something to laugh about later. I didn't know it would stir up stuff for me."

Shelby proceeded with caution. "Like what?"

"I can't ever seem to see my way clear of the past." Instead of looking at Shelby, Fiona glanced in the rearview mirror. "The whole thing that Mademoiselle said about protection. I'd never thought about how much a part of my nature it is."

"It is, though. Isn't it? You take care of others. Even today. You are looking out for David, but you are also staying by my side, even though you've got your own set of troubles."

"You'd do the same for me."

"But that doesn't make it any less true, right?"

"Yeah." Fiona smiled. "Maybe."

"Do you want to talk about it? Andrew, I mean." The two had been together for a while, and Andrew had easily fit in with their small group.

"I guess you could say he brought a lot of complications to my life."

"In what way?" Shelby wasn't sure what her friend meant. "Was he demanding? Controlling?"

Fiona stopped for a traffic signal. "No. Not really. He just wanted more than I was willing to give."

Now it seemed a little clearer. With care, Shelby chose her words. "Did he want to protect you?"

"Where's the line between trying to protect and not honoring my need to take care of myself?"

The answer confused Shelby. "But you said he wasn't controlling."

"He wasn't. At least not in the way you might think." Fiona accelerated after the light turned green. "It's just that he wanted to assume some financial responsibilities. He was at my place quite a bit, and he felt he should help out more. Take care of me a little. He'd never let me pick up a check in a restaurant. Then he started buying gifts and such, like a new television that I didn't need." She slid a glance toward Shelby. "I can pay my own way."

And she took care of others too. Including her sister, if Shelby remembered correctly. "Do you miss him?"

"Sometimes."

"Isn't give-and-take part of a relationship?" Shelby's question echoed inside her head. It applied to her as well. "Would it be so bad to have a protector?"

"Maybe not for other people. But to me, being self-sufficient matters."

"Relationships are complicated."

"Speaking of that."

"Let's not," Shelby implored.

"Are you doing better?"

No. The closer they came to the law offices, the faster her pulse beat. "He stopped calling."

"You sound hurt."

"I shouldn't be. But yes. I am…at least a little." She glanced out the window before looking back at Fiona. "It's what I wanted. Right?" The truth Shelby didn't want to see was there, bright and unavoidable. She wasn't over him.

"You asked me if it would be bad to have a protector. It's a good question, and a version of it applies to you, as well. Would it be bad to trust someone? Lean on them?"

"I see divorces all day long. Not to mention my own craptacular and short-lived marriage."

"Did Trevor propose to you?"

Shelby blinked. "Uhm… Of course not."

"So all of this is you freaking out about something that didn't happen and might never come to pass?"

Put that way, her reaction sounded ridiculous.

"Isn't that what dating is for?" Fiona's voice was not as forceful and animated as it usually was, as if she understood, really understood, what Shelby was going through. "That's where you learn more about the person you're with. You see if they have integrity and can be trusted. See if they have addictions, find out if you're compatible once the first rush of pheromones has settled down and you have to pick up his dirty clothes from the floor. Or fall into the toilet in the middle of the night because he forgot to put the seat down."

"Eww." But the image made her laugh, which was something she needed.

Fiona turned on her signal and changed lanes. "What's really going on?"

"The problem is, I was starting to fall for Trevor." And his kindness, as well as the mind-blowing sex they shared.

"Did he discourage that? I mean, some guys are right up front that they don't want to be in a relationship."

"Trevor wasn't like that." Shelby shook her head. "Not at all."

"From what little you've said, I got the impression that he was into you."

"He was." The *was* reverberated in her mind, sending pangs of sorrow and aching loneliness through her. Before she'd spent time with Trevor, she'd enjoyed her life and solitude. But the companionship she shared with him had enriched her so much that she realized how dark things had been before him.

"I asked Hannah this question when she left Mason. Were there any red flags during your week together? Is your intuition trying to give you a warning that you're ignoring?"

"Everything was fine. Honest."

"He was safe when you played? Treated you well?"

Shelby turned the question around. "You visited us at his house. What did you think?"

"That he's crazy about you. From what I know—and what I saw—he's the real thing. A man who can be trusted, one who would rather hurt himself than the woman he loves. There are good men out there. I know you see the absolute worst of the worst. You know…"

"Go on."

Fiona slid her a glance. "You won't want to hear this."

"I'm listening." She exhaled, trying not to be defensive.

"Maybe you should consider another line of work or at least cut back on the number of divorce cases you take."

Shelby wasn't sure she was capable of taking a step back. Her commitment to ensuring kids were not used as pawns between their parents was too strong for that. Even if it reopened her own wounds.

"You've got to take care of yourself the way you look out for others." Fiona's voice softened. "I think you're so caught up in what you do that you see the world from a skewed perspective. There are success stories. People who fall in love and grow together. Partners who are there for each other. Look for them. Find them. Let them serve as inspiration and guidance." She shrugged. "Mason's mom, for example."

Judith and her husband had been high school sweethearts before marrying. They'd endured massive hardships that strengthened their bond, and they'd remained deeply in love until her husband passed. And now, her commitment to Norman, the man she was engaged to, was every bit as deep and abiding.

"All relationships have issues. It's how we deal with them, right? If both partners are determined, it can work. Right?"

Fiona made an excellent point.

"You'll just have to decide what to do about your fear. Face it? Take a chance?"

To deal with the sudden flood of nerves, Shelby fiddled with her purse strap. She had spent a lot of years mucking around in other people's divorces. Maybe it had affected her outlook. But still, there was the fact that Trevor had stopped trying to reach her. "What if he's moved on?"

"I can damn well guarantee you that he hasn't. He's as mopey as you are. Looks like hell too."

"Are you serious?"

"He was at the Quarter again last week. Didn't look like he shaved. He stayed in the bar the entire night, not talking to anyone, looking as if he'd lost his best friend." Fiona shrugged. "Maybe he has."

They turned onto the street where David's offices were located, and Shelby's heart constricted, as if wrapped in steel bands.

Fiona pulled up in front of the building where a valet stand had been set up.

As two young men headed toward them to open the car doors, Fiona grinned. "This is going to be fun."

When they were in front of the law office entrance, Shelby pulled her shoulders back. Unbidden, memories of Trevor flashed through her in frantic, kaleidoscope-like images, making shivers race down her spine. In one image, he was smiling at her. In others, his eyes blazed with intent before he leaned in for a kiss or ordered her to her knees. She saw herself before him, filled with trust as she was helplessly bound in his dungeon. That was replaced by a picture of her standing over him on the couch as he purposefully moved his mouth toward her naked sex.

With a gasp, Shelby reached for the wall to steady herself.

"You've got this," Fiona promised.

A final, haunting portrait shattered all the others: his blue eyes, stark with pain when she shut him out of her life.

"It's showtime, my friend. Hold your head up high. Behave however you want, but for God's sake, look like a badass while you do it."

CHAPTER 13

Unable to hear much of anything over the sound of her internal warning system blasting a siren in her ear, Shelby followed Fiona into the building.

The main room was filled with people, most of them in small groups standing around bar-height tables. Frantically she scanned the room, but she didn't see Trevor. She exhaled relief that was mixed with profound disappointment.

"There's David." Fiona pointed to the far corner.

As if he'd heard her, he detached himself from the conversation he was having with a tall blonde. If Shelby wasn't mistaken, the woman was a lawyer with the district attorney's office.

"Damn, Shel. I'm glad you're here." David dragged her into a huge hug. "I was afraid you wouldn't show up." He pulled back but kept his hands on her shoulders.

His smile was enormous and so heartfelt she couldn't believe she'd been so caught up in her own fears that she considered skipping his big event.

"Told you I'd get her here by any means, fair or foul."

Fiona reached over her own shoulder to pat herself on the back.

"You're a hero." David released Shelby to look at Fiona. "Heroine. Whatever you want to be called."

"Goddess will work, and yeah. I am. And I've spent most of the afternoon on the road to ensure that Shelby was here for you. And that means I've worked up a powerful thirst. Which way is the wine?"

"Back there." David released Shelby and pointed toward the kitchen area. "And I think Mason's mom is manning the bar. She seems to enjoy making people happy."

Fiona waggled her fingers as she sashayed away.

"She's something," Shelby said.

"For once, I'm glad she's such a powerful force of nature."

Shelby glanced around, pretending a general interest when she was focused on looking for Trevor. "You've got a great turnout."

He grinned. "Better than I hoped for. Mason promised the Getting Hammered people would show up, and they did. A couple of members have already made contributions to the building fund."

"Are you kidding me? That's fantastic. I'm so happy for you. And joining Barney and Scheck?" She smiled. "Your star is rising, David. No one deserves it more. Really."

"None of it would have happened without you. You know that, right? None of it."

"That's ridiculous. It's all about you." She shook her head. "From the beginning, Shaughnessy Community Law Offices was your idea. You honed the vision and did whatever it took to make it come true."

"Without you, Lawton would never have looked at the proposal let alone set up a meeting with me or bring in his mentor."

"You'd have figured it out. I have confidence."

"Ask him."

"What?"

"Ask Lawton yourself. Now, even." With a grin, David shrugged.

"Hello, Shelby."

At the unmistakable sound of Trevor's rich, sexy voice, her heart plunged into a freefall.

"David's right. You're responsible for all of this."

"See?" David gloated.

Her knees wobbled as she turned to face the man she hadn't been able to stop thinking about.

His eyes were every bit as haunted as they'd been weeks ago. His face appeared more angular, as if he'd lost a few pounds. And he was the most handsome man she'd ever seen.

"I'll, er, go and greet some new arrivals?" David suggested.

Trevor never took his gaze off her as he responded. "Yeah. You do that."

Suddenly they were alone. The noise around them receded, and the world seemed to right itself on its axis for the first time in weeks. But she didn't know what to say. *Why haven't you called? I can't live without you.* All of that was too personal for a public place, but one of them needed to break the tension-filled silence. So she settled for something polite and inane. "David can't stop talking about how much you've done for him."

"It's a worthwhile project. I'm glad to be involved in it. Can I show you around?"

"I'd like that." And it would give her something to do, other than stand in front of him sorting through and discarding the millions of things she wanted to say.

"Would you like a glass of wine?"

"Yes. Thanks."

He cupped her elbow, jolting her with electricity. It was something he might have done when they were lovers. Even though she had no idea what they were to each other now, she didn't attempt to pull away. This was as right and as natural as the turning of the tides.

Fiona and Hannah were near the bar, and Trevor left her with them and excused himself to fetch her drink.

"How's it going?" Fiona asked. "Are you doing okay?"

"It's, uhm…" *Wonderful. Awkward.* "He's going to give me a tour."

Fiona didn't try to hide her grin. "Let me know whether you'll need a ride home or not."

"I'm sure—"

"Here's your wine," Trevor said.

Shelby's hand shook, and she almost spilled the drink as she accepted it.

After everyone exchanged greetings, Trevor looked at her. "Shall we?" He then glanced at Fiona and Hannah. "If you'll excuse us, ladies." Though his words were polite, they weren't really a question.

In that instant, he sounded like a Dom. So much so that her insides became molten.

Fiona grinned before taking a sip of her wine. "Have fun."

Trevor's first stop was the kitchen.

Shelby glanced around at the much smaller space. "What a difference." The vast area was now only big enough to be a break room with a small refrigerator, a microwave, a sink, and a small round table.

"It's about a quarter of the original size, which gave David enough room for another office."

"Good choice."

She followed him to the conference room. "Wow." The transformation was staggering. On many occasions, she'd met with clients in the dingy space. The last time she was in here, the paint had been an awful blend of tan and gray, and the carpet had been threadbare in spots. Once, she'd even caught the leg of a chair in one of the holes, nearly toppling over when she leaned forward to pick up her pen.

Now the walls were a soft pastel, and the lighting was bright but not overpowering. The honey-colored hardwood floor gleamed. The old rickety table had been replaced with a long, polished one surrounded by chairs that swiveled. At the back of the room was a credenza with bottles of water and a coffeemaker that brewed a single cup at a time. There were mugs with pictures of the building on it. The door had been replaced, and a window had been added. Everything was trimmed out with period-correct woodwork. Artwork depicted the Mississippi River and New Orleans courtyards in spring. A side table had a bouquet of flowers on it, set in a vase made from a material she'd never seen before. "It's not just professional; it's a place that invites cooperation. That sounds strange, maybe?"

"Not at all. Hannah was thinking in those terms when she designed it."

"The blues and greens in the color palette is soothing."

Upstairs, Mason was showing people a completed office that hadn't yet been leased.

Trevor invited her to the large window that overlooked the building's backyard, complete with a beautiful fountain. "If I didn't live so far away, I'd consider renting it myself," she said.

"John Thoroughgood, Mason's real estate adviser, has had no trouble securing tenants."

"I can see why. The renovation is amazing."

Mason and his group moved from the room.

"Have you ever seen the third floor?"

She frowned. "As far as I knew, it was closed off."

"Originally, there were additional bedrooms up there. Presumably for the nanny or governess, whatever they had back then, along with an open area for the family's kids to play."

"Where they could make as much noise as they wanted without disturbing the rest of the family?"

"I'm sure that was part of the reasoning."

"I'd love to see it." She followed him up the staircase at the rear of the house.

At the top was a closed door with a brass knob.

This was definitely a work in progress. There were plenty of pieces of antique furniture, along with some that appeared to be military or government surplus. Numerous cans of paint and construction supplies sat against one wall. "So this is where everything is stored?"

"All the work is done at night and on the weekends so as not to impact David's clients. So, yes. Storage is needed." Trevor closed the door, cocooning them from the rest of the party. "I've missed you."

The wobble of emotion in his voice streaked through her, and she turned toward him.

Raw pain was etched in his eyes. An echoing hurt squeezed her heart. "Oh Trevor."

"Have you missed me?"

"Trevor, we... I..." She stopped herself from uttering an instinctive, protective lie. In showing his vulnerability, he was taking a huge risk. Could she be any less brave? "Yes." She lowered her head.

He closed his eyes and rolled his shoulders forward. "Do you miss me enough?"

"Enough?"

"To tell me why you ran?"

Because her mouth was suddenly dry, Shelby worried her lower lip. In blocking his calls, she'd ensured that she didn't have to answer his probing question. But if she wanted to move forward, escape the pain she'd been living in, she had to expose her innermost fears. The moment was every bit as harrowing as she'd imagined it would be, filled with fear-inducing anxiety. Blood pounded in her ears, making her dizzy.

He pressed his shoulders against the door, keeping his distance. Giving her space?

In confessing that he missed her, he'd taken the first emotional risk. And as she looked at him, the image of the anchor returned to her. From the first moment she was alone with him, Trevor had been nothing except calm and patient. He'd been there for her, sensing what she needed, even when she hadn't been able to find the words to express her feelings.

"Shelby?"

She turned away to slide her untouched glass of wine on a table behind her. It was a tactic to buy a few extra seconds to sort through what she wanted to say. "I was scared." Then, as she turned, she corrected herself. "I *am* scared."

"Of…?"

"The future."

He nodded, as if he understood, when in truth there was no way he actually could.

Because he remained silent, she gathered a little more strength. "I was starting to count on you."

A frown burrowed its way between his eyebrows. "How is that a problem?"

"After my divorce, I promised myself that I wouldn't fall in love ever again." Now she wished she hadn't put down the wineglass. She needed something to distract herself from the force of his steely eyes.

"And…?"

"Divorce stinks."

"Which you see every day. Relationships that didn't work out."

"Yes."

"Which one of us don't you trust?"

Shocked by his question, she pulled back a little.

"Are you're scared you can't count on me? That I'll never commit? Maybe I'll let you down? Cheat, maybe?"

She shook her head. "What? No." All of his suggestions were absurd.

"Do you trust yourself? When you make a promise, do you keep it?"

"Of course."

"You're capable of having long relationships, right? Your group of friends proves that."

He was addressing all of her fears and dismantling them in a gentle yet relentless way.

"Do you have any reason to suspect we can't communicate? Or that we aren't compatible?"

Their time together had been amazing. They'd negotiated scenes easily, and they'd enjoyed spending time in the same ways. "I… No."

"Then…? Help me out, Shelby. Tell me what I'm missing."

"I'm afraid of being hurt." His honesty sparked the same inside her. "I told you I was counting on you, and then I realized I was falling—" She pushed a hand over her mouth, terrified that the truth she was trying to bury from both of them would spill out.

"I'll always be here for you, Shelby Maria Virginia Salazar."

How had he remembered her whole name?

"Everything about you is important to me. And I love you."

Her knees buckled, and she reached behind herself to grab hold of the table to steady herself. "You…"

"I love you." He hooked a thumb through a belt loop. "Yeah, it shocked me too. From the moment I saw you, on your knees, unable to keep your gaze from wandering, I was intrigued. Then I got to know you. I saw how dedicated you were to your clients, especially the kids. Then there's your loyalty to David and his law center. I wasn't looking for a relationship, but there it is."

"You stopped calling." She hated the hurt that softened her words.

He gave a half grin. "I thought you had me blocked."

"Until I saw Mademoiselle."

"Ah. Did you? So did I."

She blinked. "Really?"

"Agitation."

Shelby remembered the exchange the two had shared. "The distance between where we are and where we want to be?"

"Yeah. It was worse this time."

"Because of me leaving?"

He nodded. "Yeah. It showed me how much you meant to me. Helped me understand that I love you. As for calling and getting your voice mail?"

She waited.

His voice was gruff. "I spiked my fucking phone on the kitchen floor."

"You didn't!"

"Not proud of it. Pieces everywhere. Agitation? That's an understatement. At Mademoiselle's urging, I focused on my work with Mason and David, and I did my best to make sure I saw you again. I figured I'd be difficult to resist in person."

"You're pretty confident of your powers, Trevor."

"Is it working?"

How was it possible for him to make things so easy for her?

"You don't have to love me. I'm just asking you to give us a chance. Let me prove that not all men are like your ex. That relationships can work out. You don't have to give me anything more than the moment we're in."

He was brilliant. Each second they were together would lead to the next. And he'd offered her something she could agree to. Not forever, not even a year or a day.

Without another word, he extended his hand toward her. So far, he'd taken all the steps, and he wanted her to take the next one.

The first time she met Mademoiselle, the woman had spoken about the beauty that lay beyond pain. At the time, Shelby assumed the reference was to BDSM. Now she knew it was greater than that. If she wanted to experience love, she had to be willing to transcend her emotional fears.

Even though she was afraid her legs wouldn't support her, she released her hold on the table and took the first tentative step toward him.

"Come to me, precious Shelby."

Within seconds she was wrapped in his reassuring embrace. He didn't hold too tightly, but enough to let her know how much he cared. Gently he kissed the top of her head.

"I love you, Shelby."

She rested her head on his strong chest, surrendering to him. To trust. "I love you, Trevor."

"And I will cherish that."

Long minutes later, the sounds of the celebration way off in the distance, she pulled back a little to look at him. "Kiss me?"

A slow, sensual smile lit his face, making his eyes brighter than they had been. "I thought you'd never ask."

He released her long enough to lock the door.

A tremor lanced her spine. Not from fear but from anticipation.

Catching her off guard, he swept her from her feet and

carried her to the desk where she'd left her wine. He moved the glass to one side, then sat her on the top.

"Put your legs around my waist."

This wasn't what she expected. Then again, nothing with him ever was.

"Shelby."

The growl of command shot straight to her submissive responses. "Yes, Sir." Immediately she parted her legs and scooted forward.

He hiked up her skirt and slipped a finger inside the gusset of her panties to find her clit; then he pressed against it, hard.

She squirmed. "Sir!"

"How long since you came?"

In his terrible, usual way, he didn't stop playing with her. "I can't think."

"How long, sub?"

"Weeks." She caught her breath. "I haven't at all since I left."

With a long, triumphant growl, he sank to his knees and closed his mouth on her. As he teased her with his tongue, she whimpered. When she asked for a kiss, she hadn't expected this. Maybe because she'd denied herself any sexual satisfaction, this was overwhelming. "Oh. Fuck. God. I need…"

"You can come. Now. Then again as often as you want. I've been fantasizing about getting you off up here."

"You haven't."

"I assure you I have."

Trevor was all things at once—relentless, demanding, seeking, giving, taking. She arched her back and lifted her bottom, giving him everything she had to offer. He plunged two fingers inside her wet pussy and unerringly found her G-spot. The exquisite pressure shoved her headlong into a stunning climax. Mindless of their surroundings, she screamed his name.

Instantly he was there, lifting her upright, digging a hand into her hair and tugging her head back so he could claim her mouth in a hungry kiss. She tasted herself on him, sex and satisfaction.

Against her, his cock was hard. "Should I fuck you here or at home?"

She was ready for him, but she didn't dare take a chance that they'd be interrupted. "Let's leave."

"I was hoping you'd say that. Did you drive?"

"No. Fiona picked me up."

"Excellent. Do you need to stop by your house?" His eyes blazed with promise. "You won't need clothes. In fact, we get started by having you remove your panties."

Delicious hunger danced through her. There was no doubt he meant what he said.

He took a step back, then reached beneath her skirt. "Lift your hips."

The idea was easier in theory than execution. For leverage, she placed her palms flat on the desk while he worked the silky material over her buttocks. He took far longer than necessary, and he purposefully abraded her clit with his thumbnail. Wildly she wondered how she'd manage to make it home before she came.

When her pussy was nude, he slipped her underwear into his pocket.

"That feels…" A little strange. Very naughty. Perfect.

He kissed her forehead, then wrapped his arms around her. "That will have to hold both of us."

"Maybe we should get a hotel?" she suggested.

"We'll go to my place. After dinner."

"Dinner?" She didn't want to wait.

"You'll need nourishment for the night ahead." His eyes

darkened. Against her, his dick throbbed. "I promise you that."

"I'll hold you to that, Master Trevor." Turned on, she wiggled suggestively.

He growled as his cock jumped. "You'll pay for that, precious sub."

"Oh Sir." Then she succumbed to her joy. "Bring it on."

"You're being bold, Shelby. Reckless, even."

Yes. She wanted him to know how much she wanted to share her life with him. Once again she thought back to the tea leaves and the storm clouds she'd seen all around her. And now… They were gone. For the first time, the idea of a future with him didn't frighten her. Peace seeped through her, and she couldn't hide a grin. "I'm in love." Her confession was pure and straight from her heart. "So in love."

"You have no idea how happy that makes me." He traced her jawline in a way that was reassuring as well as possessive.

As always, his reaction to what she said made her feel safe.

"I will warn you, however. I have a detailed ledger in my head. Pretty little words won't get you out of the debt you owe for your teasing."

"I certainly hope not, Sir."

"My precious, precious sub." He helped her from the desk, then smoothed her skirt. "We'll sneak out the back and make our apologies later. I'm not waiting one minute longer than I have to."

Trevor wrapped an arm around her shoulders and led her toward the door and their new life together—one she was suddenly very much looking forward to.

EPILOGUE

Trevor pulled open the door to the restaurant that had been rented out for the television debut of Mason and Hannah's show.

Noise—excited talking and loud zydeco music—crashed into them.

Shelby leaned his direction, so she could be heard. "What an amazing turnout!"

Not that they should be surprised. Their friends were now local celebrities. Originally Mason had planned to host the watch party at his house, but when over a hundred people requested an invitation, his adviser, John Thoroughgood, had sought out a larger venue and settled on his favorite neighborhood haunt. In Trevor's opinion, it was the perfect choice. The restaurant, renowned for its down-home cooking, was a historic treasure and a fitting place for a renovation show.

From a spot near the largest television, Fiona waved to them.

"She said she was going to save us a place," Shelby said.

Trevor nodded and reached for her hand, determined not to lose her in the crush of people.

Winning her back had been the best thing that ever happened to him. She was now spending most weekends with him, and on each visit she left more of her belongings at his place. If he had his way, she'd move in permanently.

Early on, he made the mistake of pushing for that, and it had led to one of their very first arguments. Since then, he'd focused on celebrating the small hard-earned wins, including the fact that she was actively seeking out more corporate work. She never intended to stop mediating divorces, especially if there were children involved, but she wanted to focus less time on the messy endings to marriages.

They passed an enormous buffet filled with fried goodness—shrimp, okra, hushpuppies, even oysters. There were even huge plates of bread pudding swimming in brandy sauce.

Because the people Hannah and Mason had been speaking with walked toward a vacant table, Trevor and Shelby took the opportunity to join the couple.

"Congratulations, Mason. Couldn't be happier for you." Trevor shook his friend's hand while Shelby hugged Hannah.

"Glad you were able to make it."

"Wouldn't miss your big moment." He knew how hard his friend worked, from early morning to late night, seven days a week. Mason didn't even stop for weekends, and he recently made an appearance at David's law office to be sure the work on the third floor had been completed to his company's standards. "You should be damn proud."

Mason glanced at Hannah. As he smiled, she cradled her stomach. "We are proud. About a lot of things."

"Oh?"

"Are you kidding me?" Shelby squealed and swept Hannah into another huge hug.

Trevor blinked in confusion. "I'm missing something."

"We've got a second production underway."

"Another show?"

"No. We're expecting a baby." Mason grinned. "It was a surprise, but a damn happy one."

"Congratulations, once more." He shook Mason's hand again. "Definitely a night for celebration."

"Now that Hannah's designing the nursery, maybe she'll damn well agree to a wedding date. I thought getting her to accept my proposal was a challenge, but that was nothing compared to getting her to commit to the actual ceremony."

That, Trevor could relate to. He looked at Shelby. Her expression was hidden by her long hair, but her actions were animated.

Even though he was happy, he was greedy. Restless... Agitated.

Once again.

No other woman had ever brought out this depth of emotion in him. He knew he needed to be patient, but each day was becoming more difficult.

As if sensing his scrutiny, Shelby turned toward him. She brushed back her hair, and when he perused her, lingering on her belly, something hot and primal seared him. He wanted her pregnant with his child.

Jesus.

He'd thought about kids before, but it had been in vague terms—but now it was real, a demanding need.

Shelby frowned, and she reached out to gently touch his arm. For the moment, he was soothed.

They were interrupted by the arrival of Philip Dettmer, a fellow Titan. As always, he dressed well, including a tailored blazer. Because of the hour, he'd skipped a tie and opened the top button on his shirt.

"Lawton."

Trevor stood to shake Dettmer's hand. "Good to see you." He introduced the man to Shelby.

"My absolute pleasure, Ms. Salazar."

Primal possession lashed through Trevor, making him snarl. "We don't want to keep you."

"Of course." Dettmer nodded. "Enjoy your evening."

"Five minutes until the top of the hour!" John Thoroughgood's massive voice was amplified by a microphone and reverberated through the room. He signaled for the music to be silenced.

"Bar's open," Mason said. "Thoroughgood's picking up the tab, so drink up."

Cheers erupted through the room.

Other people were waiting to talk to Hannah and Mason, so Trevor guided Shelby to the table where Fiona was waiting with David.

After everyone said hello, shouting to be heard over the raucous crowd, Trevor poured them each a glass of champagne from the bottle Fiona had ordered.

"I figured it was a night for celebration."

Trevor couldn't agree more.

"Allow me to present the man and woman of the hour!" Thoroughgood continued. "Mason and Hannah!"

Among raucous cheers, the couple wended their way through the crowd. When they reached the front of the room, they flanked a gigantic television and took a bow.

Thoroughgood turned up the volume as a montage of shots flashed across the screen: homes in various stages of renovation, a picture of David's law offices, and even a brief snippet of Mason's mom marrying Norman.

The gathered crowd hooted and hollered, cheering at familiar sites throughout the city.

Then a picture of the house that Mason's mother had

purchased, and the name of the episode scrolled across the bottom of the screen: *Pop the Top.* Hannah had suggested that Judith double the size of the home by raising the roof, and the producers decided that was the renovation that would serve as the show's debut.

Once the narrator began talking and people quieted down, Shelby grinned at David. "You're famous!"

"A one-second shot in the opening credits doesn't make me famous."

"It's a start." Her protest was loyal.

On a commercial break, Trevor offered to make a trip to the bar. "Wine, Shel?"

"One."

Pleasure rocked him. Her answer indicated she might want to scene this evening, and he was suddenly impatient to get her out of here.

Fiona asked for a hurricane, and David said he didn't need a refill on the whiskey he was sipping.

When Trevor returned to the table, Shelby pulled her chair closer to his and snuggled up against him as she accepted her drink. He should be satisfied with her affection, but his earlier agitation still weighed on him.

"Is everything okay?" Shelby asked.

He took a drink of the beer he'd ordered. "Impatient to be alone with you." That much was the truth—or part of it, at least.

"I want that too. And there's something else I've been wanting to talk to you about."

"Oh?" Absently he stroked her bare arm, and that touch, the connection, temporarily soothed him.

"When we get home?"

Because this was not the time or the place to discuss anything private, he nodded. Maybe it was too much to hope, but perhaps Hannah's news had affected her as well. He could hope so, at least.

During the next set of commercials, Hannah and Fiona huddled together, and he caught snippets of their conversation, including mentions of a baby shower and whether or not men would be invited.

"Oh hell no," David said, jumping into their discussion.

Fiona tapped her temple, as if deep in thought. "The men can have a diaper-changing competition."

Shelby lifted her glass in a mock toast. "Great suggestion."

David shuddered, and Trevor took a drink of beer to hide his grin.

"What do you think, Trevor?" Fiona asked.

"Is there a prize? I helped raise twin sisters. Pretty sure I'll blow everyone else away."

"Come on, man," David protested. "How about a little solidarity here?"

"You're on your own." He leveled his gaze on Shelby. "Staying in practice is always a good thing."

Shelby's mouth opened a little, but she didn't say a word.

The television show returned, at a point of high drama. A terrible storm that swept through New Orleans caused issues with raising the roof.

At the end of the broadcast, everyone burst into a round of applause, and it was another half an hour before Trevor and Shelby were able to say the last of their goodbyes and escape into the cool autumn air.

When they worked their way free from traffic and headed toward Lake Catherine, Shelby turned down the country music song playing on the radio and faced him. "What did you mean about staying in practice? You know, when we were talking about the diaper-changing competition."

"A long time ago, you asked if I wanted children."

"I remember. We were at your house. When you were holding a condom."

After she'd had a bad day in mediation. Instead of filling the silence, he carefully considered his next words. Pushing her too far may make her pull away. "I told you then that I hadn't met the right woman."

"And?" Shelby's question was breathless, a little high-pitched.

"I've met the right woman. We just need the right time." He grasped the steering wheel harder. "No hurry."

"You…?"

"Yeah." Up ahead was a small shopping center, so he turned on the blinker and eased off the road and parked beneath a tall lamppost. "I'm ready for everything. A wedding. Babies."

"Babies? Plural? *Babies?*"

"I'm open to negotiation on the exact number."

She blinked. Generally when they talked about marriage, she changed the subject or betrayed her emotions by fidgeting. This time she didn't take her gaze from his.

"The timing has to be right for both partners. I'm willing to wait."

"You've been patient."

Even though it wasn't always easy, Shelby was worth the effort.

She took a deep breath then expelled it in a slow, steady measure. "I've been thinking about it for a while, and then this evening I saw the way you congratulated Mason. Then… You had me at diaper-changing competition. You're steady. My anchor. I'm ready to start making plans with you."

"Do you mean it?" Trevor captured her chin. "Like moving in? Marriage? Kids?"

"A step at a time, but yes."

"Fuck." Did he dare hope? "All of it? You're serious?"

"Yes." She grinned, and as the seconds passed, it became a full-fledged smile that lit up her eyes. "Everything. I want to be your wife. The mother of your children."

A vise had been on his heart, and he hadn't realized how tight it was until her words freed him. "But..." He released her to plow a hand into his hair. "This has to be done in the right way."

"I'm not sure what you mean."

This unexpected turn made him do a silent fist pump, but for one of the first times in his life, he'd been caught off guard. "We need a ring before I propose."

"Okay. I can wait."

"Tomorrow. We'll go shopping tomorrow." And then he'd find a memorable way to ask her to marry him. This was significant, and he wanted her to understand how important it was to him. Maybe while they were out on the pontoon? Or at a nice dinner? Maybe while they were out with their friends?

"Just knowing we'll be together is enough for me, Sir." The purr in her voice made his dick as hard as granite.

"It's not enough for me. I want the whole world to look at your hand and know you're taken."

"Since I met you, there hasn't been anyone else for me."

"Shelby, I've waited my whole life for you."

She leaned toward him. For a change, she kissed him.

Before he lost control, he took hold of her shoulders and moved her back onto her seat. "I'm taking you home."

"Please, Master Trevor."

He barely managed to keep his speed low enough to avoid the attention of law enforcement.

When they were inside the house, he grabbed two bottles of water from the refrigerator. He had definite plans for her evening ahead, and they included a trip to the dungeon.

Slowly she uncapped her drink. "You said we could talk."

"Of course." He took a seat at the bar.

"My collar. I mean the one you bought at Mademoiselle Giselle's shop."

His answer was forceful. "It is yours." He'd never wanted it back, and when she'd insisted, he'd brought it home and placed it on his desk, in a place where he'd see it every day and think of her, remember how it glinted while it was nestled on her neck.

She leaned against the refrigerator, keeping the space of the kitchen between them. "Uhm, I don't know how this works."

"Go on."

"I miss it."

Her honesty struck at him, humbling him. "You want it back?"

"I'm not sure if I'm allowed to say that. I mean, I don't think a submissive is supposed to ask her Dom to put a collar on her, is she?"

"There are no absolutes. And I'd like nothing more than to see it on you. This evening?"

She took a long drink of her water. "If... I mean yes. If you want it also."

Nothing he'd like more. "Go and change into something you can wear to the dungeon. I'll meet you there."

While she headed upstairs, he fetched her collar, then went to the dungeon to prepare for her. He selected some classic rock, then set the volume so that it would provide a backdrop rather than driving the scene. Tonight was about a deeper connection.

A few minutes later, she joined him. This evening, instead of wearing a swimsuit coverup or a robe, she'd selected one of his dress shirts, reminiscent of the first time he introduced her to his private play space.

Every time he thought he couldn't be any more in love with her, he discovered new depths.

She closed and locked the door behind her before dropping the shirt and closing the distance between them, her bare feet silent on the cypress wood floor. Silently she stood in front of him, her gaze lowered. Then, with exquisite grace, she knelt and waited, so different from that night at the Quarter.

"Please, lift your hair."

Each motion perfect, she did as he requested. In seconds he closed the collar around her neck and secured the heart-shaped lock. For now it would work. At some point in the future, he'd perform a more formal collaring ceremony. For now, this was symbolic and perfect.

He helped her up and instructed her to choose an implement for their play. When she selected a tawse, he was momentarily speechless.

"I'm ready for this as well," she said, offering it to him on upturned palms. "I trust you."

He remembered her fear, that she'd be a random sub, spanked and forgotten. That she was able to put that behind her was powerful. "I'm honored." Because he understood the emotional risk she was taking, he stripped off his clothes and put on a condom before taking a seat in his oversize leather chair. Then he crooked his finger, beckoning her to him.

As she neared, he held out a hand and helped her into place. "I'll start slow." He'd chosen to be naked on purpose, so their skin would be touching, silent assurance of his love and how much she mattered.

She made a few slight adjustments before settling herself across his lap and relaxing her body.

For minutes he caressed her.

"Mmm."

He continued what he was doing, for the simple pleasure

of having his woman, his sub, his future bride where he wanted her. "Ready?" he asked eventually.

She clenched before catching herself and expelling a breath. "Yes, Sir."

Trevor spanked her, slow and soft, warming her up. She touched her fingertips to the floor for balance as he increased the pressure and frequency. Once her buttocks and the backs of her legs were reddened enough to give him confidence that she wouldn't easily bruise, he picked up the tawse.

He trailed the leather across her skin, letting her know to expect its harsh kiss.

Her breaths came in little bursts, and he rubbed her thighs until she released the tension from her body. "That's perfect."

The first few strikes were gentle, and he allowed her to enjoy them before he picked up the intensity, spanking her faster and harder.

He kept his left hand on her, reassuring her of his adoration. And when she started to whimper, he slid a finger over her clit.

She arched her back and screamed.

Relentlessly he continued his torment, alternating between the relentless pain delivered by the twin spikes of leather and the devilment of the pleasure he was giving her pussy.

"Oh Sir!"

"Are you ready to come, precious sub?" He slid two fingers inside her heat. She was wet as he moved in and out of her easily, bringing her closer to the edge as he ratcheted up the force of his spanks.

Since she hadn't answered him, he repeated himself. "Do you want to come, Shelby?"

"Yes! Please, yes. Sir."

It was impossible for him to wait another moment. This evening, she'd agreed to make their future a reality, and he ached to seal their connection. "I want to be inside you." Trevor dropped the tawse and captured her around the waist. "Straddle me." Since she was close to swimming in subspace, he spoke to her more than he usually did during a scene. "Place your arms around my neck and give yourself to me, Shelby."

With a nod, she all but collapsed on him. And that was perfect with him.

As she lowered herself over him, he guided his cock to her entrance. With a soft sound—half sigh, half moan—she took his length.

Her head was on his shoulder, and her hair spilled down his chest. Her surrender was complete. Pure male triumph ripped through him.

He supported her hips as she rode him, and he stroked faster and faster until she shattered, screaming. This was what he lived for.

After she was replete, he sought his pleasure, coming deep in her as her pussy muscles clenched him tight.

He had no idea how long they stayed joined together until she finally lifted her head and pushed a hand against his chest so she could look at him. "That was everything I always hoped it would be. Thank you, Sir."

"Everything you want, and more, I will give to you. You're mine to love, Shelby. Now and forever. Always."

"Yes," she whispered. "Yours." She met his gaze, and a sheen of tears clung to her eyelashes.

The purity of her emotion brought him to his knees.

"Now and forever." She repeated his words. "Always. I love you."

◊ ◊ ◊ ◊ ◊

Thank you for reading His to Love.

You're cordially invited to return to the Quarter to meet Shelby's friend, Emma. An unbelievably sexy chance encounter in an elevator with a gorgeous billionaire Dominant turns her life upside down…

DISCOVER HIS TO CHERISH

Would you like to receive short stories, deleted scenes, exclusive sneak peeks, behind the scenes info, sales, promos, and more?

Become a Sierra VIP Reader Today!
https://www.sierracartwright.com/subscribe

Have you met your greatest downfall, the heroes of Hawkeye Security? Dominant and delicious, for these alphas, the line of duty between bodyguard and client isn't meant to be crossed.

In Meant for Me, two Hawkeye agents visit the Quarter to celebrate the very naughty Victorian Night, adding more complications to their already forbidden romance.

★★★★★ "The sexual tension built and built until it threatened to explode." ~Bookbub Review

★★★★★ "Sierra Cartwright is killing me slowly with this series! I love those alpha male, ex-military, Dominant, not wanting to fall in love males!" ~Amazon Reviewer

- ❣ Forbidden relationship
- ❣ Age gap
- ❣ Protector
- ❣ Danger
- ❣ Suspense
- ❣ BDSM
- ❣ The Quarter's Victorian Night

- Workplace relationship
- Second chance at love
- Steamy

DISCOVER MEANT FOR ME

Turn the page for an exciting excerpt from HIS TO CHERISH

HIS TO CHERISH EXCERPT

"Which floor?"

"Twelve, thanks." Emma exhaled her relief. The gentleman in the elevator had patiently held the door open while she hurried across the lobby of the New Orleans office building. She'd been at lunch too long—the quarterly gathering with her college girlfriends had been too scandalous and delicious to leave. As the waiter had brought a second glass of wine for each of them, they'd shared stories of their sex lives—the thrills and droughts—and now she was in danger of running late for a meeting with a client.

The man pushed the button for the twelfth floor and then fifteen—presumably his—as the compartment closed.

"How's the book?"

"Umm. This?" Self-consciously she moved the bestselling paperback behind her. "I just borrowed it from a friend." Borrowed it? Pried it from Kathleen's unwilling fingers was more like it. Everywhere Emma went, people were talking about the novel, and after some of her friends' confessions over lunch, Emma had been desperate to read it. Though she had a couple of friends who were into BDSM, she knew little about it. What she did know intrigued her. But where would she find a man into that kind of kink? Her last boyfriend, Aaron, had called her a freak when she'd bought a couple of scarves and asked him to tie her up with them. Later, she found out that was only the beginning of their problems.

"Do you know anything about the novel?"

She took a second look at the man next to her. He was taller than her, by at least a couple of inches, and that said something. In heels, she wasn't used to looking up at many people.

He appeared to be in his mid-thirties, and his thick dark hair had a hint of gray at the temples, which added to his dangerous and distinguished good looks.

Even though she knew she was staring, she couldn't look away. His eyes were a startling shade of green, dark and intense. She had an odd, feminine sense that he saw through her tough exterior into her innermost secrets.

"So, do you?"

Stalling for time, she pretended to misunderstand. "Do I what?"

"Do you know anything about the book?"

He captured her gaze. Instinct told her to look away, but she couldn't. Unnerved, she tightened her grip on her purse strap. "It's hard not to. It's being talked about everywhere." Realizing she was in danger of babbling, something she did *not* do, she changed the direction of the conversation. "Have you read it?"

"I haven't read it, no. There's no need."

"No need?"

His scent seemed to brand the air—something crisp and outdoorsy, a stamp of primal male power and intrigue.

He reached inside his suit jacket.

Emma made a decent living as a financial adviser, and she recognized quality. The suit that had been exquisitely tailored to fit his toned body cost at least a month of her salary.

"I live the lifestyle."

"The lifestyle? Meaning?" A bell dinged, indicating that she'd reached her floor.

"I'm a Dominant." He extracted his wallet, then offered her his business card. "Look me up if you're curious."

Without looking at it, she accepted his offering and tucked it into her purse.

The doors slid open. As if hypnotized, she remained rooted in place.

Because she hadn't moved, he reached out to press a button to prevent the car from closing. As he did, a wink of gold flashed from his cufflink. What kind of man still wore those to work?

"I look forward to hearing from you. Ms....?"

Automatically, maybe foolishly, she provided it. "Monroe. Emma Monroe."

He smiled, and something warm passed through her. "Very soon." This man, tall and broad, had an air of easy command, as if he was accustomed to issuing orders and having others obey. She had an insane urge to treat him with respect he'd yet to earn. Her entire body warmed beneath his attention.

He stepped aside, and she exited the elevator. Wondering what had happened, Emma just stood there.

"Oh my Lord! You were on the elevator with Philip Dettmer? Hello...? Earth to Emma..."

She looked at Lori, the firm's receptionist. Lori had been with Larson Financial almost as long as Emma had been. "That was Philip Dettmer?" Though it was fruitless, she looked over her shoulder.

"Yeah. The one. The only." Lori sighed. "The unbearably sexy."

Emma knew his name—who in Louisiana didn't? He was legendary when it came to buying businesses, whether or not they wanted to be bought. He owned stakes in the local football team and was rumored to be a billionaire. From his air of confidence, she certainly believed it. Of course she knew the name, but she didn't follow the local media enough to have recognized him.

Lori was making an elaborate show of fanning herself with a file folder. "Every time I see him, he makes me want to do things that are immoral."

Tingles still raced through Emma's body. "Does he come here often?"

"He has a business associate in this building. Gavin McLeod."

Another name she recognized.

"Anyway, you know Marjorie who works in the lobby? She sends a text to a few of us when Mr. Dettmer walks in. I do my best to catch a glimpse of him. Maybe I should just start riding the elevator when she messages me."

"He saw my book." Emma held up the paperback.

"Whoa. Seriously?"

"And, uhm, he asked if I'd read it."

"Holy shit. You talked about *sex* with Philip Dettmer?" The manila folder swished to the floor. "Get *out!*"

"Not about sex exactly."

"Just about kink?"

She didn't tell Lori that he'd passed along his business card and invited her to look him up.

"I'd get naked and do the nasty with him in under a second. The jealousy monster has colored me green."

The phone rang, and Lori moved to answer it, chirruping a professional greeting, even though she gave Emma a wide smile and a big thumbs-up.

Emma continued to her office and shut the door. For a

moment, she leaned her shoulders against the wood. Her heart was racing, and she couldn't seem to banish the scent of him.

Good God, she had this kind of reaction, and he hadn't even touched her.

She took a deep breath, then smoothed her skirt as she walked to her desk to hide the book. As she closed it in a drawer, she told herself to focus. Her client was due to arrive in less than five minutes. Her voicemail notification was blinking madly, and she still had investments to research before going home. She didn't have time to think about Philip Dettmer, or having him do delicious, naughty things to her.

Despite her determination, she struggled to keep thoughts of their interaction at bay. Her concentration repeatedly wandered off, and as a result, she had to stay at the office longer than anticipated to finish her projects.

Once she arrived home, she kicked off her pumps, then changed into leggings and an oversize T-shirt bearing a map of the French Quarter. After grabbing a glass of wine, she hurried into her office to power up her computer to learn everything she could about Philip Dettmer.

Page after page of information appeared, covering everything from his business dealings to his charitable endeavors. But then she couldn't resist opening *Scandalicious*, her favorite online gossip magazine, to read stories about his failed marriage. His ex—Anna Lively—had made a number of vague but awful allegations of marital misconduct. She'd never given any details, saying a gag order prevented her from discussing the proceedings. But she'd painted her husband as the villain among villains.

For the next year or so, there were no mentions of Philip. But then articles about him began to pop up, along with rumors of romances, a few of them with actresses or models, and even an heiress. Emma leaned forward to study the dates on his recent pictures. Since his divorce, it seemed as if none of his relationships had lasted more than a single date.

He looked heart-stoppingly hot in a tuxedo on the red carpet. He was fuck-me gorgeous in jeans and a brown leather bomber jacket. And, oh God, the one of him emerging from the Caribbean-blue surf? As she'd already guessed, Philip Dettmer worked out. The picture was grainy —probably a *Scandalicious* paparazzi shot—but she noticed a small amount of tantalizing chest hair that arrowed downward, disappearing into the waistband of his swim trunks.

And he wants me to contact him?

Dare she?

She shook her head. *What's wrong with me?* She shouldn't be contemplating a hook-up with a billionaire. A hook-up? More like a scene where he tied her up and spanked her.

He was out of her league, and she knew next to nothing about the kinky lifestyle he professed to live.

Before she could change her mind, she closed her web browser and powered down the computer.

With a sigh, she returned to the living room to pick up the paperback before heading to the master bathroom to turn on the bathwater. Tonight a shower wouldn't do. She needed a long, leisurely soak with bubbles, wine, and her book.

An hour later, she'd read a hundred scorching pages that had left her feeling restless. She'd finished the glass of wine, and she'd reheated the bathwater twice.

Emma slammed the book closed, dropped it on the floor, leaned back against the bath pillow, and closed her eyes. Part of her wished she'd never started down this path.

Until now, every one of her sexual experiences had been ho-hum and boring. Her last relationship had ended more than six months ago, and clearly the drought was getting to her. How else could she explain the fact she was fantasizing about Philip Dettmer tying her hands behind her back and bending her over the bed? He'd use one of the scarves she'd bought, or maybe handcuffs... He'd tell her, in detail, what he was going to do to her before slapping her ass hard.

She opened her eyes. It was almost as if she could feel the pressure of his open-handed strike on her buttocks.

What the hell was going on? Emma had always been practical and realistic, never given to flights of fancy. She'd studied hard, graduated with honors, and secured a great job. But now...?

She climbed from the bathtub and wrapped herself in a fluffy towel. Maybe it was because she'd read the book, or from the risqué lunch conversation, but she was more turned on than she remembered being. She grabbed a vibrator from the nightstand drawer and lay down on the bed.

After turning on the switch, Emma parted her thighs and placed the egg-shaped toy against her pussy. She finally admitted the truth to herself. Her arousal wasn't from the novel or from the discussion with her friends. It was the chance meeting with Mr. Dettmer. The scent of him, combined with his aura of authority and bold words, had made it impossible for her to have a single rational thought.

The vibrator's humming, pulsing sensation pushed her to the edge. Even though she dug her heels into the mattress and continued to move the egg against her swollen clit, the orgasm loomed out of reach.

Frustrated, she turned the toy to its highest setting and pinched her right nipple. The pain was exquisite. Would Mr. Dettmer do the same if she scened with him? Or would he use clamps on her? In her fantasy, he tormented her ruthlessly, showing no mercy even though she begged for it.

Would he be like the hero in the book, using bondage

gear to tie her up while he ripped orgasm after orgasm from her poor body?

In her fevered imagination, she submitted to him. Emma had no idea what that really meant, but she wanted to find out. She wanted to kneel for him, to follow his orders, to get rid of her inhibitions with a man who wasn't afraid of her sexuality. For her, that was what it was really about. Even when she was in a committed relationship, her sex drive was never satiated.

Her pussy got wetter and wetter as she imagined Philip Dettmer's hands on her body. His touch wouldn't be gentle, but it would be what she needed.

Enough to actually call him?

Before today, she might have said no.

But the lunch with her friends had been liberating. Talking about the book had allowed Emma and her friends to share their innermost desires.

One of her best friends, Shelby, was in a lifestyle BDSM relationship with her fiancé, Trevor. According to Shelby, he'd helped her get past her awful hang-ups about commitment, and she seemed even more confident now than she ever had. Emma knew her friend occasionally visited a club in the French Quarter with Trevor.

The idea of being with a Dominant in public made Emma tighten her grip on her nipple. As she squirmed, she pictured Mr. Dettmer slapping her pussy *hard*.

The combination of her thoughts and the slight pain was enough to make her cry out. Then she imagined him naked, his cock erect, digging his hand into her hair before forcing that big dick inside her needy pussy. The thought of him relentlessly fucking her pushed her to the edge.

Wave after wave assailed her. She'd never had an orgasm this sustained. Shock waves of sensation flooded her pussy. This was what she'd always wanted, dreamed of.

Soon the intensity from the vibrator became too much, and she dropped it, leaving it humming on the mattress while she drank in gulps of air.

It took a full minute for her to breathe normally again. Finally, she sat up and switched off the small egg. Her legs were wobbly as she stood to pull on a nightshirt.

The climax had been good, and yet the odd restlessness persisted. She usually fell asleep after an orgasm, but tonight she tossed and turned as scenes from the book teased her. In her imagination, she was the heroine of the story, and Philip Dettmer tied her, spanked her, tormented, and clamped her. He administered the pain she craved, until she screamed her pleasure and begged for the relief that he repeatedly denied her.

It was well after midnight when she drifted off, and she was awake again before her alarm clock rang. Her heart beat quickly, and her blood hummed as if she'd already had a pot of coffee.

Sometime during the night, she'd reached a decision to get in contact with Mr. Dettmer.

She wanted the experience he offered, at least once. He might be disappointed in her, but she'd have the memory to last a lifetime.

Before she could change her mind, she grabbed his business card from her purse, then picked up her phone. Needing fortification before taking the leap, she shuffled into the kitchen and made a cup of coffee from her single-cup brewer. After a long sip, she opened her email program and typed in his name.

For minutes, she struggled with what to write before settling on something mundane. *"It's Emma Monroe. I met you in the elevator yesterday. I'm curious."*

Her hand shook as she hit Send.

Over the next hour as she got ready for work, she

agonized, alternately wishing she'd never sent the email and obsessively checking for a response.

Emma was on the way out of the door when her cell phone signaled an incoming email. Curiosity wouldn't allow her to leave it unread. What if it was from *him?*

She juggled her to-go cup of coffee, her purse, and her tote onto the hallway table. Her heart momentarily stopped, then raced on madly when she saw he'd answered.

Call me.

Read more of His to Cherish

ABOUT THE AUTHOR

I invite you to be the very first to know all the news by subscribing to my very special **VIP Reader newsletter**! You'll find exclusive excerpts, bonus reads, and insider information.
https://www.sierracartwright.com/subscribe

For tons of fun and to join with other awesome people like you, join my Facebook reader group: **Sierra's Super Stars**
https://www.facebook.com/groups/SierrasSuperStars

And for a current booklist, please visit my **website**.
http://www.sierracartwright.com

USA Today bestselling author Sierra Cartwright was born in England, and she spent her early childhood traipsing through castles and dreaming of happily-ever afters. She has two wonderful kids and four amazing grand-kitties. She now calls Galveston, Texas home and loves to connect with her readers. Please do drop her a note.

- facebook.com/SierraCartwrightOfficial
- instagram.com/sierracartwrightauthor
- bookbub.com/authors/sierra-cartwright
- amazon.com/Sierra-Cartwright/e/B008H5WF76
- tiktok.com/@sierracartwright

ALSO BY SIERRA CARTWRIGHT

Titans

Sexiest Billionaire

Billionaire's Matchmaker

Billionaire's Christmas

Determined Billionaire

Scandalous Billionaire

Ruthless Billionaire

Titans Quarter

His to Claim

His to Love

His to Cherish

Titans Quarter Holidays

His Christmas Gift

His Christmas Wish

His Christmas Wife

Titans Sin City

Hard Hand

Slow Burn

All-In

Titans Captivated (Ménages)

Theirs to Hold

Theirs to Love

Theirs to Wed
Theirs to Treasure
Theirs to Corrupt

Titans: Moretti Mafia

Vengeful Vows
Savage Vows

Titans: Reserve

Tease Me

Hawkeye

Come to Me
Trust in Me
Meant For Me
Hold On To Me
Believe in Me

Hawkeye: Denver

Initiation
Temptation
Determination

Bonds

Crave
Claim
Command

Donovan Dynasty

Bind
Brand

Boss

Mastered

With This Collar

On His Terms

Over The Line

In His Cuffs

For The Sub

In The Den

With This Ring

Collections

Titans Series

Titans Billionaires: Firsts

Titans Billionaires: Volume 1

Titans Billionaires: Volume 2

Billionaires' Quarter: Titans Quarter Collection

Risking It All: Titans Sin City Collection

Yours to Love: Titans Captivated Collection

His Christmas Temptation: Titans: Quarter Holidays

Hawkeye Series

Undercover Seduction: Hawkeye Firsts

Here for Me: Volume One

Beg For Me: Volume Two

Run, Beautiful, Run: Hawkeye Denver Collection

Printed in Dunstable, United Kingdom

66083097R00157